The Diary of
MARY TRAVERS

A Novel

EIBHEAR WALSHE

SOMERVILLE PRESS

Somerville Press Ltd,
Dromore, Bantry,
Co. Cork, Ireland

First published 2014

This is a novel based on true events,
see author note at the end

Designed by Jane Stark
Typeset in Adobe Garamond Pro
seamistgraphics@gmail.com

ISBN: 978 0 9927364 22

Printed and bound in Spain
by GraphyCems, Villatuerta, Navarra

For Celine Walshe and Donald O'Driscoll

APRIL

Mitchelstown
County Cork
Ireland
Friday 5 April 1895

Sometimes, unbidden, pictures of my young self rise up before me. Unexpectedly I am assailed by moments from thirty years ago or more, unsettling glimpses of myself stalking along a night-time pavement or in the courtroom. Now, I marvel at the life I lived back then in the city, all that destructive energy whipping me onwards in a frenzy to find that which seemed always to evade me. Call it desire or acceptance, somehow it was just out of my grasp. In this quiet town, where I am liked by many, I can go about my decorous life for months at a time without any memory of the city. I look well-behaved and, outwardly at least, I have tamed myself. Then suddenly, in my mind, I am forced to see an inward image of my young self prowling like a panther through the streets of Dublin, night after night, watching the Doctor's big house on the corner of the square, consumed by a desire to hurt him or her or them both. Can one life contain two such different existences? All I know is that I am thinking of Dublin far too often these days and it is beginning to unsettle me.

I don't know why I keep thinking back to the city. Perhaps it is the beautiful April evenings, the lengthening nights, the sound of birdsong and the cry of the peacocks in the trees below the Castle terrace. When I was young and trapped in my mother's house in Dublin, I hated and feared the sound of birds on early spring evenings. It seemed to me to be a reproach, a reminder that I was outside desire, outside the call of young life to other young life. Now, a fifty-seven-year-old woman and yet still within desire, when I hear the April birdsong starting up, it simply brings me pleasure, with its promise of summer sunlight, and all I can remember is the raw bewilderment and anger of my younger self. That is why I return to those days with the Doctor and his wife. Or is it?

No, it is not! I must be honest, if only to myself in the safety of my room and in writing these pages. It is the newspaper reports. The Doctor's son is in trouble. It seems he has brought a libel action in London against some Marquess, but the precise details are unclear. I can tell him now that even if he wins, he will lose, but he wouldn't listen. I would tell him that his heart's blood will be used up in a vain attempt to gain the perfect rose, the rose of justice, and a favourable judgement. Justice doesn't exist, I would tell him, but his ear would be stopped up, filled with his own self-justification.

When Emily came up to our bedroom yesterday to give me my share of the rent money from the Dublin shops, she left a copy of the *Cork Examiner* on my work table. She left it there without comment or allusion to the report. It was in an old copy, published three days before, part of a bundle of discarded local papers and magazines sent down from the Castle. Maybe a warning shot? I understood that I was to read the report but not speak of it. There I found the report about the Doctor's son and the London trial. Nobody here knows of my troubles, except Emily, and she won't speak of it to anyone. It splashed her with mud too and spoiled her one chance to marry, although she never complains of it. I have learned in this past year in the College that I have underestimated my sister. She has unexpected reserves of tact and understanding that her pretty, apparently artless, countenance belies, and I have finally learned to trust her. Trust is perhaps the wrong word. She and I share a blighted surname. She must protect me as she must protect herself. I can only trust to the fact that we stand or fall together if my past is ever revealed to the Dean, the Board of Trustees or the Countess. Most of all to the Countess.

Saturday 6 April

Last night up at the Castle, I had some moments alone in the drawing room before the music recital commenced and I read as quickly as I could through the London newspapers and their accounts of the trial of the Doctor's son in the Old Bailey. Even from this backwater, I can sense that he is in some further difficulty. Acute danger even. All the papers are full of his trial, but exactly what kind of trouble nobody seems prepared to state. It is mystifying. The Dublin papers were not so coy about me in my time of notoriety. I could glance only hurriedly before the Countess and Emily came back from the work room to exclaim over some knitted garments for the poor and deserving of Mitchelstown. The Countess still alludes with respect to my literary leanings and my great work in the library, and so I made my excuses and asked to be allowed to check some details or other in the prized copy of Samuel Johnston's *Dictionary*. I must read these newspapers at my leisure, make sure that I am not missing some crucial facts. Perhaps the Reverend can lend me his Cork newspapers. Or, again, maybe not. I may go in to Cork city tomorrow, buy the English newspapers and read them in some quiet tea room, away from the prying eyes of Mitchelstown. Money, once the great absence of my life, is now plentiful and I can travel as I please. Again, Emily surprises me with her skills in financial affairs, the rents from the Dublin properties Mamma left us, the haggling over rights of way and leases, all providing us with abundant funds. When someone talks and talks to no apparent effect all the time, you forget to respect them and their acute instinct for survival beneath the incessant daily outpourings of trivia. In particular, when that letter came from Australia, from Arthur's widow, threatening us with legal proceedings, demanding a third of Mother's property, Emily knew precisely what to do.

'How much shall we pay to settle this claim?' she asked the young solicitor in his offices on Ely Place. He remained silent, knowing her to be the real judge of this matter.

'Perhaps one thousand pounds would silence our sister-in-law in Sydney,' she then said.

'Emily, my dear, we will see her in court before we pay one farthing. Mamma's will is perfectly clear; you and I are sole heirs.'

(I was sorry I happened on that unfortunate phrase 'one farthing'. I could see Emily's brow darken, unusually for her. It must have recalled my troubles to her and that insulting farthing I was awarded for that most elusive of qualities, my honour.)

'No, Mary. We have had quite enough of legal proceedings in this family,' she said crisply, without rancour. She turned to the lawyer and began dictating the letter of settlement for Arthur's widow to sign. She was perfectly right, of course: £1,000 down bought us both a clear title to Mamma's estate and now we each have an income of £300 a year, unknown to the College and also to the Countess, who still regards us as penniless, deserving, yet sufficiently educated and decorous for her larger drawing room occasions and for library and plain needlework duty. I often wondered what instinct came to the surface with Emily in her middle years which enabled her to be such a clear-headed businesswoman. As a girl, younger and much prettier than I, she seemed to be interested only in clothes, in guessing the income of neighbours and in talking, talking for hours about little or nothing. I was the listener, Papa always told me, the only listener amongst his four children, and the reader also, and so I was the unwilling recipient of his confidence, his troubles in Trinity College and at the library, until I, like everyone else in his life up to then, simply got up one day and stopped listening to the endless stories of defeat. Emily was a woman of so many unimportant words, but what shocked me was that in matters of finance, her wasteful words ceased and she found the few necessary words to secure our monetary independence. I suppose the years of poverty and subservience, fruitlessly badgering Papa for an adequate allowance, vulnerable to Mamma's random angers and silences, the shabby dreariness of living as a dependent gentlewoman all made steel of her kindly and pleasing face. Then the chance for freedom, the dizzy happiness and power of a full purse hidden from view.

Sunday 7 April

I sit at my desk in the bedroom and watch the lime trees break slowly into green in front of the Castle, all bud and madly singing young birds. Tonight the light from the hidden sun frames the castle with all the vivid golden blaze of an imminent revelation. This is my favourite time since we moved here and our bedroom is my place of refuge. The County

Cork is so much gentler in climate than my own Dublin, a scarcity of frost in January and February, all the camellias and magnolias in flower in early March, the full gentle glory of spring flowering through early April. Emily would enthuse about the splendours of her gardening if I allowed her; a well-placed snub can always quell her endless horticultural anecdotes but, although I am loath to admit it to her, I too waited for the camellias and the magnolias with pleasure this year.

When the Warden first showed us this narrow little limestone corner house last year, we appeared all demure gratitude and Protestant reserve, the truth of Emily's Papish faith well hidden by the drab hats and our respectable Protestant surname. At first, we modestly held back. We were politely refraining from a too hasty appraisal of our new charitable home. It seemed almost too good to be true: a home for the rest of our spinster lives, free from any financial burden, our final, unlooked-for refuge. However, Emily was unable to refrain from a cry of pleasure when she saw the cobbled kitchen yard at the back of our new stone home. Despite herself, she bolted through the narrow downstairs kitchen, running outside with a giddy energy and delight, exclaiming at the fruit trees and the tiny kitchen garden within sight of the mill by the small river. I stayed in the hallway, keeping the Reverend company in the chill air, murmuring with a kind of humble admiration at the large single drawing room and the old fireplace, the large window, and the side view of the Castle looming over our little square, the squat stone houses of Kingston College (a pompous name for what is really a set of almshouses for deserving and impoverished Protestant gentlefolk) and the green lawns in front of us. My heart sank as I saw the steep stairs leading upwards to the single large bedroom. I ascended in some gloom, the Warden discreetly allowing me to view the bedroom alone.

That first day, I was in my fifties and as strong in my body as I had ever been, but I knew that this would be our final home and that each passing year would make those stairs steeper until the day when I would lose heart and stay upstairs in bed, only to travel back down again in my coffin, four strong local men cursing the steep incline, yet grateful for the lightness of their burden.

We have been here for more than a year and our days are perfectly ordered. After our shared, mainly silent breakfast, Emily will make her way down to the kitchen garden and onwards to the dairy and from there to her hen house by the mill, and I will climb back upstairs and read and write but mostly stare out along the neat line of College houses and the trees and lawn in front of us. In the afternoon, when she returns laden, to begin preparing our evening meal, I fetch my hat and my reticule and make my way up to the tower room in the Castle to resume my ordering of the Kingston books. I am reminded of that line in *Pride and Prejudice*, of the careful ordering of the domestic routine so that Mr and Mrs Collins can spend so much of their day apart! Growing up in a house of active domestic warfare, my sister and I value our mutual indifference.

I sit most mornings or early evenings here alone at my table, writing and looking up at the Castle. In the panic after Papa's death, and the discovery that he had left nothing but debts, we tried to sell his books to the Royal College of Surgeons in Dublin but the Governors wanted nothing to do with us, Papa's name reeking of bad finances. I did sell some of his medical books to an old peddler on Capel Street, but the novels and the poetry books were not wanted and now I am glad that I kept them. I have them here in the room with me. I also have a few old newspaper cuttings from thirty years ago hidden away in a small valise under my bed. These I open from time to time. Emily knows what they are and so will not want to see them. I keep them out of view, but I think of them constantly these days as fear has begun to grow, lurking around corners in this small County Cork town. I also record my thoughts in this diary from time to time. I write to keep my mind clear of incipient fear and to justify myself before this journal. I had thought my writing days were over. Once I wrote feverishly – poems, pamphlets, words of poison and hatred which filled my days and flew everywhere until finally they struck *her* and she struck me back, as I wanted her to. Jane. The Doctor's wife.

The newspapers do not mention her. She must be alive still, for surely her death would have merited laurels in the newspapers and I would most certainly have seen them. The Reverend is an Irish revolutionary in a genteel way and keeps Jane's poetry and her stories in his small library. What would our Countess say if she knew that I was once the dearest friend of such a patriotic poetess? She will never find out, if I can manage it, because she must not know the broken, unhappy end of that particular friendship.

Jane would be seventy if she is still alive. Has she aged as well as she promised to?

Yes, I am a published poet. What would the Reverend say, with his love of fine words and the endeavours of authoresses? Would I go up in his estimation? I think not. Those poems were sent out like darts of poison. Some day I will read them again. For now, they nest under my bed, like dread waiting to burst into full flower. Sometimes they come back to me, whether I like it or not, at four in the morning, listening to Emily's stolid, unconcerned breathing, turning around and around like a song in my heated brains. 'Your progeny is quite a pest/ To those who hate such "critters"/ Some sport I'll have, or I'm blest/ I'll fry the Wilde breed in the West.'

Such hate, such a waste of my youthful energy. Did I even think, as I wrote, of the children I was menacing, those young girls in their uncle's vicarage, sweet little Isola at play, real children, not simply smart phrases in a hate-filled poem? In my defence – and I have very little defence in this matter – I wrote without any sense of the greater world, of readers, of other lives. I wrote with the sole purpose of publication, not to share my thoughts and words with others, to reach other souls, to uplift and elucidate readers with my poems. No, I wrote solely for the purpose of becoming a famous writer. I wanted to escape from being myself, to step into a fast carriage that would take me away from Mamma's house and my few grim frocks and hats and the eternal trudging in and out of bookshops and cafés without money, and into a world where I was wealthy, admired and accepted by others with fame and money and a liking for themselves, something that now, I suspect, no writer actually achieves. In short, I wanted to be her, Jane, the Doctor's wife, pointed out on the street, the friend of other poets and politicians.

Now I write this diary, my only place to speak freely.

Tuesday 9 April

When I was young, I longed so much for my mother's love that I strove to hate my father as much as she did, just to retain her approval and her affection. Now that they are both dead, I find I think much more of him than I do of her and perhaps understand his plight more than hers. Perhaps that is why, after his death, I decided to take up the pen again and write that short pamphlet about him. I have it here in front of me. *Herbert or 'Tis Forty Years Since*. I dedicated it thus: 'This mournful recital is printed in memory of a beloved parent, who was too self-sacrificing in all his relations of life to have been worldly-wise.' That would have made him wince, but I suppose at the time I was writing it for myself and not for him. I can see that now. I sent it out to a few publishers in Dublin, confident that it would be taken up and made a great success of. Not one replied. Well, just one did. Hely and Son offered to print 50 copies if I paid them £10. I had some money Mamma had left me and I did so, much to Emily's puzzlement when she discovered what I had done.

'What will you do with fifty copies?'

I hadn't thought of that.

'It is my tribute to Papa; my atonement,' I told her grandly.

'A few words of tribute in his lifetime would have cost less and achieved more,' she replied tartly. In the end I gave her a copy, sent one to Arthur in Australia, and donated copies to as many libraries and institutions as I could. That left me with these five. I might smuggle another into the Castle library. I sent one to Marsh's Library and some woman, a secretary to the Keeper of Manuscripts, wrote back. She works for Jane's silky smooth cousin, William Maturin, her beloved 'Coz Wills' as Jane always called him, and she returned the copy with a starchy letter pointing out that Marsh's Library accepts only donations of rare manuscripts. In a postscript, she expressed disappointment that Papa had not seen fit to leave any of his valuable books to the institution he had so loved in his lifetime. What did they expect? He had slaved for the good of that library for forty years and they had never promoted him beyond Assistant Keeper.

All this afternoon I have been re-reading *Herbert* and, I can see, with some hindsight, that it is not without some literary value and that, yes, Papa and indeed Mamma would have loathed it. I decided to set it in 1840 and it tells the story of one Edward Herbert, a suburban physician, a shy, withdrawn man: '*Whatever he may have been in youth, Herbert had for many, many years been fonder of silence, solitude and study than of human conversation.*' Yes and so have I, dear Papa. I have become you in so many ways, taking refuge in books and writing and feel much the happier for it all. I continue with Herbert's encounter with a patient, a Mrs Smith, '*A lady of advanced age, and having the appearance of a reduced gentlewoman,*' as I describe her. She is now, as we meet her, a lady twice widowed, but she claims that once, forty years before, she had been Herbert's long-lost beloved Caroline Aston. As I arrange the encounter, he fails to recognise her, avowing '*If you are that lady, you are greatly changed; I cannot recognise a single feature. But the voice does seem familiar to my ear and awakens memories of the past, which I thought dormant.*' Finally he is convinced that this is indeed the lady he had loved and they confess that life has been harsh on them both; a disappointment after their own early love affair had been cruelly ended by the machinations of a meddling friend.

At one point, I find that I wrote '*In the eighth year Herbert married but his married state had not been happy.*' This makes me squirm. Although both Papa and Mamma were dead when I published *Herbert*, neither would have appreciated the public airing of the marital discord that filled our home with daily clamour. In all those years, when Mamma was so liberal with her criticism, Papa never spoke one word against her, even in the face of her cruellest jibes. She had been always ready to attack him for his shortcomings as a husband and father but even she had never told us the story of his earlier love. It was Jane who told me, discreetly, over tea in Merrion Square one afternoon, about the poverty that my father had endured when his family went bankrupt, his scholarship to Trinity College, his early struggles, the love of a wealthy English girl, her family's disapproval for this penniless student, the broken engagement. 'Your dear mother could never stand a chance against such a spectre. The great love affair cruelly ended,' Jane murmured sympathetically and I began to wonder: Did Papa cling on to the memory of this early love to avoid Mamma? I loved the Doctor body and soul thirty years ago and thought I would die of anger when I realised that William wanted nothing more to do with me, but now his memory is nothing but a curiosity to me; that I could have ever loved him is of little concern to me now.

When did love first fail between my parents? Indeed, why did Papa marry her, this fashionably educated Catholic girl, with money but without any true respect for books, for his learning and eventually for him? That she loved him, I am now certain, and Mamma had charm when she bothered to exert it. In addition, she was pretty. Emily is her double in this, even at fifty-three and, like Emily, Mamma kept her looks right into late middle age before the pain from the cancer began to gouge lines on her lovely face. I don't think Papa cared for her good looks. In that letter I found in his desk at home after he died, a draft of one he wrote to his librarian friend in Manchester during my trial, he did confess his domestic misery.

> I did think that there was but one person in the world who understood my real sentiments, and was inclined to do me justice. It is unhoped-for good fortune to find there is another – the assurance of sympathy will mitigate the sense of pain, it will diminish misery, though it cannot remove it. You should not wonder that I avoid the speech and sight of human beings. In my own house (for I cannot call it home), I am a despised, unwelcome wretch, the object of religious bigotry and unrelenting jealously: a tyranny against which there can be no resistance, and from which there is no escape. I sink under the sense of injustice.

Poor Papa, passing each day without a hint that he felt the repeated lashes of Mamma's contempt. I used to wonder if he would have been any happier if he had married his first love, the rich English girl? Surely not. Was he capable of love? As I think about it now, I blush. How could I ever have doubted him? He endured without reproach all the sufferings I heaped on his head, understanding better than most the origin of my dark, wild anger. He tried, in his dull, bookish way, to talk to me, to make me a companion when Arthur and Emily and even young Bobby had all made their indifference clear. Of all the things I have failed to do, I regret most my anger at Papa's timid overtures towards a kind of bookish friendship between us.

The Countess has invited us for tea later this afternoon. Since the travails of the land wars and the killings, known as the 'massacres', ceased five years ago, her rents and also her guests have been severely curtailed and now she must resort to the College and its inhabitants to eke out her regular tea parties. I suppose our name marks us as being unshakably of the right pedigree, with perhaps a hint of a connection to Timoleague and the poet Edmund Spenser and beyond. Neither Emily nor I will disabuse her of her misapprehension. Indeed, to do so would be to lose our free and comfortable nest here and so we accept all invitations to the Castle without demur and put on our drabbest dresses and drink tea with the Countess. Correctly speaking, she is not a countess, merely Mrs Naylor since her remarriage last year to her second cousin, Mr Naylor, at present away on an extended journey in the Levant. No one, especially those of us who were permitted by her grace and favour to take up residence in the College, will insist on such correctness of form, and so she remains the Countess.

I feared that when Emily and I moved to this backwater in the County Cork, we would find it dull, but little did we know the tempest we were moving towards, the killings and riots, the police charges, the jailing. Mitchelstown in the past ten years has been a veritable battlefield, with shootings and public disturbances, and the peace that has been re-established is an uneasy one, the Castle and its inhabitants at sea in a landscape of mistrust. I sincerely pray that my own past will never track me down here, but if it ever does, even more I pray that those around me remember that their own recent past is less than glorious. On reflection, this will serve only to make them even more prone to judgement, or such has been my experience.

When we arrived here, the Lady Dean brought us to the Castle for inspection and my initial sight of this unnatural absurdity in close proximity made me doubt my own sanity and the evidence of my eyes. Who had conjured up this engorged pile of limestone to tower over a small market town, and stare defiance at the nearby, bewildered Galtee Mountains? Later I was told that it was Big George, the Countess's ancient father-in-law, who had bankrupted his estate at the beginning of the century to build this arrogant folly with over eighty bedrooms, believed to be a replica of Buckingham Palace. Emily, who has gazed on the palace on one of her frock-hunting expeditions to London, says she cannot see the resemblance. Big George had hoped to house King George IV here for one night on his Irish progress sometime in the 1820s. The King then changed his mind and stayed in Dublin, leaving eternally bereft the enormous bedchamber built especially for him, with the marble pillars and vast canopy and the three white steps up to the royal mattress. Sickened with disappointment and pressed into cloudland, Lord Kingston, now 'Mad' George, had to be locked up for the rest of his life, but something of this madness and arrogance remains in the stones and turrets.

On that first evening in the Castle, as Emily and I made our way up the long terrace and into the vast, idle emptiness of the hall and the gallery lined with dank, discoloured hangings, I wondered about this crazed universe we had plunged ourselves into when we fled Dublin with Mother's money and set up in temporary lodgings in Cork city. We sent those letters of supplication to the board of Kingston College on the advice of the Royal College of Physicians of Ireland, anxious to unburden the responsibility of Dr Travers's two aged daughters on any purse but theirs. My letters to Lady Kingston were wonderful, pure invention – my finest moment of fiction. Our situation was perilous, our father a sainted scholar and physician who had spent all his fortune on Marsh's Library and on the relief of the poor and ill of Dublin, leaving Emily and myself stranded and practically starving. I forbore to mention our private income and our regular meals in the dining room of the Imperial Hotel in Cork, and thus we were made welcome in the College, rescued from our indigence by the kindness of Kingston charity. Now that I think of it, Cork city and county being so small, she, the Countess, may have known and chosen not to know, as she does with so much of her life.

In the huge drawing room, agleam with silver, the Countess awaited us that first day, and the Reverend made his way towards her with us in tow, delighted with the formality of the occasion. I had expected an ancient woman, the widow of the last Lord Kingston who had been born, or so his tomb in the college chapel told us, nearly 100 years before, but, in fact, the Countess is younger than I, merely in her early fifties and looking even younger.

'Miss Travers and Miss Emily Travers,' the Reverend announced, stressing my status as older sister as we approached the Countess. 'May I present Lady Kingston.'

We dipped suitably and the Countess was kind enough to give us each her hand and press it with some warmth. We sat down and accepted tea, a cheap blend in precious thin cups.

The Countess said pleasantly. 'I'm so very pleased to make your acquaintance. You are both welcome to Mitchelstown. Welcome indeed, and I hope you will bring some of your erudition and liveliness to our simple country town.'

Her eyes were light blue, and her soft brown hair only somewhat touched with silver, and agreeably so. In the short time that I have known her, it is clear to me that the Countess is one of those fortunate women whose girlish prettiness in youth translates into a middle-aged softness, where wrinkles and grey threads seem only to suggest a mild fatigue and melancholy, rather than the remorseless advance of years, and where old age seems impossible.

'Mary is the literary one, the erudite one, my lady,' Emily piped up, before I could say anything, 'I'm afraid my simple talents run merely to plain needlework and other such trivial occupations.'

Clever Emily had noticed the elegant black work case in front of her ladyship and so marked herself out for preference. The Countess looked up at me with something approaching dread, her eyes seeing the feared bluestocking looking back at her reproachfully.

'Indeed, Miss Emily. Then perhaps you might lend me some assistance with my charitable endeavours. As to our literary resources, I'm afraid the library in the Tower room has been lamentably neglected since Lord Kingston's death, but please do make use of it as much as you wish, Miss Mary. I would feel less guilty about its neglect if I knew someone were using it.'

Something of relief was also visible on her face as we talked. Perhaps she expected to find the maiden daughters of the late Dr Travers to be withered old ladies. Turning to the Reverend, the Countess made a timid yet assured plea, the pretended entreaty of a polite woman who knows she has the greater power in all matters but chooses not to exercise it.

'Perhaps you might show Miss Travers the library, my dear Reverend, when we have had our tea.'

Later, after tea, the Reverend grew passionate as he described the excesses of the recent Land Campaign and the local violence. One story in particular had him enthralled.

'Yes, indeed, Miss Emily, it was poor Mr Mandeville, a farmer from near here, who was arrested and had his clothes torn off; everything he was wearing violently ripped from his body by the police in the barracks that night. His poor widow told me that they left him in a state of perfect nudity, apart from a simple towel around his waist, and even this they threatened to confiscate.'

Emily paid the Reverend a great deal of attention that night, before she realised that he would remain unmarried despite any ideas she might have had. Emily has an instinct for attracting the kind of man who would never marry. It started with Mr McCabe, that fellow who worked with our brother Arthur and would insist on calling around to our house on Sunday evenings, anticipating some moment when he might be left alone with him, a moment that Arthur was careful not to provide. Arthur was the only one of us who had inherited Mamma's undeniable good looks.

To stem the flow of the Reverend's eloquence, the Countess stood, and so the Reverend offered to take us up to the tower room to see the library. To my relief, Emily pleaded an interest in some flannel workings for the poor and so it was only myself and the Reverend who made our way through a long corridor at the far side of the drawing room, up some cold, dank stairs and over to one of the turret rooms where Big George had decided to locate his library, or so the Reverend told me, wanting all that learned stuff away from his living quarters.

The library is situated in the tower room, a circular, vast space right at the top of the Castle above the drawing room, with long narrow windows overlooking the town. It smells strongly of Kingston familial indifference, but my delight on that first visit was the pleasure of those volume-filled mahogany cases covering three sides of the room, from floor to ceiling and glassed in with mullioned panes. Slow with self-importance, the Reverend showed me through the room, with its low writing tables, many carelessly scattered with opened volumes. There were heavy, leather-backed chairs, and a wooden sliding ladder for one to reach up to the highest shelves. All I wanted to do was to make him stop talking and leave me there to open the cases and begin reading the titles. One of the larger books had been left open face down on a table, its many pages crumpled like a broken accordion, and it was all I could do to prevent myself from snatching up the book, smoothing out its rumpled pages and then placing it under a pile of weighty tomes, pressing it back into shape, repairing the violation. I remembered Papa speaking of the criminal oafishness of his predecessor in Marsh's Library, who had used a precious manuscript to block a leak in the guttering over the front door. Suddenly I understood Papa's sense of outrage, from a man habitually meek in the face of Mamma's violent insults. 'Yes, Papa,' I told him, or his dead shade, 'in this, I am indeed your daughter.'

The Reverend talked on and on.

'Observe, Miss Travers. If you look out this side window, you can see your own humble dwelling.'

I glanced down. As he had said, the College was visible far below, the white line of house fronts mellowed and slightly pink in the late afternoon sunlight, the neat squares of grass under the trees dramatically darkened by the retreating light. There, tiny but sharp, our own windows glinted back at me, rendered strange, no longer mine by this new way of seeing where I lived. What surprised me most was that, from the tower window, our house seemed peripheral to the great mass of trees behind it, masking the river and the mill, the tall dark green vegetation being in possession of the landscape, our small houses an irrelevance.

When I had returned to the drawing room, the Countess asked me if I would assist her.

'My late husband loved his books greatly and, as I say, it has always weighed on my mind that I have somewhat neglected the library. The various collections are now disordered. Could I prevail on you to call there from time to time and perhaps attempt to restore some little order? Mr Naylor speaks with much admiration for the work your dear father undertook at Marsh's Library.'

'It would give me great pleasure, Lady Kingston,' I replied, dazzled by the permission to spend as much time alone with her books as I wished. It was only later at home that a thought struck me and made me uneasy. Mr Naylor? Our dear Papa? How much did Mr Naylor know of my past?

Saturday 13 April

Now that I am nearly old, in years if not in mind, I begin to alter my ideas about love and about the loves I have known. It came to me yesterday as something of a violent revelation that Mamma, for all her complaints and grievances, even though she left home and separated herself from Papa, must have loved him much more than he could have loved her. Love. I use the word without precision, carelessly. She cared for him, even in hatred, more than he could ever have thought about her. That's why she poisoned my girlhood with her tear-filled confidences about his ill-treatment of her, his iniquities, and his many sins of omission. Maybe that is why I felt towards the Doctor as I did, when all physical pleasure had ceased between us. *He* had other cares, other loves. I had none.

Earlier today Emily came in from the mill, all aglow, wiping her hands on an old cloth, her eyes abstract with mental calculations about domestic matters.

'Her ladyship has sent down Kenneth Fogarty to say that the carriage is to go into Cork tomorrow morning, early, to collect Mr

Naylor from the London boat. He is making his return to Ireland and has telegraphed to say so.'

My eyebrows must have betrayed me since I discourage Emily from running up to me with every trivial happening from the Castle. She has become akin to the Court Circular, coming up the stairs, breathless with excitement, to tell me that it has been confirmed that the Countess has a slight cold. She hurried on with the important part of the message:

'He says that we may travel into the city if we wish.'

Emily knows me too well to expect a direct answer. I can hear her downstairs bustling around, packing bags, but I have decided that I will go into Cork with her and finally read some of these newspapers and see what exactly the Doctor's son has done and if my name is mentioned in them. A fever to find out has possessed me.

Sunday 14 April

Hateful, hateful Mr Naylor! He knows! I pace this room and read my newspaper clippings. I send out my beams of hate, praying that they might singe his silky little beard. I should never have agreed to accompany Emily into Cork, but my own weakness and curiosity overcame me. I had been anxious to read those newspapers, but to do so away from all inquiring eyes.

Kenneth came and collected us early this morning, just after six. He is the Countess's coachman and I trust him over the other men working in the Castle: a young man with a handsome figure, heavy face, and beautiful, gentle eyes that make you forget the hard bones of jaw and cheek. Just this year he married Louie, the Countess's maid, a fair-skinned little thing, tough as they come but no fool and, I suspect, sensible enough to know how well she has done in getting him for a husband. He helped us into the carriage and soon Emily was asleep. When we stopped along the road, I climbed up and chatted to Kenneth about the foggy early morning landscape, the changes in Mitchelstown and Fermoy, and he identified the various houses as we passed. The Countess remained at home to receive her visitor, Miss Townsend, who arrived from the County Carlow this morning for a week's visit.

We stopped for tea in Glanmire and then arrived in the city a little after eleven, the main streets pleasantly busy in the strong April sunlight.

I went with Emily to her dressmaker, the heavy old Mrs Dunlea, a quiet woman in a respectable shop near the Imperial Hotel, and stood patiently while they fussed over my new summer dress and hat, the smart navy one, and for an hour they debated the cut, the length, the amount and size of buttons on the front. Why all this bother, I cannot understand. Indeed, why new clothes at all? I have sufficient, indeed more than sufficient, clothing but I leave all that to Emily, who draws on our joint account, and the result is that I am better dressed than I have ever been in my life, with ranges of winter and summer clothes at apparently very little cost. I remember all those years ago begging Papa for the money for a new winter coat – my old dark brown cloak an embarrassment, a visible sign of my poverty – and finally, with some shame, accepting £10 from the Doctor for a new coat and dress, a detail his lawyer made much play of in my court case and which the Dublin newspapers pounced upon with great glee. When he wrote to me, sending me money, the Doctor would ask about my petticoats, knowing how such a letter would thrill me. Of course, that detail also made its way into the grasping fingers of the Dublin newspapers years ago. I paid for that money with every sneering line.

Money is now plentiful and something of a mystery to me. Emily orders the best of tea, butter and flour from the general store in Mitchelstown and trades the eggs to get us prime cuts of beef from the abattoir beyond the mill. Our fruit trees and bushes overflow in late summer, thanks to the warm, inland climate, and this will keep her busy with jam-making all through the autumn, more goods in her intricate system of bartering for the best produce from the neighbouring farm. I have grown pleasantly stout under Emily's new regime of spending and trading and sometimes see myself unexpectedly in shops windows: a prosperous, well-dressed woman nearly sixty, so far removed from the restless girl I still believe myself to be. When Mamma moved us out of Dublin to Greystones in the County Wicklow after my trial and when I was again well enough to be moved, her mind turned inwards and she began to practice stringent economies. Despite her ample income, she curtailed all our expenditure on food, fuel and clothes, allowing that grim house near the seafront to become cold, cheerless and unkempt, and now I wonder if it was the beginnings of the illness that unhinged her mind. Emily's prodigality with money, her insistence on the best foodstuffs and materials, is understandable after those years of spartan rule with Mamma.

As soon as I could, I made it clear that the afternoon in Cork would be mine alone, mentioning books to buy as well as ink and other items that I knew would bore Emily. I told her that I would meet her at the Imperial Hotel for tea in time to be collected by Kenneth in the carriage and then we would make our way to the boat to greet Mr Naylor. Somewhat to my surprise, Emily accepted my disappearance without resistance and so I was free to wander the streets of Cork, elegantly groomed, with a new parasol and soft fawn gloves, and with money in my purse.

Cork has always amused and delighted me with its idea of itself as a city, so near to green pastures and hills that you could almost touch them, the country courtesy of the shop people, everything on a hill or by the river. The thoroughfares are so different from Dublin's stately streets, and I miss the glimpse of escape and grandeur of the Dublin Mountains every so often present at the end of some streets in the city centre. I longed so much for them when we first fled here and then, later, I cried at the mean lanes and the truculent, unhappy main street in Mitchelstown, but now I am content with the money and the peace that such loss has brought. I roamed the streets of Dublin in such anger, never realising that I was learning to love them as I stepped along, planning my next act of vengeance.

I bought as many of the Dublin and London papers as I could, moving from shop to shop, and debated taking them into some quiet café to peruse, but it being a fine day, I resolved to walk away from the busy city and towards the Queen's College, then directed my steps out towards the Mardyke and its leafy cover. There I found a quiet park seat in the shade to begin my reading, my search. Sitting in the gentle sunshine with the ladies of Sunday's Well strolling past, I read quickly through the *Freeman's Journal*, extracting the pages with the brief accounts of the happenings in the Old Bailey and making a small bundle for my reticule, but my quick reading elicited little new information, except that the Doctor's son was quite clearly in trouble and much of it of his own making. The reports talk about what they call specific charges against him and another man called Alfred Taylor, but as to what they are, no paper will say. The *Cork Examiner* writes that Wilde had been 'betraying tokens of the keenest anxiety' but is otherwise a model of discretion.

After I had read, I relaxed and sat in the sun. Women walked past, one or two with children; the young men from Queen's College made their way towards a match. I remember how, with my own troubles, at first I delighted in collecting the morning papers and reading each day's account of the courtroom, believing that the justice of my cause would blazon forth from the pages, filling Dublin with indignation on my behalf. Soon, as I read each day's report, I began to realise that the papers were laughing at the case, the petty details, the pamphlets and my crazed story about the chloroform, and I began to see myself as they did: Moll Travers, a dangerous woman scorned. So now, as I devoured the papers, I searched with a dry mouth for my name. But there was no sign of it. The Marquess of Queensberry has been in some sort of brawl with his son outside the Old Bailey. Each paper delights in the details of the scuffle, the punches thrown, the amused crowd gathering, the noble lord being dragged off to police custody. All this seemed to be a universe away from the dull, safe respectability of an April afternoon in Cork.

I made my way back along the Mardyke, the spring sunlight now a little more pleasant to me, less fearful that the name of Mary Travers will appear in a newspaper. A little breeze had started as I walked towards the hotel, the solid burghers of Cork waiting for trams home to villas in Sunday's Well and Tivoli. As I turned into the Imperial Hotel, I could see Emily at her tea table, with one of her friends from a sewing circle in Mitchelstown. They fell silent as I approached, and I was reintroduced to this woman, the rather dour-looking Miss Sarah Bowen. My sister assumed that I remember her, but her friends all seem much the same to me: redundant single Protestant ladies, like us.

'My dear,' Emily greeted me, and already I felt some apprehension because she was using her public voice with me, the one when she addresses me smiling, as if opening a temperance meeting. When she uses this tone, Emily tries to assert an authority she does not always feel, the practical younger sister impelled to take command of her bookish unworldly older sister. Unusually I refuse to engage with such nonsense. 'Sarah has kindly offered me accommodation in her suite here at the hotel for a week and so I will stay on. Perhaps you might give Lady Kingston my compliments and Mr Naylor my apologies for not accompanying you to the dockside?'

Only the presence of Miss Bowen prevented me from interrogating Emily directly. I had been ambushed. What was she doing? I should have guessed with all her packing and her clucking around the house last night, a veritable whirlwind of activity. Now I was forced to spend four hours with this unknown quantity, this Mr Naylor, while Emily sewed and stitched in Cork. I considered a retort, relishing the look of anxiety on Emily's face as she strove to keep everything civilised. Yet something was not quite right. I did not like the unconcerned look on her face, the unaccustomed beads of light sweat on her upper lip, so I nodded my acquiescence, ignoring the few attempts of her sewing companion, the grave-mannered Miss Bowen, to engage me in conversation. Emily pressed tea on me, all solicitude for my imminent journey, but the day had left me without appetite and so I refused, collected my things, and made my way to the Kingston carriage, waiting outside the hotel, and instructed Kenneth to drive down the docks to meet the boat.

We were a little delayed with all the carriages along the quays and so when we arrived at the landing dock, I left the carriage hurriedly, instructing Kenneth to wait. The boat had already docked and the passengers were all being greeted, so I made my way to Mr Naylor as soon as I could. I was familiar with his large photograph in the Countess's drawing room – a smooth-looking man, elegant and unsmiling – and I instantly recognised him standing at the dockside in the chill evening sunlight, his luggage all round him, and a dark-haired young porter looking harried. I say that I recognised him but, in fact, what I recognised was his resemblance to his younger self. Mr Naylor was no longer the handsome man of his portrait. Years, an increasing girth and a grey goatee, like that of the late Emperor of the French, Louis Napoleon, had altered him. Of course, his seated portrait had not alerted me to his shortness of stature.

As I drew near, I could hear him address the porter and, as I did so, the tone of his words, a little louder and slower than necessary, weighed with confrontation and importance.

'Young man, I am more sinned against than sinning.'

I halted, loath to interrupt what was clearly a moment of public humiliation for the defenceless porter. I waited, hearing more than I wished to hear.

'The porter assured me in Euston that my luggage would arrive before me.'

The man said nothing, his dark eyes expressionless and closed down, his face pale in spite of his self-control.

'You are not fit to wear this uniform,' Mr Naylor concluded, catching a button on the youth's tunic and tugging at it.

He turned and I caught his eye.

'Mr Naylor?' I asked.

He took off his hat and bowed.

'I am Mary Travers. The Countess asked me to come and meet you. I believe she sent a telegram.'

He shot a look at me over his spectacles – a direct look of intense distrust, somewhat mitigated by the soft blue beauty of his eyes. He hesitated, but I could see him deciding to be genial.

'Indeed she did, Miss Travers. My dear wife has written to me about you and your sister. I had the pleasure of some slight acquaintance with your late father and I have been looking forward to meeting you.'

He turned back to the porter and shook a finger at him.

'I have not finished with you, young man.'

I stood on the dockside, patiently waiting while he enjoyed making threats against the continued employment of the porter. The sharp April wind that had begun to rise off the river Lee was no less unwelcome than the sharp realisation that this was our new master, that our time under the benign rule of the Countess was over. Mr Naylor took my arm and, full of solicitude for me in the darkening evening, walked me back to the carriage. After a great deal of fussing around with rugs, coats and hand luggage, with Kenneth's patience stretched to the full by some deliberate wrong-footing over the luggage by his master, we began our long trip back to the Castle and I cursed Emily for leaving me in such an inescapable prison, that of Mr Naylor's eloquence.

As we moved through the darkening countryside, he spoke of his year in the Levant and his love of Rome and its classical ruins. He was all geniality. Nevertheless, I knew that something lurked behind this bonhomie and, as we approached Mitchelstown in the darkness, the blow fell.

'When I was in London, the newspapers were full of nothing but this dreadful Queensberry trial and that depraved Oscar Wilde! It became tiresome beyond belief the amount of tittle-tattle on which people are prepared to waste their time, and about such a degenerate.'

I said nothing and he fell silent. We were approaching the road to the Castle and Kenneth was drawing up the carriage to my door when Mr Naylor spoke again.

'Oh forgive me, Miss Travers, but I may have offended you inadvertently. You knew the Wildes, didn't you?'

Finally it had come, as I had dreaded: my past, like a thief in the night.

I stepped down from the carriage.

'Once,' I said, 'and only very slightly.'

Friday 19 April

It is now five days since Mr Naylor returned and Emily is still in Cork. A succession of short notes arrive in the post, pleading fatigue and putting off her return. So in Cork she remains. Each note brings with it a list of tiresome domestic tasks: small bills to be paid, plants to be watered, eggs to be collected and then any surplus brought down to Mrs Sheehan's dairy, to be counted against our milk bill. In these myriad ways does Emily enjoy her days, and it disconcerts me to realise how much of our domestic well-being is derived from her incessant labours. The kitchen has grown untidy and so I have asked Louie if her old mother might give me some hours to help with the cleaning. She has agreed because her mother would find my few shillings very welcome. These endlessly trivial duties have kept me later about the house than I would have wished but, nevertheless, I have persisted with my daily visits up to the Castle.

When I began to work in the library a year ago, the chaos was painful to contemplate: a fine collection neglected, the spines dirty, some damaged and out of shape, a place where learning was being maltreated by neglect. I began by persuading Louie to bring cloths and brushes up to the tower room. This was no easy task since she is formidable, despite her youth and delicate looks, and I have but little standing in this impoverished Castle, at the lowest rung of authority. I mentioned the surplus eggs Emily has found herself with and asked if Louie knew of anyone who might oblige us by taking some. Thus she helped in exchange for the eggs. The wages of the few Castle servants are meagre and, I dare say, irregularly paid, but employment as easy and lax as this has its compensations, and Louie, I understand, does like to be able to quote her ladyship about the town.

Thanks to Emily's hens, Louie cleaned and dusted, leaving the large windows open as the air grew thick with spicy dust and silverfish. Then, with her help, I dragged the larger volumes on to the floor and began to use them to repair the smaller books that had been left carelessly open. These books had pages that were mashed and folded into themselves, thankfully without any great damage. We used the large dictionaries and Bibles to press the smaller books back into shape, stacking them on the mahogany tables. The longer tables served as a place to line up the books and begin the long task of reassembling the main collections into proper order: the complete bound series of Fielding, Austen, Edgeworth, Burney; the natural science albums, the dictionaries, the Latin and Greek texts. Someone, perhaps Big George, more likely the land agent, a bookish man perhaps, had bought well when commissioning this library and, as I worked at the reshelving, the richness of the library became apparent. I made a rudimentary catalogue, as well as moving the desks, cleaning the lamps. Sometimes the Countess would come in and join me, asking if she could assist with the restacking, admiring as she did the red, blue or gold bindings. Rarely have I been so happy in my life as at the end of certain days in the library this past year, the twilight sunset slanted low through the narrow library windows, my eyes, arms and back tired from the work, the books at peace in their ordered shelves. Each book seemed to me to be brimming with possible life, content to await the loving hand of an avid reader, confident that such a reader will indeed come. I suspect and rather hope that Emily derives equivalent happiness from her weekly egg account.

I was reminded of my father in Marsh's Library and his years of unpaid labour there as assistant librarian. And now, finally, I began to understand why it was his refuge, his solace. Of course, all Papa really wanted was to be the Keeper of Manuscripts there and he would have achieved this, but for the notoriety I had brought on him. He never spoke of it, but at a meeting, in the years after my court case, his name was proposed and then dropped. More damage I have wrought with my infatuation for the Doctor and my savage indignation at his withdrawal from me.

The Countess kindly allowed me my own key to the tower room, and so I can make my way through the kitchen gardens, into the pantry, which is habitually open, with Hannah at work cooking or Louie ironing, and then, as quietly as I can, I ascend the tower room. However, Mr Naylor's study is in the passageway leading into the library tower and so I approach this corridor apprehensively, for, since his return, he has taken to the unsettling habit of leaving his door ajar, and I find it very difficult to get past him without being called in on one trivial matter or another. The corridor is dark, usually deserted and lined with mouldy old hangings the colour of dried blood, but Emily, who notices such things, tells me that these hangings, lining most of the corridors in the Castle and the main reception rooms, are made of damask of the highest quality. One evening, as we were making our way up to the drawing room, she stopped by a window and examined the material.

'Look, Mary, I told you – the finest damask', and she turned the damp-looking hanging at one corner and caressed the soft fabric with her thumb. There, on the reverse, was the original design, a beautiful deep crimson, shot through with threads of gold – a glimpse of oriental beauty, cloth for a Pasha. After that, I could never look at the musty old hangings with quite the same contempt.

Most of these afternoons Mr Naylor is elsewhere around the Castle but, on the one or two occasions he has been in his study, his soft voice called to me as I attempted to glide past and I have been forced to make conversation with him. It is never any matter of importance, but I sense that he is toying with me, waiting to strike. He has been making mischief amongst the few remaining Castle servants, hinting at the need for retrenchment and dismissals, quietly slandering each of them to the other in a bid to make favourites, hoping to set them at odds with each other. This has failed because they all need each other more than they need him and so, now, a tighter ring of dislike has grown around him. I need that protection and to let the servants know that I am not Mr Naylor's ally.

My chance came when, yesterday, Hannah, who has worked for the Countess for many years, decided to follow me up to the tower room on the pretext of bringing me some tea. I accepted the tea and allowed her to linger with the door closed while she pretended to admire the books. She is a discreet woman of my own age, who works continuously without complaint, but her eyes are direct and unflinching in a face worn with work. Their honesty is part of their beauty.

'Such an array of learnin', Miss. The whole place is a credit to you,' she said, in reverential tones. 'Her ladyship is only delighted in the great interest you're takin' in the place.'

She paused and turned towards me.

I smiled and raised my eyebrows slightly, a clear invitation to her to talk about Mr Naylor, as discreetly as we could dare.

'Yes, indeed, Hannah. Her ladyship has been so kind to me; this is the very least I can do. I only wish I could do more. I can only imagine how difficult a responsibility the Castle has become for her.'

Hannah sat down and relaxed into a complicity based on the fiction that we were united in our concern for the Countess. The truth was that both of us felt threatened by the interloper's resumption of husbandly authority and needed all the attendant support we could muster against his meddling.

'Sure, there isn't a spare penny for the poor woman.' She dropped her voice, even though we were alone in the vast room with the door closed.

'And Mister Naylor has done his level best – doin' all the books and accounts himself, but the estate is nearly ruined.'

I needed all the information I could glean about Naylor, to protect myself against the information he had undoubtedly stored up about me. I prompted her to go on by saying, 'But, fortunately, he is a wealthy man himself.'

She looked at me and nodded, as if this was a natural progression from the earlier part of our conversation.

'Yes, the land up in Tipperary is all his, from his uncle, and some houses in Waterford too. And he's a great traveller, always settin' off to Italy or even the Holy Land last year. Such a learned man.'

Hannah stopped. Her head turned towards the door, her ear moving slightly upwards.

'Her ladyship is very lucky to have his support,' I said, and we both nodded, the real information passed, the wife living in penury in this barracks, the husband flitting off whenever he could from the financial mess he had created within her affairs. And she never complained.

Later I made an unpleasant discovery in the library. I was clearing out an old box of books left mouldering under a table when I came across a familiar green-bound volume. Jane's poems, embossed with a harp in a sturdy binding. I had had my own copy once, with her inscription written on the flyleaf, in the early days when she was beginning to befriend me and dazzle me with her intelligence and her talents. I have it no longer, burnt in a rage with all her other gifts that final day when she snubbed me in her own house. I picked up the volume and held it. That was a book I regretted burning. In fact, it is the only book I have ever destroyed. The inscription read, 'To Dearest Mary, a sign of the future and a signal of hope for Ireland's young womanhood, from your true friend, Speranza.'

I opened the abandoned volume of her poems and turned to the flyleaf. I blinked. There it was: the same semi-illegible writing, the same words of dedication. But this time it was her dearest Anna who was a signal of hope for Ireland's young womanhood. So the Countess knew her too; knew her well. Why did she never mention this to me? I glared at the book, wanting to commit my second murder of a book. Then a thought occurred to me. I got up, fetched my writing case and put the book down on the desk. Preparing the nib, I crossed out 'Anna' and wrote 'Mary' instead. Then I put the book away in my satchel. It was mine again.

Sunday 28 April
Mr Naylor, having dropped the name of Oscar Wilde like a tincture of venom into my ear, has given it a week or so to fester and today decided to reopen the subject. I was coming down the stairs from the library late this afternoon when, to my dismay, I saw that the door of his study was wide open and light pouring out. I stopped, like a guilty child, in the dark corridor, and waited, considering retracing my steps back up to the library, as quietly as I could, but he called out my name. I cursed, silently, and then made my way smiling into his room, pretending to fuss with my bag, to cover up my momentary hesitation. I have never liked that room; it is dark and stuffy, with one window overlooking the stables and furnished with heavy tables and chairs with green velvet upholstery.

'Miss Travers.' He greeted me with his sweetest smile, his blue eyes shining with a tender regard. 'You have been labouring again in the library. Really we are greatly in your debt that you can spare so much time and come to our home so often. Please do sit down; you must be tired out from your Herculean labour of restoring order to the collection.'

'Not at all. It is my great pleasure. My sister and I have been so welcomed here that it is the least I can do.'

I was still smarting from the sting, the implication that I was making free with his home and without his permission. I was relatively sure that the Countess was still the legal owner of this albatross of debt and old silver, but Mr Naylor was above such niceties.

'And we are fortunate to have you both here and to be able to provide such entertainment as the library may afford you, although, with rents as they are, our agent has been making dark noises about the upkeep of both the Castle and the College. My dear wife is quite unsettled but, as I have reassured her, the College must be maintained, as long as my own meagre resources are at her disposal.'

Again, I am being warned: I am paying for your keep. Untrue of course, but it is nothing I can challenge directly.

'However, enough of business. Here, my dear Miss Travers, I thought you might like to read the latest account from London of this dreadful Wilde case. It seems as if your friend will be sent to prison for his immoral behaviour.'

I laughed, in a favourable way.

'Friend is indeed an overgenerous term, Mr Naylor. I don't think I have seen the unfortunate man since he was in petticoats, rising four years of age. That must be over thirty years ago.'

Mr Naylor laughed, too, as if I had made a ribald remark. 'Petticoats! Miss Travers, what a wag you are. You might well have advised him for his own good to stay in petticoats and not to stray into other men's underclothes.'

The blood rushed to my face. So he knew! Moll Travers was the kind of woman with whom a gentleman need not bother with niceties. Given her history, a little club room coarseness was permitted.

He stood up, handed me the newspaper and thrust his other hand into his pocket; it stayed there, but did not stay still.

That decided me. I stood up too, ignoring the proffered newspaper and started to gather myself for an immediate withdrawal. I would have given much to have read that newspaper but these little conversations had to be nipped in the bud.

'You must forgive me, Mr Naylor,' I said, all gentle, firm politeness. 'I am intruding on your time and I must get to the post-box before five o'clock. My sister will be waiting to hear from me.'

He started to demur but I avoided all eye contact with him, pretended not to hear his concluding remarks and made my escape down the corridor and into the kitchen. What did that newspaper say

about Wilde? What was this jibe about men's underclothes? The sin of
the father, but in another form, the Greek form, as Papa would have
dubbed it. This was my conjecture but I had to know.

> The Imperial Hotel
> Cork
> *Tuesday 30 April*

I had promised myself that I would never again find myself alone
with Mr Naylor in his study but, early this morning, just as I was
preparing breakfast; a knock came to my door. It was Hannah.

'He wants to see you straight away up in his study. A telegram is
after coming from Cork from Miss Emily.'

I must have looked startled for Hannah hurried to reassure me.

''Tis all right. Maggie the postmistress told me; it came late yesterday.
It's only that Miss Emily has been taken unwell but she is better now,
thank God, and she wants you to go and visit her.'

I told Hannah that I would follow her to the Castle and, as I hurried
up the terrace, I cursed Naylor and his eternal meddling. Why would
Emily contact him instead of me? Then I remembered. As misfortune
would have it, the Countess is away this week from the Castle, on
a visit to Doneraile Court, and so he opens all her post. I made my
hands into protective fists, put them into my side pockets and made
my way up to his study.

He was waiting, telegram in hand, all tender solicitude.

'Dear Miss Travers, I sent for you as soon as the news arrived. Please
do sit down and compose yourself.'

He held on to the telegram, and it was all I could do not to snatch
it away from him. He ushered me into a seat and then fussed around,
offering me brandy for shock. I was sure that Hannah's reassurances
that Emily was now well again were true but, still, I needed to see
the telegram.

'What is it, Mr Naylor?' I burst out. 'What does my sister say?'

'Well, it's actually from her friend Miss Bowen. It transpires that
your sister has been taken ill and has been removed to a nursing home.

Miss Bowen wishes you to go into Cork today.' Finally he handed me the telegram.

It read: 'Countess of Kingston, Mitchelstown Castle. Please inform Miss Travers that sister requests her to visit Glenvera Nursing Home, Wellington Road, Cork immediately. Sister recently unwell but now recovered. No cause for alarm. Please come. Miss Sarah Bowen.'

Although Hannah had told me that my sister was now well again, why could he not have said it, too, just in case? And why did Miss Bowen not contact me directly?

He was all solicitude.

'Since my dear wife is away, please allow me to assist you. Kenneth can bring you to the Fermoy train this afternoon and, if you wish, I will telegram the Imperial Hotel and reserve a room. I shall see that your telegram will be brought straight to the post office. You might also wish to contact the Glenvera Nursing Home and assure them of your imminent arrival. You may draft those messages here while I give Kenneth his orders.'

He gave my arm a reassuring squeeze and led me to his desk. I nodded, my mind racing. I should pack and fetch some money from our strong box in the bedroom. I might have to spend some days in Cork. Louie would have to be given a key and some money, to feed the hens and keep the house in order. Emily unwell? That seemed scarcely real in the light of all this early morning haste, and so I put that from my mind.

He left and I settled myself at his desk and began writing my brief messages. It was then that I noticed it. On the floor under his desk was a sheet of notepaper. The name Wilde caught my eye. I got up and looked out of the window. I could see Mr Naylor making his hurried little way down to the coach house, waddling like the pompous little duck he was. I picked up the paper.

To the Editor of the *Cork Constitution*:
'Your recent account of the opening of the Oscar Wilde trial in the Old Bailey brings to mind, to this correspondent at least, two other encounters in the courtrooms of Dublin between members of the

Wilde family and the legal profession, and it may interest your readers to learn of a County Cork connection with one of those celebrated cases. The Wildes senior, Sir William and Lady Wilde, the noted poetess Speranza, were more than fond of a joust with the judiciary, and Oscar Wilde may have picked up his penchant for legal wrangling from the distaff side since Speranza was a central figure in two noted cases, the first involving the nationalist newspaper *The Nation.*'

There it stopped. It was dated yesterday. Did he draft it after my hasty departure? Was it to be sent? I replaced it on the floor. I finished off my messages, got up and made my way out of the study just as Mr Naylor was hurrying back down the corridor, bursting with manufactured solicitude.

'It is all settled. Kenneth will call for you as soon as you are ready and you should make the Cork train in Fermoy with time to spare.'

He took the papers from my outstretched hand.

'And these messages will go from the post office before noon. This I guarantee you. I shall see to it myself.'

Since Hannah would most likely be responsible for these, I felt disobliged to thank him too profusely, but I had to pretend that I hadn't seen his drafted letter. Was it there solely to taunt me? I shook his hand and hurried back to the house, packing for Cork and drawing out money from the safe. Emily normally doled out the money to me. I was surprised at how much was there. I took some extra bank notes. When Kenneth came for me at noon, I gave him a note for Louie, with some money enclosed, asking her to call into our house in my absence, to clean, feed the hens and keep all secure.

Only when I was safely on the Cork train did I allow myself to think of Emily. Unwell? With her strong constitution? I had been so frail in the year after the court case and had depended on her and Mamma so much. Then, later, when Mamma herself became ill, it was Emily who took much of the burden of nursing and consultation as the cancer spread and Mamma needed so much of our care. Papa had been of no assistance, troubled as he was with the disappointment over Marsh's Library and, I suspect, with secret guilt at his own lack of any real concern for his wife.

These thoughts returned to trouble me and so, as soon as I reached Cork, I resolved to walk quickly to the Imperial Hotel to leave my luggage there and then make my way on foot to the Glenvera Nursing Home, in the street above the railway station. Such walking kept me from thinking. As soon as I mentioned my name to the porter, the helpful matron was sent for, and she immediately drew me into an ante-room, and with a great deal of deliberation explained that on the previous night, in the Imperial Hotel, Emily had taken a fit, some sort of apoplexy, and Miss Bowen, who was staying with her, had called for medical assistance. The matron, speaking as if she were reading her words from a sheet, told me that a doctor had examined Emily, pronounced her out of danger but recommended that she be kept quiet.

'So now, Miss Travers, your sister is at rest, sedated in fact, by the doctor's orders and should be kept in seclusion. However, she is anxious to see you. Could you return early tomorrow, when her strength has come back?'

The matron then struck her head in mock anger. 'I have a head like a sieve. I forgot to give you this.'

She handed me a paper with a handwritten list. I recognised Emily's neat writing.

'She needs a few things for herself and asked if you could bring these in the morning.'

I agreed to do this and left. I stood outside in the strong sunlight and read the list. Grapes, sewing thread, a Mrs Braddon novel (what else!), face powder, stockings, a small bottle of lavender water, a sleeping draught, chloroform. I stopped. Why did she write that down? Was she mocking me? Then I realised that the sordid details of my court case were not ingrained on Emily's memory.

I walked for as long as I could around the busy streets of Cork, drawing out each purchase, then lingered to watch the shops being closed up and shuttered. When the streets were finally darkened, I made my way back to the Imperial Hotel, ordered a light supper to be brought to my room and here I sit, trying not to think of that letter or of Emily and her sudden fall from health.

MAY

Jane's son was arrested in London last week. Mr Naylor was correct. It is in all the newspapers and, since the ladies' lounge was deserted this morning, I was free to read away from prying eyes. One account of the case says that Oscar had ample time to escape when the libel case collapsed but, instead, he sat waiting to be arrested, drinking hock and seltzer and reading a French novel in the Cadogan Hotel. I had no such luxury when my libel case ended – just a flight back to Mamma's unwilling arms and a collapse into months of sleepless anxiety and living dread. Another newspaper tells of three hundred men crossing over to France last night on the Dover train, all terrified of a witch-hunt and more arrests. In the same newspaper, it describes the scene where Oscar's mother, here called the poetess Speranza and said to be living in Chelsea, came to the Cadogan Hotel yesterday afternoon as her son sat drinking and told him that if he stayed in London and even went to jail, he would be her son for ever, but that if he fled to France, she would never forgive him.

So she is alive. That sounds just like her, all ringing passion and conviction and full of the worst possible advice. No one but a fool would stay where there is a risk of a prison sentence. From what I can tell, the evidence is damning and a conviction certain. A man like that, well-brought up, a scholar, living in such rooms as this comfortable Cork hotel bedroom where I sit and write, such a man would perish and die in the hell of prison.

Did she learn nothing from our battle in court, where she and I were the losers, and Mr Isaac Butt, the lawyer, was enriched by our foolish squabble?

I went to see Emily this morning after breakfast. She was lying on a day bed, looking much as she always does, a little pale from her medication perhaps, but otherwise well. I put down the various parcels on the table at the foot of her bed, making sure the chloroform was upright. On her night table, next to the expensive flowers, I noticed Mamma's rosary beads, the dark ruby set with the black enamel detailing. Where had they come from? They had disappeared after Mamma's death and I presumed that Emily had given them to the night nurse who had tended Mamma, Old Mother Anna, but no, here they were. Before I could ask about them, she began.

'Mary, I need to speak to you about money.' She struggled to sit up but then changed her mind. 'That is why I asked Miss Bowen to send for you.'

'Money? I have some here, brought in from the safe at home, if you need some. We seem to have a great deal of cash at the moment.' I glanced around. 'This place must be expensive.'

She shook her head. 'Keep that money for yourself; I have ample funds with me. You must settle some of our affairs for me because I am unwell.'

She nodded downwards towards a leather case on the ground. It looked new and expensive.

'Hand me that, please.'

She was unusually curt, not unfriendly, but seemed to be in something of a hurry. I handed her the case and she took out some letters and a large blue bank book.

'It is necessary that you travel to Dublin, to our solicitor on Ely Place. This document must be handed directly to him. I have written to him and he is expecting you this week and will have some papers for you to sign. Can you also call to the Munster and Leinster Bank in Cork today? You are to become the main account-holder while I am indisposed. I have enclosed another letter for the bank manager and I have filled out the relevant documentation.'

'But Emily, why all this rush of business? Are we short of money? I have always left that sort of bother to you. Why change now?'

She smiled, opened the bank book and handed it to me. There on the end of a page was a set of figures, recording recent lodgements. The last total, dated the previous month, was well over seven thousand pounds.

'Emily, where did we get all this money?'

'I have been lodging the rents from Mamma's Dublin houses directly into this account. That is why you must become a named account-holder while I am unable to conduct this business. The solicitor will have over two hundred pounds for us in Dublin for this quarter alone.'

'But what have we been living on? The money you draw each month?'

'That is our stipend from the College.'

'What stipend? Have we been taking money from the Countess? She is poor.'

'Not the Countess. The trustees of the College have a fund for each resident, a hundred pounds a year.' She smiled, faintly. 'The Kingston estate cannot touch it or else it would have been squandered years ago.'

She lay back in the bed, tired from our conversation, and closed her eyes. So much letter-writing and yet I was told that she had been sedated for the past day. And this other revelation: so much ready money and all of it ours.

Emily seemed unwilling to talk further and so I unwrapped the grapes and placed them in a dish by her bedside. Mamma's rosary beads lay on the table, near my handbag, and I picked them up, slipped them into my purse as I was gathering up the documents, then kissed Emily goodbye and made my way out and down into the city. I would be in Dublin before she noticed and then could blame some nun or orderly for the theft. As I stood by the bank doors, a thought struck me. Our money. I could almost hear it. I would go to Dublin, conduct such business as Emily required and, with all those banknotes in my purse, I would find out what I could about Jane.

Finn's Hotel
Dublin
Thursday 2 May

In the Imperial Hotel, as I packed my bags for Dublin, it occurred to me that I knew no reliable place to stay there and so I requested the hotel manager to reserve me a room in some quiet establishment in the centre of Dublin, suitable for a female travelling alone.

I have never before stayed in a hotel in Dublin and therefore the true power of those folded banknotes in my purse soon became apparent, the first-class railway ticket, delicious tea baskets brought on at Mallow, the luxury of a covered cab from the station to the hotel. I had asked the manager in Cork to write ahead and secure me a good room in Dublin for an indefinite period, checking that the rates were reasonable, but it was only as the growler drew up in front of this hotel last night that I realised where I was staying. Finn's Hotel is right on Lincoln Place, near his old surgery rooms and within sight of the house on Merrion Square. Here, at my dressing table, as I write, I remember the door to William's surgery where his old servant, Barney, held sway as doorkeeper, keeping the many patients in order, and eventually, when I became desperate to see William, also keeping me out. Of course, the Merrion Square house was lost in the collapse after William's death, and Jane and her sons are long ago settled in London, but still, as I descended the stairs and was escorted into the dining room by the attentive manager, I almost expected a challenge, her tall figure blocking my way, demanding my immediate removal from this respectable establishment.

With Jane's spectre in mind, this morning, on my way to Ely Place to call on the solicitor, I deliberately went there through Merrion Square, staring down the house on the corner as I strode past in my elegant new summer coat and hat, daring the windows to frown out their disapproval. This is my first time to be at liberty in Dublin since the end of the trial and Mamma's insistence, as soon as I was fit, that we should move out to Greystones, away from all public view. Today, as I made my way here and there on the busy pavements, I was reminded again and again of Jane and of her distinctive manner of walking – that stately, unhurried progress that flattered anyone walking with her, a sense that you were with someone innately majestic and that an aura of majesty was being conferred on all around her. Her entire concentration was on you and if you said something that struck her, she would stop, maybe place her hand on your arm and smile. She was the one person I have ever met who could flatter you just by walking at your side.

Jane would walk around Dublin with me in the early evenings that first year, thirty-five years ago, when her husband and I had just begun our intimacy, and we would pace the short distance from Merrion Square to Westland Row and then make our leisurely way around by Trinity College, up to the Green and then on to Leeson Street and home again, watching the summer light linger on and on in the softly clouded blue sky. She would say, 'My dear Mary, I was born on Leeson Street. William married me from there and took me to Westland Row where both my boys were born, and now I find myself living in Merrion Square. Such tiny distances for such large leaps of faith.'

The walks I took with her around Dublin became more and more frequent the following year as my late afternoon visits to the Doctor's surgery decreased. Maybe she had been instructed to keep me away from him as his ardour cooled. In this, am I being unfair to her? Perhaps she was lonely too. When, eventually, Jane began to withdraw from me, the full force of betrayal became clear and my anger filled these wide streets of Dublin.

The solicitor was ready to see me this morning at noon as soon as I called to his chambers. I was slightly surprised at his readiness; lawyers had been none too pleased to see me after Papa's death and often kept me waiting, but then I remembered that Emily and I must be worth a great deal to him in respect of commissions. He went to some trouble to make sure that I was comfortably seated and I treated his solicitude and fussy respect for my comfort and well-being with the silence it deserved, which seemed to make him even more attentive. He had a great deal of paperwork for me to sign. Emily had written with instructions to make me a co-signatory on the bank deposit account and also to place me as co-owner on the renewed contracts for the leasing of Mamma's various Dublin properties. As I finished signing, the solicitor sanded and dried the documents and told me that I now had complete legal access to all our business details.

'Thank you, Miss Travers. I also have the annual dividends from the railway shares here for you, if you wish to retain the cash or lodge them in your own account. Since you are now a joint signatory, you may lodge the money today with the Munster and Leinster Bank, where your sister has another deposit account. Here is the receipt, with my own fee deducted.'

Another account. I looked down at the receipt. We have earned over seventy pounds in dividends this year. That would keep me in Finn's Hotel for the rest of the summer. I decided to lodge it today and see how much money Emily had been putting away here in Dublin. After all, it was my money too.

'One final matter,' the solicitor said. 'Your sister asked me to contact the trustees of Marsh's Library. She is anxious to ascertain the whereabouts of your late father's portrait, the one that you both presented to the library after his death.'

'I had forgotten about that. What reply did the library give you? Have they displayed Papa's portrait as we requested.'

He sighed.

'The Library is not known for its efficiency. My three letters and my personal call there have yielded no response as yet. The Keeper, Mr Maturin, has been ill and has been confined to his home in Howth for the past few months and some assistant is now in charge.'

Mr Maturin. Jane's cousin. Her 'Coz Wills'. The same man I had met frequently years ago in Merrion Square. I did not relish meeting him again but needs must. I stood up. With all this money and my new hat and coat, I felt equal to any challenge. We had given the library that picture on the firm understanding that it should be displayed. It was the very least they could do for a man who had expended his meagre affections on their precious books.

'I shall call there myself in the next day or two when I have completed my bank business.'

The solicitor took my hand and shook it warmly and, as he did, I debated asking him a question. After all, he worked for us. Still my caution kept me silent.

I had lunch in Finn's Hotel and then wrote some letters, one to Emily concerning our business affairs, letting her know that I would remain in Dublin for several days more, perhaps even a week or so, and another, more polite one, to the Countess telling her much the same. I sent a curt note to the Keeper of Manuscripts at Marsh's Library informing him that I would be calling in the following days to discuss the displaying of my late father's portrait. I could have deposited my letters with the hotel porter but, instead I decided to walk out and post them myself. On the way to the post office, I walked up the steps of the Munster and Leinster Bank on Grafton Street to lodge some of our money. The clerk took the documents from me and issued me with my own deposit book. We had over two thousand pounds in this account. Emily had money hidden in the safe in our dining room in Mitchelstown, in the account in the bank in Cork and here in Dublin.

On the way back to the hotel, after tea in the Shelbourne Hotel and a visit to a bookshop to extend my stock of the Palliser novels of Trollope, I walked for an hour or so out by Baggot Street, enjoying the warm country breeze rushing down from Donnybrook and then, with the evening still bright, began to make my way back to the hotel.

I stood for a few moments outside the Doctor's old surgery rooms in Lincoln Place, now a small chemist's shop. A basket of lemon soaps was on display in the window and I wondered what they had done with his surgery room at the back. Probably a store room now. I thought about the giddily exciting moments I had spent in the shabby, yet spotless, room over thirty years ago. His man Barney always kept this room clean for the patients. The late evening light slanting through the window, the smell of strong soap in the porcelain dishes, the old ottoman sofa where we lay. I could close my eyes and see the room before me as if in a painting. That handful of hurried visits here and later our time at the house in Werburgh Street and in Monaghan have been my entire experience of love-making, apart from Corney Wall's fumblings and a chaste kiss or two with poor deluded Frederick. Those do not count, in any real reckoning at all. An hour, here and there, in the course of a brief year. Put together, all those hours would hardly make a full day.

I stood for a few minutes and thought of my younger self rushing along the pavement, all thoughts of the assignation making my feet glide and almost lift clear upwards, the warm blood on my face feeling as if it was tingling, the impatient, gliding step over the shabby threshold, the ritual of pretence that each time was a further medical consultation, the Doctor politely removing more and more of my clothing and then, almost apologetically removing his. His body was the only other body I have known well, apart from my own, and even now I can see it and recognise that it was a beautiful body. In his dark clothes, he was a serious-looking, rather colourless middle-aged man, but without them he was unexpectedly youthful, each line of muscle clear as if carved from stone, the body of a man of energy and decision. He had the name of being a grubby man, according to that tiresome Mr Yeats the painter, but I knew him to be clean and sweet to all my senses.

Standing there today, in the warm evening air, I thought of those few hours of pleasure all those years ago, but all I could remember was the pain that they brought me, the sense of rage, and the court case. It seems to me now that those moments of pleasure were not at all worth the destruction they caused. I am certain that three of the women I know well – Emily, our neighbours Miss Isabella and Miss Ada – have lived and will die without knowing a lover's body, and I envy them. The memory of such lost physical pleasure stabs much more sharply than any vague regret for untasted love.

Friday 3 May
Today I was unequal to much business and so I sit here in my room and write this diary, trying to keep the riot of thoughts at bay. All my books wearied me and so now, with supper over, all I can do is write and try to put order on my frantic thoughts by setting them down on paper. It was said in court that I had first met the Doctor when my mother brought me to him to treat a chronic ear infection but, like so many of the court reports, that is not quite accurate. In truth, I first met him in Marsh's Library where I had gone one grey November afternoon to rattle my father about my dress allowance. Papa had just been appointed Professor of Medicine at Trinity College and was due to receive the

first instalment of his new salary that morning; so I decided to strike before his creditors did. My brown winter coat was in sad disrepair and my summer gloves were becoming more and more inadequate in the darkening winter days. Mamma was being unpleasant about my dress allowance since I had decided to convert to the Church of Ireland. She would barely speak to me, and so Papa was my only source of funds, and a very unreliable one at that.

I let myself in the old unpainted wooden door of the library; it was always unlocked, although few readers ever came there in Papa's time. I knew that he would be in the reading room at the back of the library, hiding behind his catalogue. When I tapped on the glass door, his loud voice bade me enter. Papa was the most ineffectual of men, though he did have a resounding voice, giving him a false air of authority and determination. He looked hunted as I entered the room, probably aware of me stalking through the library towards him but he smiled and rose to meet me. 'Mary, my dear, what brings you here?' trying to usher me into a chair. The room was, as always, neat and orderly, a stark contrast to the disorder of his own dirty little home nearby where he had gone to live after separating from Mamma, a place with broken furniture and a filthy carpet.

I stayed standing.

'Money, Papa. You promised me a dress allowance this quarter. I have three shillings in my purse and nothing else.'

That was not quite true, but Papa always needed firm prodding.

'Today is the day for your Trinity salary to be paid, is it not?' I asked.

Papa looked startled as he stood there. He grasped one hand into another and then stared at me, like a child confessing.

'My dear girl, I'm afraid it is not. It transpires that my predecessor, the late Dr Curran, was overpaid for his last three years and now there are not sufficient funds for a current salary. I must hold the post for another two years before remuneration is possible.'

Something close to rage began to make the blood around my ears grow warm. I felt a gust of impatience with him.

'Oh, Papa, how could you allow yourself to be treated like this by such a wealthy institution?'

He looked down, a protective blandness coming across his face. Suddenly, too suddenly, I heard Mamma in my tone and disliked the feeling. As always with my father and with any practical concerns, my sense was that of pitching a tent on unsteady ground. There could never be any firm foothold. I changed my tone and became plaintive.

'Papa, I have no money.'

He began to shuffle around in his pockets and I knew I was to be given some of his last few sovereigns. I braced myself against any feeling of guilt and took them from him, perhaps his money for dinner or books. I needed a new dress, that was the thought I held onto. I shut out any compassion as he counted out some money from his wallet and then added a ten-shilling note from an envelope in his desk. He was about to hand me the money when he struck his head with his open palm.

'The cage! I must release William.'

He caught up his large bunch of keys and hurried away into the side wing of the library, where the readers of valuable tomes were locked into small cell-like cubicles, chambers shut over with iron bars. I followed him, the money in his other hand my only concern. Inside one cell was a man standing over a chained-up volume, open on a table, a small, dark-haired man in a long coat. Thus do we meet our fate, without trumpets or warnings, just a small man poring over an old atlas chained to the desk.

'Dr Travers, please release this caged animal from his prison. I must discuss news of the greatest interest to us both.' He glanced at me as he made his way laughing from the small cell.

Papa gestured towards me. 'My dear William, may I introduce you to my daughter Mary? Dr William Wilde.'

He took off his hat and bowed, and I nodded, a little bored to have been trapped by one of Papa's dull friends.

'Yes, good news,' the Doctor continued, but now we were both included in his gaze, and I began to interest myself in this rather simian-looking man, with eyes deep-set. There was something at variance with his eyes, a kind of intensity to their narrow setting but, for all that, he was an attractive man. I stood politely by my father's side and allowed myself to observe him.

'Our Swift project has been approved. We can exhume the bodies as we had hoped, and conduct our research on the remains of Swift and Stella.'

The Doctor seemed anxious for Papa's goodwill in this matter. It was a curiosity to me that those outside our family circle were as respectful of our father as we were not.

'Miss Travers, you must forgive my pedantry, but this is a project we have all been waiting to bring to fruition.'

Not many men over forty took the time to include me in conversations like this, although many felt at liberty to stare boldly at me in the street when they were away from their wives.

'Swift?' I asked. 'Is this a literary project?'

'Yes, Mary,' my father answered. 'Dr Wilde and I are hoping to solve the age-old question as to Swift and his familial relation to his, well, his possible wife Stella – Mrs Esther Johnson – by exhuming their bodies.'

'Yes. I have just heard that we may begin next week and so I was hoping to send you my manuscript notes, Robert, if you would be so kind as to help me with your comments?'

I fell silent, somewhat angry at the interchange. I had heard of this Dr Wilde, who, despite his plain mode of dress, was a wealthy surgeon, with a large house on Merrion Square and a wife who was famous and clever, a celebrated poetess. So again my father would be helping this man to make his name, with not a penny in return. Something of my annoyance must have become visible because the Doctor turned again towards me.

'I'm afraid I'm intruding.'

'Not at all,' Papa told him. 'Mary was on her way out.'

He turned and finally handed me the money.

'Yes, indeed, Dr Wilde. I must return to my mother's house this afternoon. I was just leaving.'

I don't know why I said that. I had nothing to do that afternoon, except make the tedious walk to Mamma's house and sit and wait for dinner there. Furthermore, it always wounded Papa to have public reference made to the fact that he and Mamma kept separate homes and so I mentioned it when I could.

I turned to my father.

'Thank you for the money, Robert; it is very welcome indeed.'

It was Arthur, as the eldest and the first to rebel, who began calling him Robert in front of other people, and then the rest of us, Emily, Bobby and I, soon followed suit. Father disliked it but could do nothing to check us, aware of our deliberate echo of Mamma's imperious tone in the mocking rise on the second syllable.

The Doctor raised his hat to me. I walked out of the library and then down the path, pausing at the gate, undecided as to my route. I stood at the gate to the library for a full minute. Sitting here at this desk, writing, an older woman, I can see myself so clearly now, this dark-haired young woman in an old brown dress and the ill-matched blue gloves, cast-offs of Mamma's, hesitating as the afternoon suddenly gained some focus. A young clergyman passes by, glances at me. I ignore him, caught up with my own thoughts. A slight breeze stirs up some rotten straw on the road while I stand there, thinking. Whenever I revisit this moment now, that pause at the gate of my father's library, I am tempted to cry to my young self, plead with her to go away, but she is unheeding, intent on this new impulse beginning to move within her chest. That pretty, bright girl deserved so much more, I think. That impulse makes me turn right and then walk down the steps into St Patrick's Cathedral. There were few enough people in the gloom inside, a verger checking prayer books, and some worshippers kneeling here and there. I lingered. I look again at Swift's memorial tablet. Some minutes pass. Not too many. Then steps sound behind me.

'Miss Travers.' A hat is lifted. 'You and I have the same purpose today,' he says, glancing up at the tablet.

I looked puzzled.

'Swift interests you as well?'

'Repels,' I replied curtly. 'He seems to despise all humanity.'

The Doctor looked at me, surprised at the sharpness of my tone but, unlike men of my own age, men in their early twenties, who often become unnerved by such remarks, it seemed to interest him. Emily always told me that such forward intellectual remarks would keep me an old maid, but for all her wisdom about what men want to hear from women, here we both are, single and old, tethered together in an almshouse in the County Cork.

'Indeed he does seem to, but perhaps I can discover in my studies the reasons for his misanthropy.'

A prim old verger passed, made a face at our raised voices and the Doctor proposed that we walk outside to continue our talk. I nodded demurely, my thoughts becoming less demure. He was a worn-looking man but an intelligent one, with a deep voice, and he gave me all his attention, this medical man with books to his name. We stood at the entrance to the Cathedral and the Doctor spoke of his project, of the study of Swift's skull that he wished to undertake, to deduce physical reasons for his decline into madness by locating inherited physical causes.

'That is why I wished to inform your father immediately. His help in this matter has been crucial to its success and now the Academy will fund our publication.'

Something must have crossed my face -- perhaps the certainty that any funds for this project inevitably would bypass my incompetent parent. The Doctor paused.

'I am walking back to Trinity College. Might I be of assistance to you on your return to your mother's home.'

'Mamma's home in Percy Place is not a comfortable one for me,' I told him bluntly. 'Particularly in this last year, ever since I was received into the Church of Ireland. I often stay with Papa to escape persecution from Mamma, but today I must go there and repay a small debt to my sister.'

I had all the roughness of youth, but the Doctor was too adroit to notice.

'Then I am fortunate. My way and yours are the same today because I must return to Merrion Square to attend patients.'

I nodded and we set off, skirting up the hill and past Dublin Castle where the Doctor pointed out the elegant statue of Justice standing on the gate over the entrance and asked me if I noticed anything particular about her.

'She is turning her back on us, this statue to English justice,' I ventured and he laughed.

'My wife would approve of your sentiments,' he told me. 'Unfortunately Jane is away at present with our boys in the County Wicklow; otherwise, it would have been my great pleasure to introduce you.'

I nodded my assent but was glad his wife was away for more than one reason. I had never read a word of her celebrated poems and I wished to keep the attention of the grey eyes of her small, deep-voiced, attentive husband all to myself.

We found ourselves outside Trinity College where I was to take my leave. The Doctor stopped.

'Miss Travers, may I ask you something? The Academy has allocated me some funds for my Swift project, a study of the final sad years of the Dean's life, and I find I am a little pressed for time at the moment. I am in urgent need of assistance.'

He paused. Two men passed. The Doctor raised his hat. They smiled at him and then glanced at me.

'I was wondering if you might have time to spare to undertake some of the task with me, for a modest fee.'

I said nothing.

'Perhaps I have been impertinent.' He looked worried.

'No, no, not at all,' I stammered, lost for words for once. Money. More time to converse with this man. An occupation. Any one of these would seem a mirage of hope before me on this dull afternoon, but all together seemed a miraculous prospect.

'I would relish such work.'

'Good. Excellent. Perhaps we might meet in my house. Number One Merrion Square at four o'clock tomorrow? And do please give my respects to your mother.'

I assented, although Mamma was the last person I would tell of this exciting new acquaintance, and we took our leave of each other. '*Four o'clock tomorrow*'. These were the words that rang through my head as I walked to Mamma's house. So he knows Mamma, I thought. Something further to keep quiet. *Four o'clock tomorrow*. Those words even stayed in my mind as Mamma swept past me in her hallway, her ample skirts slapping against the wall the only acknowledgement that I existed, her face a blank.

I crossed by Merrion Square the next day in the glare of unexpected November sunlight, the trees alive with brown and gold, and made my way up to the front door of his house. I was slightly intimidated by the size and the grandeur of the house, but the servant girl seemed to be expecting me and led me into the large drawing room, directing me to sit on a bulky, uncomfortable sofa draped with heavy green velvet and a vast array of embroidered cushions. The room was untidy, with books everywhere and papers scattered on the tables, some were even on the floor, but the very untidiness reassured me, and instantly the Doctor appeared, his eyes warm, apparently pleased to see me. He took my hand in his. His was soft, warm, dainty. Useful for a surgeon. The day before he had been all courtesy; now he was brisk efficiency.

'My dear Miss Travers, your help in this matter has greatly relieved me. So many pressing projects but this one is nearest to my heart and may fail without your help.'

I was worried. This sounded like an onerous responsibility. My face fell. He hurried to reassure me.

'Now, as to your tasks. Could I ask you to return to the Cathedral and copy out the inscriptions on Swift's and Stella's memorial tablets? I will require you to transcribe some of Stella's poems for me. Otherwise, I need a clear young head and hand to make a fair copy of my manuscript and deliver it to your father for comments.'

I was relieved. Copying and writing. That was all.

'Can I ask,' I ventured, 'what will be the main thesis of your study of Swift?'

His face brightened and a warm sensation moved in my chest. This was an expression worth provoking.

'Simply this. That the celebrated Dean was not mad.'

I looked puzzled.

'Surely his insanity in his declining years is now a matter of public record and not simply conjecture.'

'No. No indeed. This will be my very point.' He lowered his voice. 'I have obtained the authentic death mask of Jonathan Swift and I would be obliged if you would keep this fact strictly confidential. It is my belief that the contortions of the poor ravaged face of the dead man reveal underlying medical symptoms consistent with an affliction of the inner ear and entirely unconnected with insanity.'

He looked eager as he spoke and moved nearer to me. The odour of his breath, heavy, dark with tobacco, curdled the air around me. It was an unpleasant odour, initially, but because it was his, eventually it became part of my passion for him.

He glanced around at a clock, got up and handed me a volume of verse. Then he searched on another table.

'Yes, here it is – the last of my Florentine volumes.'

I took the large leather-bound book, embossed with fleur-de-lys. I opened it. It was blank.

'For your research and may it prosper. As to payment,' he turned around and took an envelope from a table, 'perhaps you would be so good as to accept this small sum. The Academy can pay little but I was hoping that thirty pounds would be suitable.'

I thanked him but he brushed aside my thanks. I had never had such a sum for myself in my life. All I could think of was a proper winter coat. Then, all too soon, with apologies, it was made clear to me that I must leave, but I could call back at any time with any questions I might have. His surgery hours were in the afternoon and so he could be found there most early evenings, when the patients were all gone and he had notes to write up. I had been in the house no more than twenty minutes but he had paid me, set out my tasks clearly and now I was dismissed. The Doctor was a busy man who accomplished much and I was but a moment in a well-ordered day. I found myself standing outside his house with books, money and a purpose. But, most of all, I had an overwhelming desire to see Dr Wilde again.

I made my way back to Mamma's house, the warm comfortable home she had inherited from her uncle, her home since she and Papa had separated. It was in stark contrast to the chaos of Papa's house near Marsh's Library. Her own money, also from her uncle, kept the house cheerful and prosperous. Emily was at Mamma's house, sitting before the pleasant fire in the small drawing room, looking at an illustrated fashion journal. She looked up without much interest.

'I need to order a new winter coat, with bonnet and gloves,' I said. 'Can you help me?'

Her face brightened. Talk of clothes always did that for her.

'How much money did Papa give you?'

She clearly had not heard about the delayed new income.

'Ten pounds', I lied, easily.

She looked impressed.

'I wager I can get you shoes too, if you take my advice and use Madame Bannon to make the coat.'

The details were of little interest to me, but I knew my sister could dress me well for little or no money and I wanted to look more elegant for my visits to Merrion Square.

The next day, I went back to the Cathedral and copied out the inscription on Swift and Stella's memorial tablets and then made my way to Papa, intent on braving the squalor of his home for the sake of his books. That afternoon, I sat down, and with the aid of my father's dictionaries, attempted to translate the words from the tablets. I still have the notebook here, with the fleur-de-lys.

Hic Depositum est Corpus
IONATHAN SWIFT S. T.D
Hujus Ecclesiae Cathedralis
Decani
Ubi saeve Indignatio
Ulterius
Cor lacerare nequit,
Abi Viator
Et imitare, si poteris
Strenuum pro virili
Libertatis Vindicatorem.
AD 19 Octobris 1745

Most of it I could follow, but the final lines seemed a little unclear to me so when he came home, I asked Papa.

'Ah, William has given you some tasks for his Swift project. Good, good. He mentioned to me that he might.'

Papa looked over my shoulder.

'I would render these lines as "one whose heart is unable any further to be lacerated by savage indignation". A little inelegant, but to the point, I believe. Poor Swift – such a terribly sad end.'

He paused. Instead of making his way over to the wan fire and his book, he asked. 'And how is my dear friend, our celebrated Speranza?'

'I have no idea. She is away from home at present.' He frowned, made as if to speak, but said nothing further.

The next day I read the inscription on Stella's memorial tablet again. It seemed remarkably effusive. I wondered if she had written it herself.

Underneath lie interred the mortal Remains of Mrs Hester Johnson, better known to the world by the name of Stella, under which she is celebrated in the writings of Dr Jonathan Swift, Dean of this Cathedral. She was a person of extraordinary endowments and accomplishments in Body, mind and behaviour; justly admired and respected, by all who knew her, on account of her many eminent virtues, as well as her great natural and acquired perfections.

I had less respect for Stella than I had for Swift. At least he had written, influenced his nation, and known great statesmen. All she had done was share a famous man with another woman, and in the end, both women were at a loss.

My young heart was full of such dismissive certainties and so, later that day, when I continued my reading of her works in Marsh's Library, I copied some lines of her poems with something like contempt.

> *St Patrick's Dean, your country's pride*
> *My early and my only guide,*
> *Let me among the rest attend*
> *Your pupil and your humble friend.*
> *You taught how I might youth prolong*
> *By knowing what was Right and Wrong;*
> *How from my heart to bring supplies*
> *Of lustre to my fading eyes….*

I have it still. I have it here before me, in the writing book he gave me. He didn't teach me right from wrong. He taught me about my body and his body as if they were the only right and wrong. I close my eyes and I can smell his body, his breath, all sour, distilling the essence of desire.

Tuesday 7 May

Dinner has been over for two hours and now I sit at my table in my hotel room, as the last light of the sun finally drains from the ceiling above me. These May evenings last for ever. In front of me I have a pile of papers and letters, some of them Papa's correspondence with a man in Manchester, a Mr Jones, a fellow librarian. The sight of Papa's neat handwriting was a shock for which I was not prepared. A letter arrived from Marsh's Library yesterday, a polite one signed by a Miss Jennings to apologise for the Keeper's delay in dealing with the matter of Papa's portrait, since he has been ill, but asking me to call this morning because they had also found some papers of Papa's and wished to return them to his family. I was more than a little nervous. I had known William Maturin well in those days in Jane's house, when the clever-tongued young Reverend Maturin had cut such a dash in her soirées. Now, in my late fifties, and despite my sullied name, I had finally acquired self-possession. I was prepared to face him down.

Even as I made my way up the stone steps, I could see that the years had brought great changes to the library since Papa's time, and all for the better. The iron gates at the door were freshly painted and flowers grew in profusion along the well-tended green bank leading up to the front door. This had always been a weed-infested wilderness, or so I remember it. Papa once told me that the last Keeper, old Craddock, had gone away on an extended leave one summer and, in his absence, Papa had weeded and trimmed the front garden and had even succeeded in growing some summer flowers. When Craddock returned, the sight of the flowers had thrown him into a rage, a garden being, as he kept bellowing, the one thing he abominated above all others and so he went out and procured a goat to lay waste to Papa's new garden and return it to its original chaos. At the time, all I could think of was the shabbiness of his own home. I grew angry with Papa for his misdirected care of Marsh's. I told him so and he never spoke of the library again, if he could help it.

I pulled the bell handle. A tidy little woman opened the door and held out her hand in smiling welcome. She was plump-faced, a little younger than me, with faded, colourless hair that had once clearly been bright auburn.

'Miss Travers, I have been expecting you. I'm Violet Jennings. I wrote to you. I've been helping the Reverend here since his late illness. Please do come up with me. He has travelled in from Howth to see you this morning, his first visit to the Library in some time.'

So I must face Maturin again. Well, after all these years I would be ready for his jibes. We ascended the well-swept staircase and she ushered me into the main library, along the creaking floorboards and through the glass doors where an elderly man was struggling up from the desk with some difficulty.

'Miss Travers.' He took my hand. 'I don't suppose you remember me but I do believe we have met before, or maybe it was your sister. It was many years ago, at my Cousin Jane's soirées. William Maturin.'

I stared at him. Could this small, wan-faced old man be the same as that lively dark-haired young man with the sharp tongue and the ready opinions? Surely he and I were about the same age. He could hardly be more than late fifties. I walked towards him.

'Reverend Maturin.'

I gave him my hand. Something of my disbelief must have been apparent to him because he smiled.

'Yes, indeed, it is I. Much changed, as you see, since my days in Merrion Square sitting at Speranza's feet. Was it you or your sister I knew in those days? I cannot recollect; my tired old head won't let me.'

I said nothing, stared again. The young Reverend I remembered had been very sure of himself, of his sleek good looks and of his erudition. The black hair was now all gone and his face seemed in danger of being drowned by pale fleshliness. I remember several elaborate manoeuvres Jane had concocted to contrive a love match between him and myself, putting us side by side at concerts, leaving us alone in the drawing room while she attended to her children. All these attempts we firmly resisted, by me because I desired no man but her husband, and by him because he believed himself to be deserving of a much better match than an impoverished daughter of a shabby professor. Despite this, I had always liked him, maybe because we were of the same mind about any doomed idea of a love match between us. Much later I heard that he had finally married a bishop's daughter with some money and a villa in Howth, and I was pleased. Perhaps it was a sign of Jane's growing fear of my obsession with her husband that she sought to pawn me off on her debonair young cousin, but neither of us would countenance such a possibility. She might have had more success in marrying me off to Mr Henry Wilson, the Doctor's dull but worthy assistant. Mr Wilson approved of me for having abandoned my mother's religion in order to enter the Church of Ireland, but Jane refrained from making that particular match and for reasons that enraged me further when I discovered why.

Maturin ushered me into a chair and sat down opposite me, somewhat heavily himself, despite his own frailty.

'I have been unwell in the last year since my dear wife's death and find I can make the journey into Dublin only once or twice a month, but our invaluable Violet has been tireless in her endeavours here in the library.'

'I agree,' I said, 'I have never seen it ... shine so much.'

Our invaluable Violet dismissed my praise with a shrug and a laugh that made me like her more, but I could see she was pleased as she chatted happily. 'Now, enough of that. I will make us all some tea while you sit back down and talk to Miss Travers.'

She settled him down with a rug on his knees, despite the warm day, and left us alone. Behind Maturin's head, the back gardens of the library looked fecund and lively in the sunshine and the whole room of dusty old books seemed to envy the flowers their freedom and colour. I looked around the room while the old man fiddled with some papers in a cardboard box. He caught my lingering stares and smiled at me. I smiled back.

'Forgive my rude staring,' I said. 'I have not been back here since Papa's death; I had forgotten what a pleasant room this can be in sunshine. A haven in a busy city.'

'Yes. Believe it or not, although I have spent my days recuperating in Howth, each day I have longed to return to this desk and these precious volumes. I am so pleased to see you again, Miss Travers, because your letter prompted me to a matter that had been much on my conscience during my convalescence. We did indeed receive your late father's portrait and I have been making plans to have it placed on display here in the library, as a tribute to all his tireless work to save Marsh's.'

I assumed he was being polite and nodded, slightly bored. As if he knew this, he continued.

'You may not believe me but, if he had not persuaded Mr Guinness to give one thousand pounds to the library in 1860, then the building would have been shut down and the books all sent over to the National Gallery, to languish in the basement there while the board of trustees squabbled. We would not be sitting here but for your father's timely exertions.'

I had known nothing of this matter, or of Papa's unexpected facility to attract such a large sum for the library and I would like to have asked more, but Violet had returned and much fuss was made with cups and plates. When we three had all been safely provided with our tea, I brought the conversation around to the matter most pressing to me.

'May I ask: did Papa's portrait arrive here safely?'

He turned towards Violet, a little confused, and she took command, as she had been patently waiting to do.

'Yes, Miss Travers, indeed it did, and I found it in state of some neglect in a store room downstairs, and so I've dusted the frame and had it brought up here today. Cornelius, our gardener, has prepared a setting on the wall. It awaits your approval and then we can put the portrait on display.'

Unexpectedly, I found myself a little tearful. So much care had been taken over his picture by this energetic little woman, who had never even known Papa. If there is justice in the world, particularly in the matter of infirm widowers seeking helpmates, Miss Jennings will be no more within the year and, instead, a new Mrs Maturin will reign at the villa in Howth. I wished her well; she seemed a pleasant woman, although no beauty, and certainly not a woman to turn the head of the handsome young cleric I remembered from Merrion Square. However, the years and his physical frailty had now rebalanced the scales.

'I am grateful to you, Miss Jennings. Your care for Papa's portrait is very much appreciated. I will write and tell my sister; she will be so pleased.'

Miss Jennings looked over at Maturin. 'Well, the late Dr Travers is something of a cause with the Reverend. He feels that tribute of this kind is much needed and somewhat overdue.'

'Yes, indeed. When I began my tenure here as Keeper, it was with great difficulty that I could persuade your father to stay on as Assistant and even to accept a key for his own use. He insisted on the statutes: only the Keeper should have the key to the door.'

'Papa had no key?' I was startled. 'However did he get into the library every day?'

Maturin looked grave. 'Yes, old Craddock kept him on a very short leash. Your father was forced to call upstairs to his apartment each morning and then return the key in the evening. You may read of it yourself in his letters to his friend, Mr Jones, in Manchester.'

'Letters?' I began to get uneasy.

'Oh, some old files with his handwriting on them. I found them all last week when I was clearing out your father's papers from his desk and I have gathered them together for you. Again, another task too long delayed; I thought you might like to keep them yourself. They were returned to the library after Mr Jones's death three years ago.'

'I must apologise, Reverend. My sister and I were so much preoccupied with Mamma, in the latter stages of her decline, and Papa's sudden death meant that we were unable to come here and clear away his papers. Papa had reached a great age but had been strong and well all his life, and so his passing came upon us as a great shock. And then, of course, so quickly followed by Mamma's final illness.'

He sighed and rubbed his bald head, clearly without much interest in either death. 'I do understand,' he muttered. 'I should have been quicker with these papers. I have been so remiss and now with this terrible trial happening in London....'

I began to shift in my seat, but before he could continue Miss Jennings intervened, smoothly but firmly, and stood up.

'Reverend, you might gather up the letters and the documents for Miss Travers and place them in that folder, the one there by your pocket watch. In the meantime, do you wish to see the portrait now, Miss Travers? I had Cornelius hang it this morning.'

We rose together and she took me gently by the arm and brought me into the inner hall of the library, by the cages, where I had first seen the Doctor. There it was. It was not by any means a great work of art but it caught Papa admirably. It had been done at the behest of some of his former students on his retirement and the artist had captured his reticence perfectly. The more you looked to see the man, the more he retreated. This was a painting that revealed nothing of the sitter. It was Emily's excellent idea to donate it to Marsh's, for we found that we could not live it with it ourselves.

'A fine face,' Violet murmured. 'I never had the pleasure of meeting your late father because I began my work here after his retirement, but the Reverend speaks of him with such respect, I feel as if I have.'

She looked back at the office door and lowered her voice.

'I am very anxious that we keep on pleasant topics and peaceful remembrance at the moment with the frail state of the Reverend's recovery and all this terrible newspaper commotion from London. I have managed to keep the worst of the court accounts away from him, but he does worry so about poor Lady Wilde. She is a relation, you know, and was very kind to him when he was a young man.'

'Yes,' I said, in as colourless a tone as I could manage. 'I know.'

'So all this talk about your late father is something I encourage. I may tell you, privately, that the Reverend has been getting the most distressing letters from her son.' She paused and then added, hurriedly, 'Her elder son Willie, that is. Begging letters, pleading for money and giving the most upsetting account of his mother's poverty, but luckily I have been able to intercept them. The Reverend has been making such progress lately, and nothing must hinder his recovery.'

Indeed, nothing would, I could see that. Maturin must be well enough to stand in front of a clergyman and make his vows, this was clear enough. The plight of his cousin Jane, who had been kind to him in his youth, must be resolutely shut out by Violet.

Well, I have money and Jane shall have some of it. I owe her that much at least. This I decided as I walked back to the office with Violet. But how would I contact her? As I thought about this, Violet spoke again, changing her tone abruptly, the confidence of a woman managing the man she had marked out as her future husband was making her almost pretty.

'Good news, Reverend: Miss Travers approves. The portrait is in the right place.'

'Dear Miss Travers, I am so pleased, and can you please remember me to your sister? We used to know each other in our youth in Merrion Square but I always thought that she disapproved of me and found me too frivolous for her own earnest tastes.' He laughed. 'You can tell her that I am no longer capable of frivolity. My poor cousin Jane, I really should write to her….'

Violet and I exchanged understanding glances and I stood up.

'I am most grateful to you both,' I said, playing along with her, 'Forgive me, I must return to my hotel and write to my sister. She has been unwell and so will welcome the good news about Papa's portrait.'

Maturin began to struggle to get up and make his farewells but Violet restrained him with one hand while swooping down to collect the folder of papers with the other and nodded to me to take them from her.

'You stay right there and continue with your correspondence. I shall walk Miss Travers to the door, and you can get on with that great pile of demands and questions.'

She took me by the elbow, and we made our way down the long room and out into the sunshine. I shook her hand and thanked her for her care of Papa's portrait and she thanked me in return for my tact concerning the vexed question of poor Cousin Jane's woes. As we talked in the warm sunshine on the steps outside the library, she looked down, tutted and knelt to pull away some weeds.

'Bindweed. So infuriating!'

No bindweed would flourish in the life of the Reverend Maturin as long as Miss Jennings had breath, I thought.

I resolved: as soon as I could, I would travel to London and bring Jane some money.

As I walked down the steps, Papa's folder under my arm, a piece of doggerel came back into my mind, from all those years ago. It was said that some Trinity College students had composed it, but now, it occurred to me that the young Reverend Maturin may have had a hand in it:

There's an occultist living in Merrion Square
Who had a skill that's unrivalled and talent that's rare?
And if you will listen I'll try to reveal
The matter that caused poor Miss Travers to squeal.

Now here I sit, all sleep vanished. There are too many papers and files in the folder for me to read but I do have Papa's letters before me. I long for laudanum, but Mamma insisted when she nursed me back to health that it was dangerous for me and so she weaned me off it, with her customary firmness. So I read. Mr Edward Jones was Papa's friend in the library in Manchester: many of the letters are tedious accounts of rare editions and book auctions, but I found what I was dreading: Papa's one mention of my trial.
He writes to Mr Jones:

2 March 1865. It is so long since I wrote to you that you must have supposed I had altogether abandoned letters nor would you have indeed been very far astray. For several months past I have been in a fit of almost complete inertia, disinclined to every effort of mind. I have had much of domestic and other annoyances and have perhaps yielded too much to its disheartening influence.

That's as much as he dared complain: 'domestic and other annoyances'. All Dublin laughing at him and at his daughter Moll. I was the cause of it all, and was then in a state of collapse in Mamma's house.

I read on. Not a mention of his separation from Mamma, the troubles at the library. But, later I found it. A rare moment where he told his friend Mr Jones about Bobby. About that terrible year when Bobby ran away and enlisted in the army, to prevent his being forced back to that cruel boarding school. Papa recounts the whole painful tale as if it were happening to someone else's bright, vulnerable sixteen-year-old son; Bobby's posting to India, his death at eighteen from typhoid, in an army hospital somewhere outside Calcutta. Dead at eighteen because he was afraid to return to a school where he was beaten regularly, a school so brutal that the Army seemed to him a haven of gentleness in comparison. Poor Bobby, the youngest of us, the merry boy who was always waiting on the doorstep for Papa's return when he was a child, a boy who lost his way because his father was a parent only in name. Looking back, I cannot blame Mamma for it all; she was so maddened with anxiety about Bobby's future not to see that his school was a torture and so she insisted that her boy return there. All Papa could do was shake his head sadly, and Mamma needed more, much more from him than that. I read the words Papa had used to tell his friend of Bobby's death: 'sad but inevitable'. It struck me that death and time can work dangerous effects on our memory, that they can gild the absent ones with unexpected kindness and virtue and that the real man is not that reticent portrait on the wall of Marsh's Library but the man who closed his ears to the sobbing of his beaten son and the despair of his hard-pressed wife, forcing her younger son back to a school of torture because she could see no other way to save him from the abyss that Papa was allowing us to fall in. Poor Mamma. In this, she has my sympathy. I have her rosary beads here in my hand. How often did she pray for forgiveness for her complicity in her youngest child's sad but inevitable end? I can be sure that Papa never saw any need to beg forgiveness for his own negligence.

Friday 17 May

Today I went into one of those fashionable ladies haberdashery shops off Sackville Street and bought a few fripperies to send to Emily, who wrote to tell me she has left the nursing home but will stay a few more days in Cork before returning to Mitchelstown. Her friend Miss Bowen will stay with her at the Imperial Hotel and they are engaged on a new embroidery. I sent some spools of expensive silver and gold threads and a yard of good lace trim and, as I packaged them, it surprised me how pleased I was to see the neat brown parcel, and I thought of Emily's pleasure in opening it. Such is the renewed delight in family life that absence and distance can engender.

Jane's son is on trial again, and the newspapers report on his ordeal. Here in this hotel, I may read them as I please. The charges are still unnamed but the Cork papers made mention of Wilde 'betraying tokens of the keenest anxiety'. That seems to me to be an inadequate expression for what he must be enduring.

Tuesday 28 May

I have stayed away from my journal these past days. Too many memories. Jane's son Oscar has been sentenced. Two years' hard labour. It will kill him. I found one account in yesterday's *Freeman's Journal.* Full of the familiar high moral tone of the press, a tone to which I was once subjected.

As to the horrid character of Wilde's crime, it is quite superfluous to add anything to what Judge Wills, who held the scales of justice with scrupulous fairness, said in passing sentence. The remarkable thing is to discover now that Oscar Wilde was at the centre of festering corruption and seems to have been known in the artistic and theatrical circles in which he moved. But it is satisfactory anyway to feel that even the most brazen effrontery in the pursuit of such abominations does not bring immunity from punishment. It is even said that the police could lay their hands on fifty men well known in society who are equally guilty with him and whose connection with this odious scandal has been notorious for years. Some months ago I saw Oscar Wilde at the first night of 'An Ideal Husband'. He was then in the zenith of his fame….Wilde himself was in a stage box, being flattered and lionised by a party of most distinguished persons – men and women whose praise he condescendingly accepted. He was dressed in a last note of fashion, faultlessly groomed and assuming airs of semi-royal graciousness to an admiring audience. He strutted in from the wings with an air of contemptuous indifference, one hand in his trouser pocket and an opera hat in his other. The object of this ovation responded with a shrug of the shoulders, suggesting a feeling of deprecatory boredom. When silence had been restored, he drawled out a few words of studied insolence and retired. I saw Oscar Wilde on Friday last in the dock of the Old Bailey and a more shocking contrast could not possibly be conceived. The aspect of sleek, well-fed luxuriousness had vanished, the cheeks were lined and flabby, and wore a most unearthly colour. His eyes were bloodshot and expressive of the last stage of acute terror; the eyes of a man who might at any time get a fatal seizure from overstrain. His hair was all in disorder and he crouched into a corner of the dock with his face turned towards the jury and the witness box, his head resting on his hand so that it was almost hid from the public.... The general impression he conveyed was of a man filled with a vague hopeless terror, not of one filled with shame at the dreadful ignominy of his position.

I do not recognise the man they describe. I can only see that well-behaved boy in Merrion Square when they speak of Oscar, always at his mother's side. Was Jane in the court? She did so love the drama of the court room. Not so now, I suspect. I am sorry for her; truly sorry if the venom of the newspapers is an indication of the level of public delight in attacking Oscar in London this week. Perhaps I could write to her. Or would that seem like gloating? No I will go to London. Would she meet me now?

Wednesday 29 May
The papers are coming in with judgement thick and fast. I sit and read, appalled. He has been sent to prison, his house closed up, his wife and two sons fled, but that Lord Alfred Douglas seems to have disappeared. Not all the papers hate Oscar. This is an extract from the *Cork Constitution* yesterday:

All who heard the trial of Wilde say the sentence passed upon the prisoner is not a whit too severe. These persons – I will not call them privileged – describe the evidence as revolting. The sentence, as a matter of fact, is the most severe known to the law. It is not confinement only which indeed might be borne with equanimity. It is in the complementary infliction of hard labour that the sting, the misery, the degradation exist. The interpretation of the term in prison covers all that is demoralising and crushing. The maximum of loathsome and humiliating labour has to be borne by a system reduced through the thinnest and most rigid diet to a point just above actual collapse. Such a life, even for two brief years, to a man of luxurious habits crowds by a refinement of skilful pressure all that is conceivable in exacting toil and shameful degradation supplemented by associating with the scum of the earth, quite ready themselves to heap upon this particular criminal the unspeakable loathing aroused by his offence. A leper would not exchange places with Wilde.

A rare moment of compassion from the newspapers. No such compassion for me in my time. Young women at the centre of public scandals are much more enjoyable as the focus for innuendo from journalists than from middle-aged men in some vague criminal bind. How will that poor boy do? I must remember to stop thinking of him as a boy. He is a forty-year-old man, with a wife and sons and, if the newspapers are telling the truth, a taste for some unnamed hidden worlds. Oscar was a gentle child when I knew him, but Willie was my favourite – bright, imaginative, full of questions. The newspapers barely mention him. Perhaps I can write to him.

Oscar seemed to have had everything to live for up to this. The papers say that his plays alone were earning him over £200 a week. Now all that he had – a house in Chelsea, wife, children – thrown away for a whim of the body, the drug of desire. I understand perfectly. The needs of his body, so long denied, becoming of paramount, un-assuageable importance. Even though I said in court, under oath, that the Doctor had ravished me, in truth I wanted him as much as he desired me. It was by my own intention that the seduction took place. I was nearly twenty-five and wanted to know what a man was like. I can sit here at my desk, a woman in my late fifties, and if I close my eyes, instantly I am back in the surgery room, slowly undoing my dress as he watches. As I wanted him to.

In the week after he gave me the money, I worked on the notes, made a fair copy of the manuscript and called to his house. He was away in the West of Ireland, they told me, attending to family matters. I surrendered the notes and manuscript and, as I stood outside I realised that I had no reason to return; no literary reason, that is.

The following week, when my new clothes were ready, late one gloomy afternoon I made my way to his waiting rooms around the corner in Lincoln Place. I knew he would eventually be free of patients, as he had been careful to tell me. I wanted something more to happen. His surgery was an open one and always busy, the vital source of wealth maintaining that big house and all its pomp. He kept a set of rooms across in Lincoln Place for patients; entrance could be gained by pulling a long dangling bell at the side of the heavy dark door. On that first day, a surly manservant, elderly but strong-looking, came out, looked me over and then wordlessly ushered me in. I learnt later that the Doctor had brought Barney with him from the west and that he knew all the Doctor's secrets and kept order for him. Barney was the only one in that house whom I feared; the only one I knew who would not hesitate to use physical force to keep me out if ever I grew angry.

That first day he brought me into the waiting rooms and gestured at a seat. In the dim November light, the last few patients made their way one by one at the beckoning of the taciturn countryman into the Doctor's inner room. The waiting room was plainly furnished but comfortable, with firm chairs and a table with a porcelain ewer and basin, dishes full of soap and thick white towels. In such unremarkable, utilitarian rooms are our sparse moments of paradise on earth known.

Finally, Barney beckoned me in and the Doctor stood up and took my hand in his, motioning Barney to leave.

'Mary, a pleasure to see you. Not a medical crisis, I can tell, for you look the picture of good health.'

He looked pleased to see me, offered to take my coat, thanked me for my work on the manuscript and then asked how he could help. 'I'm sorry to intrude, but I have been troubled lately with a drumming in my left ear and I was wondering if you might....'

He smiled, his medical manner coming to the fore. 'Of course, let's see what the matter is. If you could seat yourself here, I'll prepare the instruments.'

I sat down on the flat, heavy wooden stool and he turned to his cabinet and began to take out some small medical devices. He came and stood over me. The pungent smell of tobacco was on his clothes, the dark materials of his sombre suit rustling next to me, but his breath that day was clear. Not that I minded his strong breath.

'If I might ask you to remove your jacket and unbutton your upper garments. I would prefer not to splash your clothes.'

I began to do so as he turned and busied himself at a side table. My neck was bare by the time he turned and my mouth began to feel dry. His fingers touched my neck, gently, hesitantly, and he stooped to look into my ear, asking me questions as he did, his tone serious.

'Tell me, does this drumming take place at any particular time?'

'At night only, and for an hour at most, but rarely lasting for a week or more,' I replied. His fingers stayed around my neck, lightly, moving a fraction hither and thither as he peered into my ear with the small, cold steel instrument. The sensation of cold within my ear was not unpleasant and at one point, his leg came to rest against my thigh. For a small, lightly made man, his limbs felt warm and muscular and I shifted slightly towards his heat and firmness, without any sense that I had meant to. All my consciousness had focused onto that body heat. Abruptly, after a minute of this, I made myself move away again. Just as abruptly, he straightened up, with a noise of approval. He seemed to have come to a decision.

'As I thought.'

I must have appeared worried in my glance upwards because he hastened to add. 'A simple problem with a simple solution. You have an excess of fluid in that ear. Draining will remove the problem.'

'Will that be a lengthy procedure?'

He laughed. 'No more than ten minutes. If I could ask you to make yourself comfortable, I will have Barney fetch some hot water. I can end all your woes this very day.'

He left the room and I sat there, breathing deeply. After an age, when it seemed as if he would never return, I heard the door open and close and the splash of water as he busied himself over a basin. Already I was anticipating the renewal of our close contact. He turned, and came near me again with a small basin and a syringe. I had loosened my dress further, to protect it and now my neck was exposed. He tut-tutted.

'Mary, may I look at your neck? You appear to have a rash.'

The curling tongs! I had forgotten. I blushed and hurried to explain.

'Oh, that is nothing. Simply an old burn mark, a trivial accident.'

I had tied a broad ribbon, of dark green, around my neck, but it had slipped down and the burn was now visible. Without asking me, he untied the ribbon and drew it off my neck, the silk sliding across my skin like a blunt knife. He touched my neck, softly, softly, and stroked the scar.

'This should have been treated. When did this burn occur?'

When? The spat with Mamma, her insistence that I should pay more attention to my appearance, her jeers at my straight, lank hair, the attempt to curl my fringe ending in another quarrel and a burning at her angry hands which may or may not have been an accident.

'A year, maybe more.'

He frowned. 'That scar tissue has not entirely healed. It must cause you some discomfort still. When I have treated your ear, I will attend to your neck.'

He placed the small silver syringe in my ear and warm water gushed in, causing my shoulders to shiver in a mixture of discomfort and pleasure. Pleased with the result, he drew back and checked the contents of the small basin he had me hold next to my ear.

'And now, your poor neck.'

He rummaged around in a drawer and drew out a large gleaming tin.

'This has excellent healing properties', he told me. 'The Balm of Gilead. Why such pompous biblical names for simple unguents? Still, I think it will be of use.'

He got me to hold the tin and dipped his fingers into the smooth, greasy mixture inside to build up some on his fingertips. Then he turned and began to dab some on my neck, gently at first and then with a greater firmness. It was more direct physical pleasure than I could bear and, as if he understood, he moved his other hand towards my open blouse and his hand slid gently downwards on to my breast. He let out a deep breath which ended with my name, and his fingers, as I had wanted, arrived at my nipple. Slowly, as he had caressed my neck, he began to caress me there and my body began to feel his slight movement, in thin lines of tingling excitement in my veins, at the base of my throat. As he made the tiniest of movements with his fingertips on my breast, I moved my hand towards his leg and slid the back of my hand along his knee.

Then I turned my hand, opened it and put my middle finger briefly on my tongue and then reached up and touched his cheek lightly with my wetted finger. This lasted for less than a minute and then he stood away from me and said, 'My dearest Mary, my dear, we must not.'

I nodded, unable to speak with the blood pressing against my cheeks and the choked air in my lungs, and he turned away, and, placing his hands flat to lean against the wall, bowed slightly and took some deep breaths. I looked down; my breast feeling as if he was still caressing me there, and then I stood up and hurriedly began to button up.

He came back and, when I was fully dressed, took my hand in his and kissed it.

'Thank you, my dear, for becoming my friend. It would distress me greatly if that were ever to cease. Please let what happened with us today here remain our own private moment?'

I nodded.

'And do please call and see me again.'

I hurried out through the waiting room. Barney was there dampening down the coal fire and turned silently to watch me leave. I made my way home through the darkened streets, anxious to return to my room and sit down in the dark and relive the feeling of his hand on my body and his breath choking out the air all around me.

The next day, a letter arrived from him, the first of so many that first year. It accompanied a small parcel. A novel: *Ernest Maltravers* by Edward Bulwer-Lytton. It came with a short note.

My Dear Mary,

Please permit me to share with you one of my favourite books at this moment. Yes indeed, the pun in the title has already suggested itself to me but I will dub you 'Earnest Moll–Travers', with your permission, as I know your studious ways and believe that you are indeed an Earnest Moll. Pray read the novel and then come and visit me some dark evening when I am worn out with care and medical duties and brighten up my day with your Earnest musings and opinions. On a matter of business, I am bound to visit my brother Ralph in his home in Monaghan early next month and I was hoping you might be able to accompany me there, as I require some scholarly assistance with my catalogue of ancient Irish antiquities. My brother, the clergyman, lives in a quiet way with his nieces, the Misses Emily and Mary Wilde, my two pet Marmosets as I have christened them, and he would be glad to offer you his hospitality. Pray do ask your dear Mamma and let me know if you are free to travel.

Yours
'Earnest Maltravers'

I began reading the novel that day, puzzled as to why he should think this story would interest me. Lord Lytton's work had little or no charm for me, and, besides, how could I trust a writer who had his own wife locked up in an asylum, for no other reason than the fact that she objected to his possession of a mistress? It told of a fifteen-year-old girl, Alice, alone in the world except for a criminal father, and also of the handsome young Ernest Maltravers, eighteen, wealthy and idealistic, who saves Alice from her father, arranges for her to learn how to read and write and believe in God and then realises that he has fallen in love with her. This Alice, who seemed to me to be insipid to the point of simple-mindedness, is pretty and good, despite the delinquent father, and she adores her saviour with a kind of idolatry. Is this really what men want their women to be? Perhaps it is, I thought, as I read. Was that what the Doctor wanted from me: to rescue me from my ineffectual father? I suppose the pun appeals to him and so I am happy, more than happy to be his Earnest Moll.

As I read on, the book interested me despite myself. All the women, the haughty Lady Florence, the French Madame de Ventadour – proud, rich, stubborn women – were smitten by the hero one after another, and each one was rejected or died piteously. All pure nonsense and melodrama and yet this is what a man with education and talent like the Doctor chooses to read and to send as a love token. I suppose he fancies himself as Ernest and me his innocent, child-like Alice. Ernest and Alice do have a child, something that Lord Lytton makes plain. So Alice is not so innocent.

I devoured the book in the days after my visit to his surgery, and when I was not reading it, I paced the streets of Dublin, hoping to meet the Doctor accidentally, but also dreading doing so. I was making my way down towards Papa's house one afternoon to leave some letters for him that had been posted to Mamma's address by mistake, thoughts of the Doctor filling my mind when I turned a corner, just below Dublin Castle, and there he was, making his way along, a bundle of books under his arm.

'Miss Mary Travers – the very woman. I am on my way to Marsh's Library to return these books to your father. His own volumes, long overdue.'

I beamed to see him.

'I'm afraid Papa is away from Dublin this week. He left for London yesterday to attend some parliamentary committee on the future of Marsh's Library and will be gone for several days. May I help in any way?'

'Indeed you may,' he said, smiling down at his burden. 'Can I ask you to take some of these books and walk with me to your father's house? I promised to return them months ago and perhaps you can let me in and I can deposit them in his study. I've never been to his home, so you can direct me.'

I nodded and, in the manoeuvres to give me some of the heavy volumes, I felt his hands on mine and, at one moment, pressing against my breast. I could think only that we were walking together towards an empty house and could speak very little while he talked of our forthcoming trip to the County Monaghan and of the train journey and of other such matters until we arrived at the shabby little house near St Patrick's Cathedral. The Doctor seemed a little surprised when I stopped at the terraced house but said nothing and followed me as I unlocked the door and made my way up the grubby staircase to Papa's study. Since the house had been unoccupied for a few days, the peculiar smell of damp that seemed always to issue from beneath the stairway was overpowering. I motioned to the old mahogany desk where Papa kept his letters and books and we deposited our burden there. He looked around again and, this time, spoke.

'Such disorder.'

I blushed.

'Is the entire house so derelict and uncared for?'

I nodded, ashamed.

'You should not have to see your father live like this. Something must be done.'

I had hoped to be kissed, but to be rescued was more than I had hoped for. I was still young and foolish enough to believe that words spoken in such circumstances, by a man desiring a woman, are more than merely words. He looked around him again, and then took me by the shoulders and we began to kiss, for the first time, as if we had been kissing all our lives.

Thursday 30 May

I must see Jane. I have made my preparations, booked the boat train to London, and the manager here has secured me a hotel, in Russell Square. I sent a telegram to Emily to tell her about my trip to London, saying only that I will be away for a week or two. Late this afternoon, returning to the hotel, I saw a familiar figure making her way up the steps. Miss Jennings from Marsh's Library. I hurried to catch up. I touched her gently on the elbow and she seemed startled and none too pleased to see me. She had a folder under her arm. 'Miss Travers.'

'My dear Miss Jennings, will you come in and join me for tea?'

She shook her head vigorously.

'No indeed, I must not. The Reverend is waiting for me in the Shelbourne and we are due at the Archbishop's house for a meeting of the Trustees this evening. I have promised to take notes. I wanted to deliver this to you personally; the post can be so unreliable. I found it yesterday and realised that it must also have been the property of the late Dr Travers. I felt that you should have it.'

She spoke quickly, and not without some discomfort and, before I could reply, thrust a large cardboard folder into my hands.

'You are too kind,' I said, feeling that she was being less than kind. 'And now you really must come in for some tea. You deserve it after such a tiresome mission. I am leaving for London. Do please come in and bless my journey with tea cake.'

She refused tea but shook my hand again with some warmth no doubt glad that I was leaving, and it was only later, in my room, that I dared open the folder. There, on the front cover, in my father's neat hand, was the date 1864 and underneath: 'Trial – Travers versus Wilde.'

JUNE

The George Hotel
Russell Square
London
Saturday 1 June

I arrived here early yesterday morning, after a long and somewhat stormy night journey, and I have settled myself into this comfortable hotel, with a long and a deep sleep last night after my travels. I have been sleeping little these past few nights and this was a welcome respite from the unceasing industry of my thoughts.

My last visit to London was my ill-fated attempt to get away from Dublin and the Doctor's growing coldness by joining Arthur in Australia, thirty years ago. I was staying in a terribly hot, noisy hotel near King's Cross when Arthur's letter caught up with me, forwarded by Emily from Mamma's home. He wrote bluntly that he had no space for me in his home, that his wife's mother was unwell and had moved in with them and that he could not afford another dependant, a penniless sister. Faced with such brutal clarity, I was forced to slink back to Dublin and, on my return, I discovered that the Doctor and Jane had added to their family in my absence. Then my rage became titanic. *I promised my wife no more children.* Months before, the Doctor had told me this, with a look of agonised, beseeching entreaty. *No more children, except those conceived within wedlock* was what he meant to say. Rather, it was what he had omitted to say. And to tell me that he and Jane were expecting another child. Unto us a child is born. Isola.

I have made the room my own with the few books brought from Mitchelstown, Mamma's rosary beads threaded over the mirror on the night table, and the sturdy writing desk set up by the window. Yesterday

I sent Emily a telegram from Dublin to inform her of my London address. Swift as ever, she replied and so there was a short letter from her waiting for me at breakfast this morning, telling me of her continued recovery, and that she has decided to stay on in Cork in the Imperial Hotel, to enjoy some shopping. Another, from the Countess, newly returned to Mitchelstown Castle, came this afternoon; Emily must have given my address, and the Countess tells me that all is well in our own little house since she sends Hannah to inspect it regularly. She finished her letter by mentioning her worries for my sister's continuing ill-health and her hope that I will return soon to the County Cork. I will write and give my excuses, send a small gift of money to Hannah and plead my need for more time away. I do not plan to mention her former friend, Speranza. I will visit her, and give her money, but I find I am strangely reluctant and so will take my time. I am my own mistress now.

Now that I have settled in, I have opened the folder of Papa's papers and spread some of them out on the desk in front of me. The contents so far appal me. My trial, the newspaper details, kept in neat order, hidden and festering in his desk for years. I had kept a few of them myself, in that old valise, along with a letter or two from the Doctor and also that notebook he gave me, but nothing as thorough and as professional as Papa's collection. During the trial, Papa said little or nothing to me, finally protesting when I had him called into court as my witness, but here they are, every sordid newspaper report neatly cut out, dated and filed as a good librarian should. All the putrid spewing of Corney Wall in his grubby rag the *Dublin Daily Sentinel*. Did Papa read them all, even the nasty references to his own reputation for eccentricity and the misery of his house near St Patrick's Cathedral? I have done wrong in my life and, if I believed in an afterlife, then I would sincerely hope that some place of punishment awaited me. If so, such men and women, journalists who are happy to write like this, certainly deserve their place in hell too, perhaps the eternal torment of being rendered mute and having their venomous prose read out to them again and again, Corney Wall being the most roasted, the most tormented, his fat cheeks boiled up like a chicken in a pot. The man who betrayed me for a few cheap newspaper articles and took his pleasure from his fumblings, my payment for his help. Of course Miss Jennings certainly did look through the folder. It was little wonder that she refused to have tea with me. Has Papa's portrait been taken down? Another unexpected link with the dreaded court case in the Old Bailey: another outbreak of bindweed to be rooted up and destroyed.

I have decided to take the file of newspaper cuttings and read the contents every day in the main reference room of the British Museum. I attempted to read some last night here in my hotel room, but the thought of all those memories returning was too painful and I need some sleep to get through each day. I read these loathsome pages while others are present. It is curious, but few memories survive of that whole period of my life, those months of restlessness and planned attack and then the days of the trial, with the packed courthouse and the heat of the stuffy room. Looking back, all I can clearly remember is the look of disdain on Jane's face when my lawyer, Mr Butt, her own former paramour, asked her directly if she thought there had been an illicit relationship between myself and her husband.

'When Miss Travers complained to you of your husband's attempt upon her virtue,' Mr Butt asked, his dark, flabby face lit up with the innocent wonder of inquiring moral rectitude, 'why did you not answer her letter? What was your reason?'

Jane turned to look directly at me before replying, with studied indifference and, underneath, a kind of pleasure in this chance to make public her off-handedness.

'Because I was not interested.'

'Do you really mean that?' Mr Butt asked, delighted with the success of his attack.

'Yes, I do mean that.'

I remember the pleased look on the face of my solicitor after she had spoken, the look of true dislike towards Jane on the judge's face and my own anger that she had known all along. I also recall the feeling of dread that made me want to run from the courtroom and the thickening feeling in my throat, the first intimation that I was losing my sanity.

Tuesday 4 June

I am glad that I know no one in London, as I reread the story of my younger self in these old newspaper pages, a self that was so angry, so foolish, so determined. For the past few days, I have been making my way every morning in the bright sunshine through the summer blossoms of Bloomsbury and then I take my seat in the lovely domed reading room of the British Museum, open the folder and read through these reports, appalled and spellbound. This Moll Travers is another woman, full of her own righteousness and wrath. At times she horrifies me, but at other times I want to protect her. Sometimes I glance around, afraid that some venerable reader in the library will have overheard the drama replaying in my head and will order me to leave.

At lunchtime, outside in the sunshine, I eat the cold lunch the hotel housekeeper has prepared for me, drink some tea from a kiosk at the main gate, look at the other readers on their break and wonder about their lives. The bearded men, all grave and weighty, the young men and women, unsmiling, bookish, oblivious of their own beauty, or so it seems to me. Here and there are women like me, older, respectable, and confident in their learning. I look in the mirror and, like them, I appear sane, healthy, well-nourished and acceptable in any public institution or hotel, safe, invisible. Maybe I could live such a life, move here to London, rent a small flat in nearby Gordon Square or Gower Street and make study my occupation, taking courses at the university, attending evening lectures, even sending an essay or two for consideration to a literary or scholarly journal.

But no, my publishing days are over, and a good thing too, if the evidence of these newspaper reports is to be believed. We have only one chance or, at most, two to remake ourselves, to escape, in any life, and my chances have gone. In my late fifties, I am old. Every morning my body creaks and complains when I arise from my bed. Last year, on an icy morning, I slipped and knocked my knee against the low garden wall outside Mitchelstown Castle and now daily, my knee reminds me with a sharp twinge of that encounter with the wall. That blow to my knee will remain with me to my death. It seems as if my youth was filled with angry yearning but the years have simply replaced that yearning with a grim recognition of time lost irrevocably.

My day's reading over, I go back to the hotel, have dinner and then take advantage of the sunny evenings to walk around Bloomsbury for an hour or so, up through Gordon Square, across Tavistock Place and sometimes along the Euston Road towards Regent's Park. I need that walk to clear my head of all the thoughts that my reading engenders. How can I continue to walk, eat, sleep, write, enjoy the sunshine when I read of the poisoned life of that harridan Moll Travers, her illicit relationship with a married man, the false friendship with his wife, the campaign of harassment, the lies she told in court? Because, to me, Moll Travers, Dr Wilde's Earnest Moll, is dead, as dead as he is, as dead as his daughter, Jane's child, as dead as those poor girls in the County Monaghan. Moll is dead and now Miss Travers lives, a fifty-seven-year-old spinster, a member of the Church of Ireland, the owner of several houses and shops in the Liberties district of Dublin, and a respectable reader in the British Museum. She lives and Moll is dead and that is how I can read these newspaper reports and then sleep at night. I return to my room, more and more anxious to write. This diary is my sole companion in this unfamiliar city.

It has just occurred to me. I do know someone in London. Jane.

Wednesday 5 June

Last night I was looking over the old Swift notebook that the Doctor once gave me, all those years ago when I began working with him, and it occurred to me that I have never read the final version of that book, our relationship at a point of estrangement when it was finally published in the same year as my trial. Today I checked the catalogue of the British Museum and there it was. *The Closing Years of Dean Swift's Life* by William R.W. Wilde. I requested it and spent the rest of the day reading it, losing myself in the lively intelligence of the writing. It is a fine book, full of energy and wit, yet compassionate and fluent in his argument that the late Dean of St Patrick's had not been mad but merely afflicted with a disorder of the inner ear, leading to an unbalancing, a derangement of his physical sense, but not of his reason. The writing is clear and uncluttered, as well it should be, with all the corrections and editing I made to the original manuscript. The Doctor wrote rapidly and with little thought for correct spelling or punctuation, and so it was my task to edit and make smooth and I enjoyed the challenge, particularly because the story itself seemed to me to be a compelling one. This book was the pretext for our journey to the County Monaghan, the purpose of our train journey where we worked together on the manuscript, and I look on that trip as perhaps the happiest weekend of my life.

It was not without some difficulty that I managed to evade Mamma's all-seeing eye and meet the Doctor at Amiens St station. Mamma could be dangerously discerning in relation to my comings and goings, even though she had already stopped speaking to me. This happened when I announced that, after months of covert instruction from an elderly clergyman attached as prebendary to St Patrick's Cathedral, I had been received into the Church of Ireland. This was sin enough in her pious eyes, but I had also written to her confessor, Monsignor Roche, to inform him of my conversion, or, perhaps as he would have seen it, my perversion. She was livid, as I had hoped, and I came home to find her standing in the parlour with Monsignor Roche's letter in her hand.

'Mary, if you do not desist from this foolishness, then you and I will have nothing further to say to each other.'

I shrugged, not believing her to be serious, but she did keep her word, as only Mamma could, with all communications made via Emily, the handmaid of the Lord, and all attempts on my part to speak directly to her blocked with her raised hand. Eventually I stopped and so we settled into a truce of non-communication, sharing the same table at breakfast and supper without a word passing between us. Still, she could convey much with her face and with the set of her shoulders, and I feared banishment from her comfortable house and perpetual exile to Papa's dreary home. I told Emily that I was staying at Papa's for a few days to work on the Swift manuscript and also to try, while he was away in Belfast, to drive out some of the damp by keeping a fire alive in the downstairs parlour. Emily looked a little sour, but I knew she would tell Mamma and that would keep them both at bay for the five days I needed.

The Doctor and I met as arranged at Amiens St, on an early February afternoon. All the travel arrangements had been made, the first-class seats to Dundalk and onwards to Ballybay, the carriage to meet us there. I was surprised at first that his servant Barney was in attendance, but he made himself invisible in third-class, emerging only to deal with luggage and to fetch the carriage for us. Besides, he was never to be seen in the house in Merrion Square. As I sit here, remembering, in another city and more than thirty years later, those hours on the train to Monaghan are still precious, have a kind of protected, almost heaven-like air around them that William's later polite indifference and my own demented rage can never taint. I see us, the young woman and the man, sitting together close on the busy train, working on the manuscript, and nothing has tarnished the glow of expectation around us for me.

I took notes and listened while the Doctor talked with energy about the relationship between Dean Swift and Stella, particularly the story that, on her deathbed, Stella begged Swift to acknowledge her as his secret wife, but he refused in anger and stormed away from her bedside. In revenge, she changed her will and gifted her fortune away from him and to a hospital instead. It was if all obstacles had melted miraculously as we worked side by side at our table, while those around us dozed or read their newspapers. Every so often, he would press my arm into his, a delicious conspiracy of intimacy in a public place, the reassurance of his warmth near me. I knew, without needing to tell myself, that by the end of the day, we would be together as lovers. Knowing nothing would prevent that, I was unhurried, at peace.

When we arrived in the small railway station, it was already dark and Barney went out to collect a carriage to drive the hour or so to the vicarage. As we settled ourselves into the comfortable interior, and began our journey through the dark, unknown night, he mentioned that his brother, the Reverend Ralph, as he called him, was away from home, collecting his two wards, Miss Em and Miss Mimi, from their school in Belfast and that we would have sole possession of the house during our visit. Understanding what that meant for us, I took his hand and settled it on my breast. The motion of the carriage soon put him to sleep on my shoulder and, as we drove, I watched him, looking so much younger, his face smooth and unlined, his expression almost innocent. From time to time, as we travelled slowly through the unlit countryside, I would touch his lips as gently as I could or trail a finger through his hair, marvelling at the lines of his sleeping face and the soft fullness of his lips.

Tiredness and hunger had made me pleasantly light-headed by the time we arrived in the dark house, and I allowed him link me into the front drawing room, clearly his lover, and settle me down on the sofa while Barney and he bustled around, lighting candles, building up the fire. The housekeeper had left out supper for us under silver dishes, and a tureen of soup with a spirit lamp underneath. William cut bread, opened wine, carved cold ham and beef and insisted on bringing the heated soup and the food on a tray to me. Content that the fire was blazing, Barney withdrew for the night and William joined me to eat and drink and sit close in the dim candlelight, watching the fire crackle. We sat silently, when we had finished eating and drinking and I was afraid that he or I would fall asleep again and so, determined that the moment had finally arrived, I moved my head over to kiss his face. I worried that we would clash, that our mouths would not fit together, that he would find me clumsy or lacking in some way. Instead, as our mouths came together, I found myself tasting the tang of tobacco on his tongue, and, fainter again, the florid scent of red wine. As if by some unknown accord, our tongues, stealthy, pliant, caressed each other with a confidence and an energy that startled me. Despite myself, some knowledge was taking me over, an unerring instinct, and the cushions on the sofa were moving and spilling as we kissed and struggled together, our clothes becoming unbearably hot and unnecessary.

Once, when my hands rested on his thumping chest, he whispered pleadingly, 'Please, may we stay together tonight?' and I nodded, wondering why he needed to ask me. This decided him and, taking my hand, he raised me up. As if in some kind of daze, or waking hallucination, we quenched the sole candle, put screens up against the bright fire, and then he opened the door and led me up the short stairs to the narrow first landing.

'This is to be yours, I believe,' he said, pushing open a door already slightly ajar and drawing me into the room with him. A large double bed was prepared, already turned down for me, and my travelling case and small trunk placed next to the dressing table. We stood, still breathing deeply, smiling a little awkwardly at each other and he took my hand and kissed it. It was unnerving to have to return to the words of everyday exchange after this whole new way of being with each other had occurred, but he asked, 'Have you enough courage for this?'

I thought it a peculiar question. Courage to take a lover, another woman's husband. Yes, I had. Of course, that was not what he meant. He was concerned about a more commonplace risk.

In answer, I began to unbutton his shirt and he stood breathing deeply while I undressed him in some haste, afraid the moment would pass. Without his clothes, his body seemed younger, slighter even, unused to light, yet by the glow of the fire almost unbearably beautiful to me, sculpted and muscular. I turned and he put his lips to my neck, kissing and even softly biting while his hands slid down into my open dress and he completed the undressing he had begun downstairs. Without our clothes, our skin seemed unbearably alive and the powerful aroma of his breath and the other scents arising from his body and mine, the scents of heat, fresh sweat and arousal, rose up around us and he turned me, cupped the small of my back and drew me against him. I felt a pleasurable choking pulse in my throat that spread downwards with each drawn-out breath deep into the centre of my body as his skin moved against mine and his fingers traced light touches over my breasts and down my stomach. The vulnerable beauty of his body was unexpected, somehow touching, and the renewal of our kissing was like a familiar conversation resumed. All this made me courageous. I found that I could kiss him and touch him as I wished, with increasing confidence. When he moved me towards the bed, I felt no fear and there, when we lay down, and he moved closer and closer towards me, my body welcomed him and our bodies joined with care and, eventually, with focused pleasure.

It was only later, with Corney, that I realised how fortunate William and I had been on that first night. I know now that William was no low seducer of young women. Rather, he was something more dangerous, a middle-aged romantic, seeking to cheat time with this infatuation for a young lover. Separately, we both found something, something we had waited for and we were each, for a moment, lifted out of our habitual selves. We were lucky, I suppose, but only he understood that our luck was all that we had to link us and that it would pass, and that when it did pass, it would mean little or nothing for the idea of 'us'. We were never together; we were merely in the same place. Had I been old enough to understand that, I would have been grateful for that alone. He was experienced enough to realise that this was a miraculous accident of chance and nothing more. He should have told me this. Perhaps he tried to. If he did, I do not remember. My ears would have been closed to such realism.

The next morning, when I awoke, to my disappointment he was already dressed, his beautiful body covered by drab brown cloth, somehow now intimidatingly worldly. He had opened my small hand case and was looking through the contents. He became aware of me, watching him, and carried the case over to me, kissing my brow by way of apology.

'Forgive my furtive search amongst your belongings. I wanted to know more about you. I wasn't planning to steal your watch chain. Am I forgiven?'

He kissed me again and I had hoped that he might rejoin me in bed but he held in his hand my little notebook, the one I carried in my pocket, for scribbling.

He held it up. 'May I? Or am I being over-familiar?'

I hesitated. I tried to recall what was in this book. Nothing about him, as I remembered. He noticed my hesitation and handed it to me.

'I have been too familiar. Forgive me.'

'Not at all. It is nothing, a few jottings.'

'A diary? Full of sensational confessions.'

I smiled.

'Nothing so interesting. Just a commonplace book. Sometimes I write down fragments of poetry, phrases that please me. Nothing else.'

He stared at me, a light blush coming to his face.

'What a strange young woman you are, so quiet and reserved and yet so full of hidden surprise.'

He took back the book and opened it, flicking through the pages until he came to my last entry. He began to read it out.

> *'But I have lived and have not lived in vain:*
> *My mind may lose its force, my blood its fire,*
> *And my frame perish even in conquering pain;*
> *But there is that within me which shall tire*
> *Torture and Time, and breathe when I expire....'*

He looked up at me, a glint in his eye and, wordlessly, reached down, took out a small book from his waistcoat pocket and handed it to me. *Childe Harold.*

'I carry it with me everywhere. How could you know that he is the voice, the sole voice of my own maddened soul...?'

He stopped talking and I tried not to stare at this unusual, passionate man.

'Now I must leave you alone to prepare yourself for breakfast. We have more work to do. My brother arrives in two days with Mimi and Em and when the Marmosets arrive, their ceaseless chatter will disrupt our work and drive us to distraction and insanity.'

I was dressed and leaving the room when I encountered the housekeeper, a comely, grey-haired woman on the stairwell, and I nodded pleasantly and moved forward to introduce myself. She stopped, raised her hand as if to halt me, shook her head and then turned away abruptly, leaving me standing there alone. I was a little shaken but I joined William in the library and decided not to mention the encounter.

Later that morning, we resumed our work. The abrupt transition back to the world of Dean Swift was a peculiar one, especially because he would break off from time to time and stare at me, long loving glances that disconcerted me and made me utter some dismissive remark to make him stop staring. Still, this house was ours, to do as we wished, and after lunch, again provided by Barney, we went for a walk around the small lake near the house, a dreary steel-grey body of water with a few ducks fluttering up in our path. He held my arm very lovingly and we strolled back in the gloomy twilight to the house, a fire already visible in the front room and food left for us on the table. We had a full day of this solitude and the freedom to kiss where we would, all around the old house.

The next day, after tea by the fire, I had gone upstairs to my room for a sleep, and awoke from something of a feverish sleep to hear the sounds of voices in the hallway. I looked out and saw that another carriage had arrived. Dressing for dinner, I heard the sound of girlish voices in the hall and a running up and down the stairs. I waited until all had gone quiet and then made my way downstairs. The study door was open and I could hear William's voice raised.

'Really, Ralph, how much of this must I listen to? Your damned housekeeper had no business sending for you.'

Another voice, deep and pleasant as his, but rising higher with annoyance, interrupted him.

'You will listen to as much as I need to say. This is my house and you must....'

Unwilling to keep listening any longer, I knocked loudly and then, after a moment or two, I pushed opened the door and entered, to see William sprawled on the sofa by the fire, while an older man stood over him, looking like thunder. There was a strong resemblance between him and this older man, Ralph. It was an unpleasant resemblance, as if William had had all his vitality and energy drained away by the years. Looking at Ralph and the lined, wasted face and grey hair, it was as if I was seeing William in later life, and it was unnerving. Nevertheless, something of the family charm surfaced when Ralph saw me. William got hurriedly to his feet.

'Mary, Miss Travers. Can I introduce you to my brother, the Reverend Ralph?'

The older man walked over to me, a smile on his face, took my hand in his and pressed it kindly. He held on to it as he spoke.

'Miss Travers, you must forgive us the lack of any proper welcome. My foolish brother had forgotten that I and my wards would still be away from home until today and so let me apologise for the cold, solitary house and for our absence. You are most welcome, most welcome indeed.'

The warmth of his apologies rebuked William and, by implication, myself. William stood there, looking politely bewildered, as if he were somehow apart from all this.

'Reverend Wilde, thank you indeed for your kind hospitality. It is such a beautiful situation here and I am so grateful to you for inviting me.'

'Now, now, we must be Ralph and Mary. Do tell me of your father. We were at Trinity together, you know, and I have not seen him for many years.'

Each word of kindness was like a needle jabbed into my skin, and William was of no assistance, wandering around the room and picking up books as he went, clearly anxious to leave. Fortunately we could hear steps on the stairs and the sound of voices laughing. William's face lit up.

'Those little monkeys! Where are you?'

Two young girls entered the room behind me, holding hands and then advancing to mock-curtsey to William. He grabbed them up from their curtsey and roughly embraced them, the two clearly enjoying the attention. They were young, the elder around thirteen, and the younger no more than eleven, and clearly sisters, both pretty with russet gold hair, the elder darker than the younger. The kinship to William and Ralph was also evident at first sight, the same slightly simian features translated into girlish prettiness, the deep-set eyes, the strong foreheads, all made delicate and appealing. William was a great favourite, and they enjoyed his mock rebuke as he brought them over to present them to me.

'Now, Miss Travers, I have the regrettable task of introducing you to two of the silliest Marmosets in the kingdom of Ireland, Miss Mimi and Miss Em. Miss Travers is a serious young woman from the city of Dublin who is helping me write a book and she has no patience with giddy girls, no patience at all.'

He laughed, as did Ralph, but I could see the Reverend had little credence for the idea of me as a serious scholar. The girls shook my hand. The older girl Mimi, spoke up, a confident manner that made me like her instantly.

'Miss Travers, please do not listen to Uncle Doctor. I am a fine scholar, as Uncle Reverend will tell you.'

At this, Ralph laughed and nodded.

'But I cannot answer for my sister Emily. Have you ever met such a provoking child, Miss Travers?'

I smiled. 'She seems much civilised to me.'

I took the younger girl by the hand.

'I too have a younger sister called Emily. She tells me that I am the foolish one and she the wiser, and sometimes I think she is right.'

'Do you live with your sister in Dublin?' the younger girl asked.

I nodded.

'Imagine another Mary and Emily, just like us but in Dublin. Dublin must be a splendid city. I long to visit. Aunt Jane writes and says we must come and see her soon in Merrion Square.'

Ralph intervened, Jane's name hanging on the air unpleasantly, for us adults at least. 'Now, no more of your nonsense and please allow Miss Travers some peace. We may as well proceed to dinner since it is almost eight o'clock. Girls, please show our guest to the table.'

We made our way to the dining room and I sat between the girls, both full of questions about Dublin and stories about their school in Belfast, while little was said between the brothers, the girl's easy chattering covering up the awkwardness.

Finally, Ralph spoke.

'William, have you made arrangements for the girls as I asked?' He smiled at me. 'I am taking a trip in the later spring and early summer, Miss Travers, one I have dreamt of all my life, all the way to Jerusalem. These girls will need minding while I am away.'

William spoke up, glad of a chance to make all well with his brother. 'Yes, indeed. Eily has promised to travel down here in the spring and keep house whenever the girls are back from school.'

Em made a face. 'Eily.'

William turned to her sharply. 'Now, I will have none of that. Eily Black is a good woman and very kind to you two.'

The younger girl looked abashed at his reproach and her mouth quivered, threatening the onset of tears, but Mimi silently took her hand and pressed it in her own and then turned to ask William, 'When will she come to us? Will you visit too?'

'I'm afraid I cannot. This new book must be ready for publication by March and already I am late. Indeed, Miss Travers and I must return to Dublin early tomorrow morning to deliver the first part of the manuscript to the Royal Irish Academy.'

He turned to me and asked somewhat abruptly, 'Can you be ready by seven? We can make the nine o'clock train in Ballybay.'

I nodded, the suddenness of our departure a relief. I was surprised at the quickness of his decision, but not sorry to hear that we were to leave the house in the morning. The sincere innocent charm of the two girls and the kindness of the Reverend's manner were, in different ways, something of a torture for me.

After supper, we sat in the drawing room, and I tried not to think back to my previous evenings in that room and on that sofa as Mimi, Em and I sat together and looked through their drawing albums and music books while the two brothers chatted by the fire, all apparently harmonious now, consulted maps of the Levant, going over household accounts and making arrangements for the coming months.

'Miss Travers,' Mimi asked, as she and her sister stood up to make their farewells before bed, 'may we ask a favour? When you return to Dublin, will you write and send your address. We should like to send you a small drawing or two, from time to time.'

I smiled.

'It would be my pleasure. I will write to the Reverend and I'm sure he will ensure that our letters pass safely between us.'

I looked over at their uncle.

'Now, silly girls, off up to bed and stop bothering Miss Travers with all this nonsense.'

I understood. No letters would pass between the girls and this young woman, who was foolish or reckless enough to allow herself to be so exposed.

We all made our good nights, promising to meet at breakfast, and I escaped as soon as I could to my room.

The next morning, after my lone breakfast in the still dark dining room, William joined me to say that Barney was ready with the carriage to drive us to the train. No Em, no Mimi and no Reverend. On my breakfast place, I found a small posy of early snowdrops, tied with white thread, with my name in careful writing on a small piece of paper on my breakfast place. I put it in my case and forgot about it. It was only later, years later, when I heard of the manner of their deaths that I remembered that posy and I cried foolish, useless tears for those two sisters, the happier Mary and Emily, united in death, as their gravestone is said to read. I should have defied the Reverend and written. Tomorrow I must write again to my own Emily.

Kew Gardens
Thursday 6 June

The beauty of the summer morning made me restless and so I abandoned my reading for a day and took myself away from the centre of London, for some green grass and trees and the sight of flowering blossoms against summer clouds. There is an expensive food shop on the corner opposite the hotel, with strawberries and other luscious fruits in the window and I went there this morning and bought fresh bread, black grapes, figs and a wedge of expensive French white cheese. I took a cab out here to Kew, to sit on a bench in the midst of this riot of flowers. I am surrounded by the intoxicating perfume of the lime trees and watch tiny fragments of white blossom drift down from some exotic trees and float past me while I eat my summer picnic. Kew. I smiled when I remembered a snatch of verse by Pope that William used to quote whenever he saw a pompous old professor from Trinity College, a man with a face like a bad-tempered old pug and a self-important drawl: '*I am his Highness' dog at Kew; / Pray tell me, sir, whose dog are you?*'

So many thoughts of William. I sit here, alone, scribbling in my diary as the perfect June afternoon floats and dawdles all around me, the light breeze, the floating fragments of blossom, the fluffy clouds above as innocent as the painted ceiling of a baby's nursery. On such a day, the purpose of living is clear to everyone, young and old. All we are required to do is admire the day. Some of the fig juice has dripped onto the pages of this diary, and onto my dress, and the sight of it makes me happy. I succumbed to this longing for the scent of full-blown roses and the taste of black grapes because those memories of William gave me a longing, however vicariously, for something of the sun, of the delight of the senses.

When I came back from Monaghan, it was to find a council of war assembled and waiting for me at home. Mamma had uncovered my deception, alerted by a letter from Ralph, and she took immediate action. I walked into her house to find Emily, Mamma and Papa there, with Aunt Belle and Monsignor Roche in attendance, all sitting uncomfortably around a late breakfast in the dining room. It was a fine spring day and, despite the early start, William's embrace at parting had buoyed me up and I was singing as I walked home to Percy Place in the cold sunshine. As soon as I entered the room, I knew what was about to happen, but I was unconcerned. William wanted me and that was all I needed. Papa looked harassed and I felt sorry for him, as he loathed the unctuous Monsignor; in fact, he had dubbed him Extreme Unction, after the sacrament. He stood near to Aunt Belle, Mamma's younger sister, whom he had always liked. Indeed, we all liked Aunt Belle and her girls, Clara and Nan, but her husband, Mr Ellis, was another matter, a red–faced little man with a permanent whiff of whiskey and a penchant for the covert pinching of pretty nieces. Mamma bullied Aunt Belle as relentlessly as she did Papa, with more result, but I knew that my good-natured aunt would be genuinely shocked and concerned for me, and I thought it a pity that Mamma had forced her to learn of her niece's disgrace.

'Mary, is it true that you travelled with William Wilde to Monaghan? I am told that you stayed there in his brother's house, and without the permission of the family?'

I shrugged. Why discuss this? Mamma would never listen, her ever practical mind already on the next part of her campaign of coercion.

'I take this for a yes, you foolish girl. If you continue this course of action, and I cannot prevent you, I tell you now that I will not support it. You are debarred from all our standing accounts in the nearby shops, unless you promise me to stop seeing this man.'

She threw a glance at Emily, who looked away. Nevertheless, she would follow her instructions, I knew.

I said nothing. Money was not important, I thought, with all the folly and arrogance of youth.

'From now on, you must rely on your father for financial assistance,' she continued, with something of a smirk, knowing that no one, not even he himself, could rely on him for that.

'Robert, you talk to her. You are her father. This is your fault: you introduced them, knowing, as well as anyone else, the nature of the man's reputation.'

What reputation, I wondered. Papa murmured something vague about how painful all this was and Mamma made a face of derision at him. I could not prevent myself from flashing out at her. 'Mamma, must we witness another fight between you and Papa?'

I was tired at the defeated look on Papa's face.

'Mary,' Aunt Belle spoke up. She looked unhappy with this threat of open warfare between us, and her gentle face was flushed pink. 'I was reluctant to credit you with such behaviour, but am I now to understand that it is true?'

I nodded. I was proud of myself. Clara and Nan could boast of no such conquest. Nan was to be married to her dull lawyer fiancé and Clara had a distant cousin on the other side of the family as her beau.

Aunt Belle flushed a deeper pink, her mouth closing into a tight bunch.

'Then please, my dear girl, please, I beg you, as you know my affection for you to be true and my concern for your welfare to be sincere, please give this man up. I know his reputation to be unsavoury and that of his wife even more so. My own girls have been terribly worried, and we are all extremely fond of you. Promise your mother that it is at an end and we will receive you as if nothing at all has occurred.'

That wasn't quite true. They preferred Emily and found me too bookish, but they were always kind and welcoming, and I had so few friends, so few houses where I could call without any question. That was about to end, I could see. This upset me, but, as Mamma was watching me closely, hoping for such a result, I remained impassive. I loved my cousins and relied on them for the sparse social life I possessed. I might be barred from seeing them, but nothing would dissuade me from seeing William.

The Monsignor spoke up. I presume he felt obliged to earn his hearty breakfast.

'Mary, child, he is a *married* man. You are in grave peril.'

'I am no longer in your pastoral care and, if I need spiritual advice, I will consult with my clergyman, Reverend Andrews.'

Mamma sprang from her chair and advanced on me, her face becoming buckled with annoyance. I hoped that she might strike me, in full view of her beloved priest. She stood before me, took a deep breath and said, 'Mary, this will be the last exchange between us for quite a while. Now go to your room. Your father will call on William Wilde this afternoon and put an end to all this nonsense.'

Papa did go and see him. William told me about it the following week when we paced the Liffey quays for an hour or so in the early evening gloom. I had called to the surgery the day after the council of war and Barney silently handed me a note from William suggesting a meeting elsewhere, because the surgery was too public. In his note, William told me that both men had gone through the charade of discussing me. Knowing them both, I can only imagine Papa's diffidence being equally matched by William's protective patina of bewilderment and so nothing was achieved there. He also asked me to meet him at the Essex Street bridge that evening and so we walked and stopped where we could to kiss, fleetingly. Generous as ever, William proposed making me a direct allowance himself. I refused this and in the end we agreed that I would be his paid assistant on the Swift book and on his newly commissioned catalogue of gold for the Royal Irish Academy. He would also seek reviewing work for me with the *Dublin Daily Sentinel* through his contact with one of the editors, an old friend, Corney Wall.

I was uneasy about calling to the surgery on Lincoln Place and, again William had an answer for this. This woman, Eily Black, was travelling down to Monaghan to take care of the Reverend Ralph's house, and she had a small house, more of a cottage, just off Werburgh Street. William was the owner of this house and it would now be vacant for the spring and summer. I could have my own keys and work there as I needed, conveniently close to Papa's house and to Marsh's Library, and so we could meet there, undisturbed by Mamma. I was not quite prepared to be expelled from Mamma's house and to be forced to starve and shiver in Papa's house and so it was essential that she remain as much in the dark as possible. William's practical turn of mind and his quick grasp of possible ways out of our dilemma impressed me. And all that summer, we were able to meet and to love in the little house in Werburgh Street.

When I think of those spring and summer months with him, and the little house next to the sewing shop, I close my eyes and smell the colours of summer heat and the house filled with shimmering excitement. It was a beautiful, sun-filled spring and then a summer of unusual heat, and I can still recall the dim reflection of golden light on the ceiling of the small front room, a shadow of the fierce afternoon sun outside, his deep voice growing lighter as his pleasure became more intense and his sobs of laughter at the moment of release, on one occasion, myself squirming fully dressed on his naked body. He told me that he owned this row of little houses and rented this one and the adjoining shop to Eily. That shop had the name Maria Amelia Blake painted in gold and white above the shuttered shop front and it was closed down while she had gone away to take care of Mimi and Em. A dusty, neglected shop it looked, unlike the neat and tidy little cottage where I spent my afternoons, working on William's manuscripts and on the reviewing work he had procured for me from Corney Wall and waiting for him to come and make love whenever he was free.

I had not met Eily at this time, but the small cottage was filled with her presence, samples of the knitting and the needlework from her shop next door on shelves, a pencil drawing of two girls framed above the fireplace, verses from Byron worked on samplers and set into glass. I often wondered about the woman whose house I had come to know so well. I was careful never to enter her bedroom but worked downstairs on a sofa by the piano, and it was here that William and I were together so many times that summer, with the curtains drawn and my desire for him making me bolder and more assertive, to his great delight.

Money ran out much more quickly than I had anticipated. Emily proved unexpectedly helpful as the economic reality of Mamma's interdict began to dawn on me and I found myself short of gloves and handkerchiefs and without the cash to pay for them. I was attempting, without much success, to repair an old pair of gloves one morning when Emily told me that she was making some purchases for Mamma and for herself in Flood's drapery, if I wanted to come with her, she would get me new gloves on account. Mamma was eagle-eyed with the household accounts but Emily knew a trick or two. Thinking about it now, I'm not sure if it was not Emily herself who paid for the gloves. I was grateful to her for this tacit support, for we never spoke of William and she had remained silent throughout the council of war. We put on our coats and bonnets and made our way to Grafton Street. The shop was busy and we were looking through some new samples of ribbons and waiting for the attention of a sales assistant when Emily silently nudged me and nodded towards a tall woman who was speaking about a dress with the head seamstress, Mrs Reilly.

'And so we are settled. The white satin and the dress will be trimmed with black lace and with bunches of green velvet made in the fashion of shamrocks. Thank you, my dear Mrs Reilly; I will indeed be a spectacle of great beauty and a credit to you.'

Mrs Reilly was wreathed in smiles and all attention to the woman and I watched her closely, knowing who she was and why Emily had prodded me. Jane. His wife. The celebrated Speranza. She was taller than I, and older, but undeniably handsome, with straight dark hair touched here and there with a becoming lock of white. Her manner to the saleswoman was without affectation, genial and lively. At that moment, our names were called loudly by the young male clerk.

'Miss Travers, please. Your mother's alterations have just come down from the workshop.'

We moved up to the counter and Emily and he were soon lost in minute inspections of the new coat and skirt. Jane had turned to leave but, as she paused over some lacework, her dark eyes met mine for an instant. Something in that glance chilled me and I feared that she would come over to me but, at that moment, an elderly woman touched her arm to catch her attention and there were kisses and embraces and 'dearest Jane' and 'my dear Cecily' and then the two women left the shop arm in arm. I turned and made to speak about her to Emily, but she had already found some gloves for me and her thoughts was now firmly on the haberdashery.

The following week, in Eily's cottage, William handed me a letter. It was from his wife. I guessed from the seal. I looked at him. 'Open it,' he said. 'Jane will not bite you.'

Had she been enlisted in the campaign against me? Apparently not.

'My dear William has been telling me about your work and your learning and I feel that I must get to know you. Permit him to bring you to me some afternoon soon and we shall clear the premises of all redundant males, including husband and small boys, and thus talk. Do promise that you will. Jane Wilde. 1 Merrion Square.'

He read it himself and then kissed me on the nose.

'You must come and meet her. You two will get along famously. Two of the most intelligent people I know.'

I was uneasy.

'Are you certain? Perhaps she will resent me.'

What I really feared was that I might resent her.

The following week, when I called into Merrion Square by arrangement, ostensibly to collect some money, the Doctor was still at home and presented me to Jane, just returned with their little boys, Willie and Oscar, from a few days in their house in Bray. He led me into her drawing room, more than a little nervously, and she was alone and about to have tea. She stood up, taller than him, and said nothing, taking my hand into hers with great energy. She beamed at me for a moment and then began.

'My dear Miss Travers, this man of mine has been telling me all about your Herculean endeavours with his Swift book. Come, come, sit down by me and have some cake. We must balance our scholarship with some frivolity, and what is more earnestly frivolous than tea cake?'

She brought me to the tea table, pressed some cake and tea on me and sat me down. Turning, she said with gentle firmness, 'Now, William, 'you have monopolised Miss Travers for far too long. Leave us. This is my chance to get to know her.'

He smiled me a reassuring smile, pressed her arm and left us to tea. I sat on the couch, my teacup in one hand and some cake crumbled up and uneaten on the plate before me, full of fear, while she talked and asked me questions, kind inquiries after my father, 'our learned Robert', said without any irony, as if she meant it and, discreetly, a little later, with slightly less warmth, after Mamma, 'dearest Anne'. All the while I watched her and said little, the large, beautiful expressive eyes and so much talk – beguiling, charming, comforting talk, caressing away all my fears.

'You young women are the hope of our beloved country: young women with intelligence, scholarship and bravery. I am teaching my two sons to revere Ireland above all else and they will do great deeds for our country when they are grown up into men, but we need our young women to be just as truthful.'

People spoke of Jane as over-theatrical, as self-dramatising, but all I can remember today as I sit here is the warmth that drew me in, as different from the reserved intelligence of the Doctor, but just as potent. Perhaps even more so.

That first day, she produced a volume of her poems and presented it to me, with her inscription: 'To Dearest Mary, a sign of the future and a signal of hope for Ireland's young womanhood, from your true friend, Speranza.' She told me that we must always be Mary and Jane to each other, and while the afternoon passed quickly, she sat there and spoke of her time in the courtroom as a young woman in her early twenties, when she had tried to claim authorship of a seditious verse, a poem that could have brought her to jail. This story I was to hear again and again, with different variations, and always, she was its proud heroine. She had written a poem 'The Die is Cast', a call to arms against the Queen, published in a revolutionary paper, and when the police had raided the offices and arrested the editor, every effort was made to trace the author of this bloodthirsty verse.

'The editor was finally brought to trial,' she told me, her face still and grave with the drama of it all, 'and when the judge taxed Mr Gavan

Duffy with the authorship of the poem, I knew my moment had come. I had been sitting quietly in the body of the court, heavily veiled, and there and then I stood up. A great hush fell on the crowded courtroom as I attempted to own up. "It was I", I called out, three times. As soon as I had begun to speak, those around me made loud noises to drown out my confession, such was the chivalrous nature of the men of revolution. Thus was the judge prevented from hearing my confession and instead it was poor Mr Gavan Duffy who was deported to Australia where he prospered and became even more celebrated!'

It was pure melodrama and probably invented, but she told me the story with the practised ease of one confident that every one of her words would be listened to, and I loved it. Despite this, I cannot think ill of Jane. Or if I do try to think badly of her, one memory alone prevents that. I once watched her recite from memory a sonnet by Shakespeare at one of her afternoon literary events. Someone, I think it was her cousin, the witty young Reverend Maturin, or maybe it was the Doctor's assistant, Mr Wilson, was decrying the pernicious foreign influence of English literature when Jane silently stood up, closed her eyes and began to recite sonnet fifty-seven from memory. The room fell quiet. She began in a soft, vulnerable tone, as if she was speaking to herself: 'Being your slave, what should I do but tend/Upon the hours, and times of your desire?' I remember her voice and that poem, in a packed room, her voice so much quieter and more intimate than ever before, as if she was confessing a secret to each one of us, one at a time, and when she came to the next lines, 'I have no precious time at all to spend;/Nor services to do till you require', she made a tiny, beautiful gesture, a half-opening of her hand downwards in a self-deprecating way, a kind of apologetic admission of abjection. A woman who could recite a poem like that seems to me to be a woman in possession of a soul of outstanding compassion. I never doubted that; even when her soul was closed off to me. It was I who raged like Caliban at the loss. She needs it all now with her son in such public disgrace.

Jane had charm and energy, with talk to bemuse me, and books, so many books, and all of them necessary for me to read. I came away from

Merrion Square that day laden down and a note arrived soon afterwards inviting me for tea again. She was always amused at my punctiliousness in returning them as soon as I had finished reading them. 'Mary, you are truly the daughter of a first-rate librarian', a compliment I wasn't certain I appreciated but some of Jane's compliments did have that slight aftertaste of doubt. Soon, she and I were meeting on a regular basis, my fears about my love affair with William kept at bay by her clear liking for me, and she introduced me to their circle, Mr Wilson, William's young assistant, some sort of cousin to the Doctor, but heavy-looking, and rather dull, with a tendency to lecture on religious matters. She always included her own cousin, the handsome, lively young Mr Maturin, who was much better value for conversation and enjoyed teasing Jane and her friends, the two Miss Flynns, older women, both lively talkers and book readers and known to be women of independent means. Jane whispered that her young cousin was contemplating marriage with the younger Miss Flynn, Adelaide, some twenty years older than he was but in possession of an independent income. I liked Miss Adelaide, but such a conjunction seemed grotesque to my young eyes; she had deep lines on her forehead and underscoring her cheeks and Mr Maturin was so elegant and winsome with his dark hair and his bright blue eyes.

She also encouraged me to befriend her own sons, and this was no hardship, particularly with Willie, my favourite, a bright little boy with a pretty smile and his father's deep-set eyes and a mind full of curiosity. Jane was comical about her maternal duties. When I first visited the nursery upstairs under the attic, she showed me the lament she had pinned up over the nursery window. 'Alas the Fates are cruel/ Behold Speranza making gruel.' But she enjoyed the time with her children and some afternoons I sat with Jane in the nursery, while she attended to the boys during their nurse's rest time, and we fed them and sang songs to them and Willie always came and sat with me and asked me so many questions about my house and my sister and if I had any little boy of my own.

With the boys sent for a nap, we would return to the drawing room and read and have tea. Jane gave me a copy of her new work, *Sidonia the Sorceress*, and asked me for my opinion the next time we met.

'Your real opinion, mind. I expect no less of you. I always believe that it is only insignificant people who say what they are expected to say.'

I read it overnight, found the poem dark, exciting and daunting in places and marvelled at her sheer energy and dedication to her work. She was pleased at my words and at our shared hunger for poetry and books.

'I take it as a compliment that you called my poem daunting. A lesser soul would suspect that you simply found it impenetrable but I disdain all lesser mortals and shall read it as an affirmation. You are too shrewd not to divine my genius at first glance.'

She smiled as she reacted to my reading of the poem, but something made me think that perhaps I should not have been so frank and I noted it for our next conversation.

In all my visits, Jane asked me a great deal about home and was curious to meet Emily, but I discouraged that, saying Emily never read a book and was interested only in fashion and in journals about the doings of London society and the progress of the widowhood of the Queen. Jane disagreed about my lack of interest in my own attire and my contempt for Emily's silly obsession.

'No, indeed. For any woman of worth, dress ought to express a moral purpose; it symbolises the intellect.'

She told me once, in serious tones. 'A woman should study her own personality, be she a superb Juno, or a Pallas Athene. When the style suits her best, let her keep it.'

To prove her point, she showed me the gown she had ordered for a reception at Dublin Castle, all bunches of shamrock in green velvet catching up the expensive satin of the white dress. On any other woman it would have seemed farcical, fit for a burlesque, but on Jane, such was her self-possession, it made her look queenly.

The day is clouding and I must return to my hotel in Bloomsbury. Jane. Suddenly a longing for her, as intense as my longing for William, sweeps over me. Jane the sorceress. Did she bewitch me with a cold heart, and charm me merely to keep her husband's latest passing fancy firmly under her gaze? Or did she come to like me, to appreciate my mind, my taste, my discernment? I cannot say. Her charm was so innate that she could not help herself in making me love her; it was her instinct as much as William's. Did they discuss me, and make arrangements about me, Monday afternoon tea at Merrion Square with Jane, the following week with William in Eily's cottage, all part of a busy week?

Friday 7 June

It has been raining this morning and so I have decided to stay in my room and write. The sun has just come out again, even though a slight fall of rain persists, but I have no wish to leave. The lunch tray has come and gone, and still I sit here and write, filled with memories of that time and of Jane and William. If I were to close my eyes, his face comes back to me with difficulty – only his deep voice, his rather wheezy laugh and the rankness of his breath; but her face, round, pale, her neat black hair, touched with white, her lively stream of beguiling wit. And, behind that, my anger at her, another moment away, her shrewd judgements, her sharp mind and wide learning, weighing me up and finding me wanting.

William had provided me with some further work with the Royal Irish Academy, but this proved to be scantly recompensed and so he took me to the offices of the newly launched *Dublin Daily Sentinel* to meet the pompously named Cornelius Farrell-Wall, Corney to all, a journalist friend of his, and I took an immediate dislike to him. Partly it was his appearance: a tall, bald, fat man with a permanent look of being overheated, a reddened face with a moist, unpleasant glisten of sweat, but his looks were only part of my dislike. He called me Mary from the start, praising my learning simply on the strength of my father's name, and gave me books to review from that first meeting but insisted that I call in person to deliver the reviews. Always he took me into his own office where he poured a pale sherry for himself and all honeyed words ended while he took a great deal of pleasure in patronising me, editing my paltry reviews, spending long minutes pondering the construction of my sentences and my chosen vocabulary while I sat mute in the stuffy office and longed to take the expensive-looking decanter of sherry and pour it over his bare, waxy pate. But I sat and pretended to be grateful, since he paid well and had contacts with all sorts of other journals, even with barristers and politicians, as I was to discover. I knew also that he would dart covert looks at my bosom when he thought I was unaware.

Emboldened by my paltry success as a literary journalist, and a pound or two coming in each week, I returned to my own verse-writing with renewed energy, rising early in the morning to revise some old stanzas. For years I had attempted various forms of literary expression, working on lyric poems and even on a Gothic tale or two, and now my pen worked harder than it ever had before, for I was determined to make money as a poet as well as as a journalist. I concentrated my energies on two or three poems in particular, resolved to show Jane these works and secretly hoping for her instant recognition of my hidden powers as fellow verse-maker. After all, she had made me a gift of a volume of her own verse, and I knew that she was working on another, produced painstakingly in the long studious mornings sequestered in her bedroom, after breakfast with William and morning lessons with the boys, when she pretended to random callers to the house in Merrion Square that she was still slumbering, that she was a languid woman, lazy even. It was a myth she enjoyed cultivating, but in truth she was a marvel of industry, composing verse, translating, teaching herself new languages. I knew how seriously she took her writing, but I also know how she preferred not to display that seriousness. She told me once, 'My heart sinks when I am asked by this person or that how exactly to become a successful writer. It is tiresomely simple. All true writers simply write, and write and write, for long, tedious hours of applying pen to white sheets of paper. In this, there is no mystery, and those who do not understand this can never be told. Those who want to write, do so. Those who want to be writers, never do.'

And so, with some trepidation, I asked her one morning if I could show her some samples of my own verse. I was expecting some exclamation of delight but instead she looked at me gravely.

'Mary, may I ask, do you want me to praise your writings or do you want my true opinion? Should the first differ from the second, it may damage our friendship.'

I grew sulky.

'Indeed, Jane, I would not waste your time with my poor verses.'

She smiled and stroked my cheek, but refused to humour me.

'If they are indeed poor, then why waste my time with them? You are out of temper with me, but I like you too much not to be honest. So do not speak to me falsely of your poor verse.'

So I copied out three of the best verses, on clean white paper, into an expensive bound notebook I had bought with my review money and brought them to her when we next met. She thanked me graciously, but, somewhat to my surprise, the notebook was placed unopened on her table and she went on to talk about some new friend she had made from Sweden. Over the next two weeks, I called in as usual, but no mention was made of my poems, although my notebook had disappeared from the table, until finally I asked, 'And my own writings? Have you had a chance to read them?'

She smiled.

'I did. Now where did I put them?'

She began to riffle through her papers.

'Here!' she exclaimed.

She opened the notebook and began thumbing through the pages. The first few pages were as clean a copy as I had given her but she stopped at the third poem, 'Refusal', and I could see it was pitted and marked in dark green ink.

'Now this one, this seemed to me to have some promise.'

And the others? I wanted to ask. Were they to be dismissed without comment? It seemed that they were.

She began to read.

Refusal

I stand alone, defiant,
refusing to sink into grief,
too proud to lose myself in forgetful waters beneath Elsinore.
No, I am no Ophelia, to be cast aside.
No cowardly surrender into the babbling madness of the brook for me.
Nor will I be a subservient Cordelia,
Kneeling at the feet of the deranged king
The author of all my woes.

Antigone's task shall not be mine,
seek thine own burial, foolish warrior brother.
I demand that I transcend all inherited duty,
I shall not play these roles.
I insist that I, and, I alone, create mine own.

Jane paused, looked at me and then closed the book.

'Promise here, indeed some promise, but smothered by too many afternoons in the library. Your anger is to be valued but it strangles your poem, brings it to abortive birth before it can have the chance to live. You need to work it again and again and burnish it until the anger is subsumed and the verse shines like a polished gem. I have marked here and there some phrases of worth, but you must return to your task of creation. It has only begun.'

'Some phrases of worth.' I burned with anger but sat still and let her chatter on about her neighbour Mr LeFanu and his latest gothic tale. Later that day I took my own verses home with me to Papa's house and burnt them. I then took down the volume of her verse, and read it out loud.

To Ireland

My country wounded to the heart,
Could I but flash along thy soul.
Electric power to rive apart
The thunder-clouds that round thee roll.
And by my burning words, uplift
Thy life from out Death's icy drift,
Till the full splendours of our age
Shone round thee for thy heritage—
As Miriam's, by the Red Sea Strand
Clashing proud cymbals, so my hand,
Would strike thy harp,
Loved Ireland.

That was true poetry, each line smooth and faultless, like a perfect battle cry. I was a fool ever to show her my pitiful work.

Papa was upstairs in his study and came down when he heard my voice. He shook his head when he saw what I was reading.

'Why so disapproving, Papa?' I asked sharply.

Unusually for Papa, he spoke out and his pleasant, thin face grew hard as he railed against her.

'I remember well when Miss Jane Elgee, as she then was, published this dangerous nonsense. Her verse was seditious and at a time when the kingdom of Ireland was like a tinderbox. Her foolish doggerel could have brought disorder and rebellion on our heads. We were lucky to have survived, and no thanks to her fanaticism.'

I shrugged. 'Jane is a brave woman and no fanatic.'

He looked at me with something approaching dislike.

'Indeed. It was impossible not to read her verse without discerning the true abandonment of self that characterised the fanatic.'

I laughed at him.

'Papa, you sound like an editorial for a conservative newspaper.'

This drew unexpected ire from him.

'Do I? The real truth is that her time as a revolutionary poetess came to an abrupt end when Mrs Butt discovered her in the arms of her husband in the offices of *The Nation*. Jane's freedom-loving friends were none too pleased about her liaison with a married man, and she was soon reviled within nationalist circles.'

I was shocked. I had never heard my mild-mannered father speak so ill of anyone or indeed pass on gossip.

'Now you sound like a scandal sheet.'

I returned to my reading. His disapproval was enough commendation to me and I read all I could of Jane's verse.

Saturday 8 June

I decided to rise early today, wash and put on my finest dress and make my way back to the British Library for another day's reading. I could feel the old dread welling up in me when sleep failed me and I remembered Mamma's strict regime when I was ill in the weeks after the trial and my voice had failed me. I forced myself to write to Emily, to go shopping for books and newspapers, to buy fruit and to walk in

Bloomsbury Square. In the bookshop, I thought I might buy a copy of her son's plays but none were to be seen on the shelves and I was hesitant to utter his name. I cannot see the grown man, the subject of such scandal; I can only see the bright-faced little boy whispering in his brother's ear in their Mamma's carriage.

The day after my altercation with Papa, I found a letter waiting for me in the cottage from William, saying he hoped I would make good use of three tickets for a subscription performance of Handel's *Messiah* to be performed in St Patrick's Cathedral to raise funds for William's small charity hospital. William and Mr Wilson had persuaded the Lord Lieutenant, Lord Carlisle to attend and the concert was an attempt to pay for an extension to the hospital. I told Emily, without revealing the source of the generous gift, and she suggested we bring Cousin Clara, recently engaged to her distant cousin, the bank manager, and now full of forgiveness towards me and thus prepared to meet me despite Aunt Belle's interdict. William had included some money in the letter, insisting that I buy a new dress for the occasion and so I did, and used some of my review money on a new bonnet and gloves.

The following week, on an evening in early summer, Clara and Emily, all of us excited to be in our best frocks, made our way to the Cathedral from Papa's house around the corner, with some considerable care for our skirts and boots but we managed to keep ourselves looking elegant. Outside the church porch, we paused and stood in the throng, the girls engaged in covert observation of the cream of Dublin clerical and medical society as the carriages rolled up to the Cathedral.

At my insistence, we soon made our way into the cool gloom of the building, where candles were already alight and the mass of lilies in front of the choir filled the air around us with a dizzy, almost unbearable, perfume. Our seats were towards the front of the nave of the Cathedral, in the centre, and I felt a kind of giddy thrill as the golden light of the early summer evening filled the vast emptiness above the altar and the lovely confusion of the small orchestra tuning up made a lively festival of the evening. We waited for the choir to file in. There was no sign of William, but he did say that he would be occupied with escorting Lord Carlisle and his party to their pew. At our last meeting he told me that Jane would be there and so I had called into Merrion Square that morning, to ask if we could accompany her to the concert, but her maid told me that she was indisposed and that the doctor had recommended a day or two of bed rest and then a trip to Bray for several days.

With something like horror, Clara looked up from her programme, nudged me and hissed; 'Do you realise: Emily says that this concert is due to last until ten o'clock tonight. I told Mamma that I would be home by eleven. How will we sit through three hours of sacred music?'

I was amused by the look of dread on her face.

'Look, we will be able to see the Lord Lieutenant's party from here. Why not pass the time by attempting to put a price on Lady Powerscourt's diamonds and then, when you get bored with that, on her daughter's lace?'

Clara was not amused and went into a sulk, but then the choir began to file into their places, the chattering and coughing died down and the music began. The overture seemed pleasant but unexciting and I was settling myself for a dull evening of worthy music when the choir began the opening chorus. They were an unpromising sight, timid-looking, pale women of many shapes and sizes and a large sprinkling of bald, tired older men but, as soon as they began to sing, I sat up straight in my seat. I knew little of church music, apart from the choir in Mamma's beloved church, and a few evening services I had heard in St Patrick's, and so was unprepared for the sensation of excitement, even rapture, that the singing produced in me. As the choir and orchestra moved from section to section, Clara restless with boredom next to me, their capacity to produce such joyful music astounded me, and when the pretty blonde young soprano stood and began to sing, she looked much too slight for the powerful sound she was creating; her voice moved through the vast body of air above us, pushing tears of happiness out of my unwilling eyes and, to my surprise, doing much the same for Emily on the far side of poor, trapped Clara. At moments, the singing seemed to become part of the golden light and the delicate perfume of lilies. Everything unsettled me in a way that only William's touch had done before.

The interval came. Emily said to me, with an air of wonder, ' I never knew such music could exist' but, unwilling to break the spell of the music, I let her and Clara make their way outside for some fresh air while I stayed seated. I saw William walking towards me. He sat down.

'I've been watching you. Were you crying during that last chorus?'

I laughed and denied it and then taxed him for spying, aware of disapproving looks from various matrons as they passed us.

'Yes, I was spying on you,' he said. 'It was my test and you have passed it with flying colours.'

'And what test is that?'

'That you do indeed possess a soul. Only a heathen or a savage could fail to weep at the beauty of "For Unto Us A Child Is Born".'

'Or my Cousin Clara. She fell asleep.'

'Then she is little better than the beasts of the field. Have you heard of the story of the first performance of this miraculous work? It took place around the corner from here and when the worthy Dr Delaney heard Mrs Cibber sing, he forgot all his reservations about her dubious past as an actress and he jumped up and shouted at her " Woman, for this, are all thy sins forgiven." I've always rather liked him for allowing his soul to overpower his moral rectitude.'

I did not want to think too much about women with dubious reputations, given some of the stares I was receiving from the female members of the congregation, and so I changed the subject.

'When I saw the choir file in, my heart sank. They seemed like the dullest, plainest people imaginable, yet the music they create is sublime, somewhere beyond mere mortal beauty.'

He nodded. 'I've always thought that humanity is at its best in a choir and, I'm afraid, at its worst in a doctor's surgery. And now, I must return to his lordship. We shall talk after the concert. Do not leave without a good night and, remember, I will continue to look back.'

He pressed my arm and I sat, happily, until Clara and Emily returned and I amused myself by telling Clara that an extra half-hour of sacred music had been announced in her absence.

The second part of the performance pleased me even more and by the end of the concert I was exhausted, but with a restless energy.

We shuffled out, after the many rounds of applause and the tedious addresses and thanks, and Emily and I agreed that we would ask Cousin Nan, who was the only musical one in the family, if she would play us some of the arias at the weekend, when we all planned to meet for tea and to discuss Clara's nuptial garments, in Aunt Belle's absence on holiday in London. Emily, who has a pretty, true little voice, was humming to herself 'I Know That My Redeemer Liveth' and looking very sweet when we encountered Mr Wilson, William's assistant, in the narrow street outside the Cathedral. I introduced him to my relations, and he and Emily began discussing the programme and the quality of the soprano with some gusto while Clara and I were looking out for her father's carriage, which was due to meet her at ten o'clock. I noticed William making his way towards us and, as he did, Emily, who missed very little, suddenly slipped away to the side of the railings, continuing her conversation with Mr Wilson but now shielded and out of sight. Clara, who was sleepy and thus less observant, stayed where she was. 'William,' I said loudly, 'thank you again for the kind gift of the tickets tonight. It is very much appreciated. May I present my cousin, Miss Clara Ellis, soon to be Mrs Eustace Price?'

Clara blushed when she realised who was standing there, but held out her hand, and thanked William most kindly for the gift. I could see Emily glaring at me over Mr Wilson's shoulder.

William bowed to Clara, and to my surprise, began asking her how she had enjoyed the concert and to give his best regards to her mother, his old friend Belle. Without warning, my mood changed and, from the delights of the music, and the glow of ownership around William, I found myself becoming more and more furious. Of course, I told myself, it is Clara he likes now; she was always the prettiest of us all, the one with the widest smile – of course William prefers her. Poor Clara, who had always been kind to me, who had defied her mother in coming to meet me and had endured hours of what was to her dull music, now became the focus of my jealousy and rage. Without a word to anyone, I pushed past them all, ignoring Emily as she called after me.

Arriving home, I rushed in the door, ignoring Papa's startled face, and went up to my bedroom where I began gathering the small gifts and tokens William had given me, the small silver brooch, the books, a sprig of lavender he had picked for me in Merrion Square, and placed them all in a parcel, with a short, sharp note to William telling him that all contact between us must be ended and that we must henceforth never meet. I glanced around my room, looking for other damage to do and my eye fell on the manuscript of his Swift book, the final proofs with all his corrections clearly marked. I moved towards it, murder in my heart. I remember thinking that it would only take a moment to walk downstairs and open the stove door, and I then found myself on the stairs with the manuscript cradled to my breast before I gave myself time to think further. I paused halfway down the stairs, then turned around and went back up to my bedroom.

That night had several consequences. Firstly Mamma's invitation to Mr Wilson to tea with her and Emily at home, and, secondly a letter of pure contrition from William: 'Don't throw over your truest friend, one you may never meet again. Don't be as rash in one way as he is in the other. Turf and thunder, cannot I speak to another woman? God forgive you. William.'

And I did forgive him, the very next day, in Eily Black's drawing room, with all my heart and my body. But I did wonder, in the long months when William evaded my every attempt to see him again, if that night was the beginning of the death of his passion for me.

In truth, when I try to place the precise moment, the silent but inexorable erosion of William's attention, I always think of Eily Black, Maria Amelia Black as her shop front proclaimed her, and I blame her. For years I resented her as the harbinger of doom, the bird of ill-omen, her contagious melancholy poisoning the air around William and myself. This is, of course, unfair to this honest woman. I presume she is long dead but I owe her something, partly for her patience with my younger, arrogant self, and partly for her attempt at friendship. She might so easily have resented me, the girl who had taken over her home for a covert love affair, but she never did. Instead, she tried to prepare me for the inevitable. I would not listen.

I was sitting in the downstairs parlour of the little house in Werburgh Street one warm afternoon, a month or so after the concert at St Patrick's Cathedral and the scene in the street outside Marsh's Library. William had written to placate me, to say that he had no further intention of talking to Clara but that he needed to go down to Monaghan to attend to the Marmosets for a few days. He asked me to write up his notes on the Catalogue of Gold for the Royal Irish Academy. He would be away for a week or so, he told me, and then he would come and see me as soon as he returned. Jane had gone to Bray with the boys and had not invited me, although that had been the arrangement as I had understood it and so I was at something of a loss without them and I applied myself to the new manuscript, the catalogue, with renewed vigour. I wanted to have his catalogue work done for him and was missing him with a kind of possessive confidence when I heard, with some delight, a key scraping at the door of the little house. I rushed out to meet him but, to my confusion, a tall woman dressed in a travelling cloak was standing in the open doorway, a large trunk beside her and some baskets and bags at her feet. I guessed her to be the occupant of the house, Eily.

I blushed because her neat front parlour was full of my papers and books, in great and untidy profusion. However, she seemed unsurprised to see me and held out her hand to greet me.

'Miss Travers, I'm Eily. I'm sorry for comin' in on top of you like this, but William said he'd let you know I was due back today. Well, I see he never did! That man has a head on him like a sieve.'

Her voice was pleasant and low, marked with a strong country accent, and her hand was likewise firm and warm, the hand of a woman used to physical work. I rushed forward to help with her luggage.

'Please do forgive me, Mrs Black. I had no idea, my books and papers are everywhere. Here, let me help you with these.'

She had begun to drag her trunk towards the stairs but waved me away, so I gathered together the baskets and followed her up the narrow little staircase. I left them outside her bedroom door and hurried downstairs to shut the front door and then back into the parlour for a hasty tidy up. I heard her making her way around the upper rooms and up and down the stairs and, in that time, I managed to get the room in some sort of order and checked for any tell-tale signs of William. I was packing my valise when she came back in, smiling broadly and rubbing her hands.

'God, it's great to be home, back in me own place, and I'm dyin' for a cup of tea. The kettle is on and you'll join me, of course, Miss Travers.'

'No, no. I have intruded enough in your home. I must leave you in peace to settle in.'

She took my hand in hers and drew me towards the sofa, giving me a playful push, but something of her strength was a little unsettling.

'You will stay for tea and that's an end to it now.'

I smiled back, her good humour and friendliness irresistible. 'Well, then, you must allow me help with the tea tray.'

'No, no. Sit down there like a good girl and take your bonnet off again; no need to rush off. It's all done, the tea is wet and I have a tasty bit of soda bread from Mrs Higgins in Monaghan to keep us from the hunger. She gave me a jar of her famous apricot marmalade this morning. I'm sure she had you stuffed to the gills with it when you were down there in the spring.'

I thought it best not to mention that Mrs Higgins the housekeeper had kept to her room in protest during my short stay, but Eily's pretence was a comforting one. I wonder what Mrs Higgins had actually told her of me.

We had our tea and Eily cut the soda bread into neat slices and urged me to sample the apricot marmalade. It looked sweet but had something of an aftertaste, a sharp sting of ginger or cloves, and I ate no more than a slice, my stomach becoming a little unsettled by the highly spiced concoction. As we ate and drank, Eily was also unpacking the latest drawings and samplers from Mimi and Em, and I supplied suitable exclamations as to their proficiency and precociousness when Eily sighed and stretched herself.

'That was grand. I'd better report back all the news to William before he travels down to Monaghan tomorrow. I'll scribble him a line now; you might put it in the door of Merrion Square for me if you are passin' that way.'

All through this, she was watching me carefully, but her words were casual.

I matched her offhand manner and said, as if it were a matter of no importance, 'But William set out for the country this morning. You have just missed him. He wanted to get down in time to welcome his brother home from London on Sunday.'

For a brief moment, the disappointment was clear on her face.

'Today? But I wrote and told him I'd meet him here.'

I hurried to assure her. 'Your letter must have been delayed; he wrote to me here yesterday and told me he was off to Monaghan today.'

I looked over my teacup as she stared beyond me, in something like distress, a handsome woman in her late forties, I imagined, dull russet hair going grey here and there, hair that must have been golden when she had been young. All her heartiness was gone and she looked deflated. Then she shook herself and smiled ruefully.

'After all these years I should be used to it. Miss Travers, William Wilde is a sweet man but he would cross Ireland rather than see me.'

I did not care for the turn of this conversation. Why should she care for William's comings and goings and why should we be co-conspirators in this matter? The aftertaste of the apricot had turned my mouth sour and unsettled my stomach and so I finished off my cup of tea and began gathering my things. This woke her from her melancholic reverie and she focused back on me.

'Miss Travers. Mary, if I may. Forgive me but I've learnt the hard way. When that man loves you, it is a bliss like the sweetness of the heavens to come, but when it stops, despite his polite good manners, I think a slap to the face would hurt less.'

I stood up. I wanted her to stop. I could not bear this naked admission that she had been William's lover, that I was now as she had been, that her house, this very room, had been our bower of bliss and that she would be sitting here all evening, longing for the man who had evaded her again.

I took my bag and began muttering my 'thank you's and farewells in as brightly polite yet frosty a way as possible, just as I had seen Mamma do with unpleasant visitors or over-curious neighbours at Sunday mass. I was edging towards the door while she sat looking at me, sadly, refusing by her silence to help me cover over the awkwardness of her words. Then she stood up, and followed me out into the hall and towards the door. Without waiting for her, I opened the door and stepped outside, thinking that the open street would put an end to her disturbing frankness, her insulting assumption of common ground. As if guessing, she stood out into the summer light and told me, with a touch of anger, 'Don't think this will be different for you; there's more than one woman in Dublin eating her heart out for him. You are just the same.'

I stuck to the blank wall of politeness.

'Mrs Black, I must thank you for your kindness in allowing me to study here. Please let me return your keys.'

She recovered and met my stare with an equally cold one.

'No need in the world. Those are William's; this is his house. You have no business givin' them to me.'

I stopped listening. A spurt of warm bile suddenly surged up my throat and filled my mouth. Then, to my horror, my stomach heaved. I leaned against the wall of the small house and I was violently sick. Eily had come quickly to my side and she held my head while the spasms of nausea shook my frame. Soon it was over, and, to my shame, I found myself crying. I stood up and leaned against the window frame, my eyes closed, while Eily went inside and got me cold water. I sipped and pretended not to hear her murmur, 'You poor girl.'

As soon as I was recovered, I was determined to bring this encounter to an end. I turned at the door and, when, for one dreadful moment, she seemed disposed to embrace me, I took her firmly by the hand and shook it.

'Many thanks again for allowing me to perch here for the summer. It was very good of you indeed, very good.'

Before she could speak again, I hurried away. I never spoke with Eily Black again, since my troubles intervened and thereafter I avoided walking down that street, but someone told me years later that a woman in a heavy veil appeared every year in Monaghan at the graves of the Marmosets, and left a wreath of snowdrops there on the anniversary of their dreadful deaths. The one time I did see Eily Black again was when I watched Jane welcome her into the house in Merrion Square to sit by William in the weeks leading up to his death, while I watched from across the road, anxious not to be seen.

Late that night my nausea grew more severe. I still blamed Mrs Higgins and her apricot marmalade for my indisposition but by the following day something of the truth had begun to dawn on me and, in growing terror, I wrote a two-line note to William and showed it to Emily before I posted it, knowing it would be reported directly to Mamma. It had an immediate result. The next day, he wrote back to say that he would be calling after eight o'clock that evening and, again, I left the note for Emily and took to my room, refusing to talk to Mamma when she tried to speak to me.

I spent most of that day lying in bed, my stomach sour, drifting in and out of a light doze from which I kept jolting awake with a keen sense of dread. At seven that evening, Emily came up to my room and told me that Mamma had sent for Papa and to ask if I felt strong enough to come downstairs. I was still a little unsteady on my feet but, determined to be there, I forced myself to dress and made my way down to where Mamma and Emily were sitting in the parlour by the fire.

'Where is Papa?' I asked, as I sat down next to Emily.

Mamma held her determined gaze on the large clock over the mantelpiece, her attention on the forthcoming encounter. Emily shrugged and said nothing, and so we sat there in silence, the occasional crackle of the fire the only sound in the room. Just after eight, we heard a knock on the front door and then the parlour door opened and William was announced by Maggie, all prim and proper in the excitement of the day's tensions. Of course, I thought to myself, the servants know as well.

William bowed to us all, and advanced as if to shake Mamma's hand. This she prevented by folding her arms firmly and nodding him towards the empty armchair next to her. He sat, heavily, smiled once in my direction but then kept his eyes fixed on Mamma.

'My husband was expected to join us this hour or more but, as usual, he is never to be found where he is most wanted. You and I alone, Dr Wilde, must decide on this sorry state of affairs.'

Again William bowed his head. 'Perhaps....' and he glanced towards Emily with a slightly raised eyebrow.

'My younger daughter will remain here. I rely on her commonsense and practical nature and she may be called upon to provide assistance in our present dilemma, depending on what we decide.'

Decide. What did we need to decide? William must take me away from here.

'So?' Mamma asked him, in a carefully neutral tone. 'This is not a happy day. In fact, all these past months this is what I have feared would happen, but we must put emotion to one side and keep our minds on practical matters. You, at least, have some experience in these matters and can assist us.'

William looked uncharacteristically grim at this remark but said nothing, shifting slightly in his seat.

'The house in Monaghan is no longer an option, I presume, as it has been in the past.'

William shook his head.

'I thought not,' Mamma continued.

'What has Monaghan got to do with this?' I asked Mamma as a terrible fear crossed my mind. 'Do you mean that Mimi and Em are …?'

'Yes', Mamma replied crisply, not meeting my eye. 'His daughters. I believe you have met their mother, the woman whose house you have been occupying all summer.'

This reduced me to a shocked silence as Mamma continued.

'So, Bruges has been recommended to me by my sister Belle. There is, or so she tells me, an excellent convent there, at some distance from the main town, run by a nursing order with connections to a sister house here in Dublin. They do require a substantial subvention, I'm told.'

William interrupted her. 'All expenses will be mine to deal with, I do assure you.'

'No, they will not,' Mamma countered. 'I have sufficient funds, thanks to the generosity of my late uncle and, besides, this is partly my fault. I have failed to protect my daughter. It would be the place of a father or a brother to take more direct action but my only son is in Australia and my husband unequal to the task. No. There is little I can do, but I *can* pay.'

I wondered at Mamma. She seemed genuine in her regret, her sense of self-reproach.

William turned to me. His voice was gentle but his eyes troubled and faintly angry.

'And you, Mary – what do you wish to do?'

I hesitated. 'Is there some place I could go, some quiet place in the country where I could live...until...and then I could remain there, continuing to work.'

I stopped. I knew what I wanted and so did he. I wanted him, and I wanted the life we had had to continue. I waited for the inevitable scolding from Mamma, but instead she sat, quietly, watching William, with a pained, sad look in her eyes, as he began his hesitant yet implacable words of kind reasonableness.

'My dear Mary, I wish the course of our lives could remain unchanged, as you do, but we must be pragmatic. My only concern is to protect you and to assist, but, as you know, my life is not mine alone. I have obligations.'

Emily looked at him, her face filled with anger.

'But that it not to say that you, and your happiness, will always be of paramount concern to me,' he went on.

Before I had a chance to say anything, Mamma broke in, speaking directly to me for the first time, but not unkindly.

'Mary, my only concern is to prevent scandal and any more loss of reputation. I propose that you and Emily travel to Bruges as soon as you are well again and that you will both remain abroad for the remainder of this year and into the next. After your confinement, arrangements can be made and then you can return home to me and continue as before. We shall say that you two have gone to study French; no one will be any the wiser. Do you agree?'

I could see it: the quiet, well-appointed convent house set behind tall trees, the discreet, unsmiling nuns, the dull bedroom at the far end of the house, away from the main road and the prying eyes of villagers, the months of endless waiting and genteel incarceration, and then pain, terror and the covert removal of the bundle, destined for some respectable Flemish farmhouse and a family grateful for the small monthly stipend. No: if I were to lose William, then such exile would be a further hell. I stood up abruptly.

'I am unwell. Pray excuse me. Mamma, please do make any arrangements you feel suitable and I will be content to obey.'

I moved quickly towards the door. William stood up, making to speak, but I cut him off, anxious to get away. Nothing important could be said now. I hurried to my room and lay down on my bed, thinking furiously, trying not to listen to the sounds of William departing, of Emily and Mamma moving around downstairs. The house in Monaghan. Mimi and Em? Thoughts chased around my head as I lay there, longing for the house to fall quiet. I threw a blanket over my head when I heard Emily's step on the landing, not wishing to speak to her.

Later, as soon as I heard her gentle snore, and after the sounds of Mamma entering her own bedroom next door had subsided, I gathered myself and slipped out of the room and down the stairs. I made my way as quietly as possible into the parlour where Mamma kept some spirits in the cabinet by the piano, sherry for her ladies of the church, brandy for cooking and for medicinal emergencies. I took down the brandy decanter and, removing the stopper, sniffed at the liquid inside. The sharp smell made my eyes water. I poured some into a tumbler and the taste on my tongue was like a kind of sweet burning. In small gulps, I allowed it trickle down my throat. It warmed my chest and, heartened by this, I drank a little more quickly, draining the tumbler. It took my breath away as it moved downwards, but, determined, I filled another measure and forced myself to drink more. By now my head was pleasantly swimming and my cheeks felt warm. I poured a third glass of brandy and sat down by the dying fire, feeling the brandy fill my body with happiness. Em, Mimi.... And Jane knew.

With this, I stood up, drained the glass and threw it on the floor, hoping it would shatter. It rolled harmlessly under the sofa. I walked back up the passage and began climbing the stairs. At the turn of the stairs, by the small window, I paused and closed my eyes. The brandy had made me feel as light as air and so when I turned around and allowed myself to fall forward, it seemed all a piece of this sensation of airlessness. There was merciful darkness and oblivion and, after what seemed an age, I came round, with Mamma and Emily frantically rubbing my temples and slapping my wrists, real anguish in both their voices as they called me back, 'Mary, Mary, answer me'. For a moment or two, I lay there, the brandy still in my veins, my body cloud-like, and then the first sharp pain caught me in the pit of my stomach and I began to vomit. Mamma and Emily got me back upstairs, anxious to screen me from the eyes of the servants, fetching the bowl and the old sheets themselves, ministering to me in my agony, and so by the time old Doctor O'Neill finally reached the house, fetched by Emily when Mamma decided I was out of danger of discovery, it was all over and there was little for him to do, except bind up my sprained ankle.

Write no more. Write no more. I cry for that poor girl on the stairs and, more surprisingly, for her mother, racked with guilt at the wreck of yet another one of her children and in agony at her unwitting, well-meaning part in that fall, that plunge into the abyss.

It is the weekend and the library has closed for the afternoon. Without my noticing, the city has been abruptly deserted, the hot sun emptying Bloomsbury, shutters down, the pavements bereft of all life, everyone gone to the country or the sea, or so it seems. I have resolved to stay here in my hotel room, keeping the windows wide open to let in a light breeze. The maid has left me a tray of food and a large jug of lime juice, and I need not leave for the rest of the day. Indeed, I do not wish to leave.

I have found something unexpected here in my bundle of papers from Marsh's Library and this has intrigued me. At the same time I dread it. In the folder, stuck in the middle of some newspapers, I found a large envelope with the words 'Travers Case' written on the outside in bold letters. The handwriting was unknown to me, clearly not Papa's fine copperplate. I opened it and inside discovered letters written between Jane and William Maturin from the time of my trial, each page alive with Jane's indignation. These letters were never meant for my eyes, but my surmise is that the efficient Violet Jennings, in her haste to cleanse Marsh's Library of all taint of the Wildes and of Earnest Moll Travers, must have bundled them unread into the folder with the rest of Papa's newspaper clippings and letters. Now I have them all.

When Jane bombarded her cousin with her well-honed missives of triumph and self-justification during my trial, her moment of crisis and eventual triumph, she little imagined that I would read them so many years later. Do I want to read them? I hesitate, imagining them to be full of her scorn and her irritation with me, and so here they sit on my desk, innocent faded letters in their neat musty pile, vipers poised to bite me. They say that we never hear well of ourselves when we eavesdrop, but I am beyond any sensitivity in this matter. Let Jane drip her venom to her cousin. I shall read them all. Thanks to the over-zealous Violet, I can spy into Jane's mind.

When I made this discovery in the library this morning, I came to a decision and therefore, on the way back to the hotel, bought paper, scissors and a pot of glue. I have resolved to order these letters and papers by date, destroy those I do not wish to keep and paste the rest into this diary. It will keep me busy. They will stay confined, safe and hidden in my diary and, when I return to Cork, they can be kept out of sight in my bedroom. Perhaps I will show them to Emily. She is the one person who might have some interest, even after all these years. They might give her some explanation of how our two lives, hers and mine, came to be so mired by my behaviour.

In reading the letters, I noticed that Papa kept all the cuttings from Corney Wall's grubby news sheet, the *Dublin Daily Sentinel,* and I was gratified to hear some years ago that Corney went too far in an editorial by slandering some old bishop or other and ended up in the debtors' court. He deserved that and more.

Dublin Daily Sentinel
1 July 1864
DUBLIN DOCTOR HONOURED
The state apartments in Dublin Castle were the scene of a conferral of honour on the well-known Dublin medical figure William Wilde, when the Lord Lieutenant, Lord Carlisle, bestowed the

honour of a knighthood on behalf of Her Majesty and the Knights of St Patrick welcomed him into their ranks. His Excellency, seated upon the throne, bade Wilde come forward and said 'Dr Wilde, I propose to confer upon you the honour of knighthood, not so much in recognition of your high professional reputation, but also to mark my sense of the service you have rendered to statistical science, especially in connection with the Irish Census.'

The newly created Sir William will lecture next week to the Young Men's Christian Association on the subject of 'Ireland: Past and Present, the Land and People', at the Metropolitan Hall at 8 p.m. A full gathering of Dublin's scientific and literary elite will be in attendance.

Rathmines
Dublin
2 July 1864

Dear Cousin Jane,
Congratulations on the elevation of the good Doctor and I will of course attend your dinner of triumph tonight. A word to the wise. I was at old Ma Fogarty's (the brewer's widow) last night for cards where the delightful Mrs Delafield took great pleasure in traducing you and your soirées, saying that no respectable woman would be caught dead at them. She is all up in arms about the newly minted friendship between William and her daughter, Sylvia. When it was pointed out to La Delafield that you and I are close kin and bosom friends, she harrumphed and muttered that she knew what she knew and no one would change her mind about your house being an 'indecent place'. My friend Stafford was witness, as am I, and we are prepared to take oath. Who can tell, you might shake a few coins from the ample pockets of her dragon husband, the merchant prince.

Yours in haste,
Coz Wills

P.S All augurs well with my application for the Marsh's Library position. Dr Trench is well disposed towards me, or so I am told.

Merrion Square
Dublin
3 July 1864

Dear Coz,
You are indeed a kind coz! Young Sylvia Delafield has become a dear friend of the good Sir William and myself and a visitor to our home and so I resent the sordid implications of her evil-minded old crone of a mother. Below is a copy of the letter I fired off. Old Delafield shall not trifle with me.

Your loving cousin,
Jane

Merrion Square
Dublin
3 July 1864

Dear Mrs Delafield,
Pray forgive the intrusion but it has been brought to my attention that you have taken it upon yourself to cast aspersions on my evening gatherings here in Merrion Square, dubbing them 'indecent' and 'a place where no respectable woman can be seen'. Apart from my horror of respectable women, I am astonished to discover that you could have such decided views on my home since I have never had the great honour of receiving you and I can only assume that reports of my simple evenings of poetry and conversation have travelled to the fair suburb of Monkstown, transformed during the journey into episodes of orgiastic excess. If I could presume to offer one word of advice: pray do not affect to despise a world you can never know and, to add another to that word, pray also be advised that I have had recourse to legal action in the past and would be more than happy to place the whole matter into the hands of my advisors, if slanderous reports persist.

Yours,
Jane Wilde

That name. Sylvia Delafield, William's newest disciple. I heard of her when I came back from London – a whisper from Mamma dropped a hint about William's latest protégée, Miss Sylvia Delafield, a deliberate ploy by her to keep me from William, and I hated this simpering little madam without ever seeing her. I heard afterwards that her mother, the dragon Mrs Delafield, packed her off to the safety of the County Wexford to protect her from the rumours linking her and William. The same pattern, I suppose: books given, kisses and meetings, and then invitations to tea with Jane, and the whole inevitable infatuation and consummation, and all this time I was wandering around the streets of Dublin pining for a glimpse of William, a glimpse with which he was careful never to provide me. I suppose talk of my own misadventures also added to Mrs Delafield's unease.

Around this time, in the summer of 1864, I wrote to William, telling him that I had returned from England and that the journey was a failure, my brother forbidding me to join his family in Australia and my hope for a new life now dashed. I let William know that I was obliged to live solely with Mamma and had resolved to return the £30 he had given me for the journey to Sydney. I told him that I would be in St Patrick's Cathedral every afternoon between 2 and 4 p.m. for a week, and begged him to come and meet me. I waited for him each afternoon, but to no avail and, at the end of the week, when I called to the surgery, Barney refused me admittance. I gave him the money in cash. I do not know if it was an accident or a deliberate snubbing when I passed William later that day outside the Shelbourne Hotel during a rainstorm. He had hurried past with his hat pulled over his forehead before I had realised it was he. Did he, in fact, recognise me?

The next day Emily told me that she had heard that he and Jane had had a new child, a daughter, born while I was in England. In a rage I stormed into the house in Merrion Square, pushed my way past the maid and rushed up the stairs into Jane's bedroom, where some young lady or another, perhaps the commendable Sylvia, was sitting with her, drinking tea. Jane was outraged and ordered me out and with her voice ringing in my ears, the maid turned me away from the house unceremoniously. It was from that day that I burst into publication, verses, pamphlets, scurrilous letters, all the fruits of my maddened pen and all published by the delighted Corney in his vile rag of a paper. Worst of all, that was the day I began writing that vile 'Quilp' pamphlet, my fetid masterpiece under the pen name of Speranza. It was about William, and I dubbed him Dr Quilp, implying that he had outraged me in his surgery. This was to be my most foolish action, performed in a white heat of energy. I wrote it over two days and, as soon as I could, I had Corney print me up three hundred copies, missiles to be launched all over Dublin, to spatter mud on the name of the newly knighted Sir William and his fine Lady Jane.

Sunday 9 June

It is early morning and the maid has just brought me in a breakfast tray and some hot water. I made the tea strong and feel it stimulate my stale mind. I attempted to sleep last night but it was a torture, my brow burning despite the cool evening and the light sheets on my bed, and so, somewhere in the dead of night, I rose, opened the windows fully and tried to fill my lungs with the fresh summer air. A light dew had fallen on the flowerpots full of geraniums on my window ledge and I dabbed some on my eyelids. The London street was deserted, dark, and a light breeze had just picked up. A few foolish birds began their chirping, believing that dawn was on the way. I stood by the window for an hour or so, hoping the night air would cool my fevered head, and watched the occasional person on the street below. At one point a young man, dark, bearded, came past the hotel, dressed in fashionable evening clothes, a little unsteady on his feet, singing quietly to himself. I watched him and hoped that he was on his way to gladden the heart of some lover, or perhaps he had just left the beloved's bed, his youth and his beauty a focus and a purpose to this beautiful summer night.

As I write, the sunlight from the deserted early morning street slants into my room, an angle of the light I have not seen before, striking my sore eyes. Yet still I am glad to be awake and free from remorseless dreams. I washed my clammy face again and again in cold water and forced myself to sit down at this desk, partly relieved to have such a task in hand. I spent yesterday arranging these papers in order, day by day, to paste them into my diary. Papa would be proud to see how methodical I am. The *Dublin Daily Sentinel* seemed to have been to the fore in bringing each sordid detail to the public eye. This was Corney Wall's proudest moments in print, all the exclusive details directly from Isaac Butt, the price of my legal services. And Corney's occasional groping of my body.

This morning I shall paste in Jane's letters first – her battle cry!

Bray
29 July 1864

Dearest Coz,

Yes, I know what you will say when you see my handwriting on this envelope! I have been a most neglectful and irresponsible correspondent in the last week or so. I beg you to forgive me but, in my defence, we have been infernally busy, and exciting events have overtaken us, both good and evil. My writing desk has been closed over with dust. Hardly had we recovered from the celebrations for William's doctoral honours at Trinity College than, as you know, the splendid news of his knighthood burst upon us. Yes, picture it, your old friend Speranza, the former Fenian rebel, the wild Irish girl, now transformed into Lady Wilde with one flick from the wrist from Lord Carlisle, kneeling in humble adoration at the feet of the throne.

Now that the fuss is over, William is quietly pleased, and all Dublin calls to our door to pay homage. Even our dour neighbour, Mr Sheridan LeFanu, the invisible prince of Merrion Square, has risen into the bright sunlight and called on us to offer his good wishes. Of course, as is inevitable in this fair city of ours, malice and envy have raised their ugly heads, and the news of William's honours has drawn forth a campaign of persecution from an unfortunate young woman, a victim of delusion and hysteria. You will remember, of course, Mary Travers. I was kind enough to befriend her last year. I was in the habit of inviting her to our soirées and now this foolish daughter of that shabby librarian Robert Travers has taken offence at some imagined slight at my hands. She called for me two weeks ago in Merrion Square, and when I told the maid to say that I was resting, she dared to make her way into my very bedroom! She was soundly reproved for her insolence. The following day, while I was out and Barney at lunch, she slipped into William's study and, dramatic to the last, made a histrionic scene, draining off a half-empty bottle of laudanum before him and fainting dramatically on the hearth rug. William was forced to run out and make Barney fetch an antidote to revive her and then, as soon as she was fit to go, he put her into a cab and banished her from the house.

As a result, she has started a campaign of persecution against us, publishing various notes and letters from William, who simply felt sorry for her and her terrible home life; you remember the scandal of her parents' very public and acrimonious separation. Now she has decided that we have wronged her and, this past week, daily she publishes loathsome letters and pamphlets, and puts up placards, purporting to be in my name, hinting at, but not daring to name, an illicit relationship between her and William.

An episode of utter vulgarity occurred last week when she tried to disrupt a public lecture of William's by employing penny boys and newspaper sellers to hawk her foul verses and slanders outside the Metropolitan Hall and we were forced to retreat. This woman is now banned from my house in Merrion Square and so I travelled with my darling Isola and the boys out to Bray this week to escape her antics. This morning, Willie and Oscar were playing in the hallway while I prepared their baby sister for our morning stroll by the sea when this lunatic girl gained illegal entry into the house and thrust one of her filthy missives into the hands of my innocent sons. They came running up the stairs into the nursery crying 'Mamma, Mamma, Mary has returned and these papers have your name on them'. I found she had given them copies of her letters from William and the boys could read out my name and said, 'Mamma, this paper says it is written by Speranza. That is your name, too, Mamma.'

I calmed them as best I could. In the circumstances I feel it best that Mimi and Em remain out of Dublin and so we have postponed their planned trip here and I have already written to Eily and to Ralph. I have also resolved that I shall write to Robert Travers and force him to put an end to this outrageous conduct. I will endure the public spectacle of this girl's madness no longer. I enclose a copy of the letter I will send to her father. I am resolved that this will call a halt to her foolishness.

Your loving cousin,

Jane

Bray
27 July 1864

Dear Doctor Travers,

You may not be aware of the disreputable conduct of your daughter Mary in Dublin where she consorts with all the low newsboys in the place, employing them to disseminate offensive verses and placards in which she makes it appear that she has had an intrigue with Sir William Wilde. If she chooses so to disgrace herself, that is not my affair; but since her object in insulting me is the hope of extorting money, for which she has several times applied to Sir William Wilde, with threats of more annoyance if money is not given, I think it right to inform you that no threat or additional insult shall ever extort money for her from our hands. The wages of disgrace she has so loosely treated for and demanded shall never be given her.

Jane Wilde

The next week I found Jane's letter hidden in a drawer in Papa's study and brought it straight to Corney. This had been a good week for him. He had published my Dr Quilp pamphlet in his newspaper, and now he was so pleased, he insisted on locking the door of his office there and then. He unbuttoned my dress and fumbled impotently here and there while I closed my eyes and imagined his clumsy hands to be those of William.

Flushed with what passed for his pleasure, Corney then sent me straight over to see his barrister friend Isaac Butt, with a note saying that I was, until recently, a very close friend of William and Jane Wilde, that I had a sorry tale to recount and, more to the point, a burning desire for revenge and legal action. Corney told me that my trump card was this imprudent letter from Jane to Papa, and instructed me to inform Mr Butt that I had, in addition, a whole folder full of sweet billets-doux from the impossibly romantic and foolish Sir William and that I was willing to sing a song of woe in court. Of course I was. The thought of justice, of public acknowledgement of the ways in which the Doctor and Jane had wronged and traduced me – this thought filled me with excitement and with conviction. Corney rubbed his hands and told me how much Dublin will enjoy such warbling. He warned me to say to Butt that I had no money to pay, but the pleasure that Dublin will get from this pretty affair will compensate him. As a certain result, Butt will be back in clover and in high demand as a prosecuting counsel, with all his monetary problems solved.

Butt interviewed me. He was very stern, demanded to see William's letters and quizzed me about the pamphlet I had written about Dr Quilp, pressing me to give details of the alleged assault in the story and asking if this was based on actual events. I hesitated, he grew impatient and was about to send me on my way, so finally I told him that yes, Dr Quilp was indeed William and that a sexual assault had taken place, that he had outraged me against my will. He smiled, shook my hand and told me that I had a case and that, in the interests of justice, he would represent me. I walked out of his office as if my feet were winged. No fear seemed to warn me. I was drunk on my sense of rightness, of my hunger for public vindication. Why did I agree to such an untruth? Because, there and then, I believed in my right to justice.

And so the case began. It never occurred to me to wonder why a leading barrister was prepared to take on such a petty case and spend hours on the papers without a penny from me. Jane, at least, understood it all, and why her former lover Isaac Butt was so quick to betray her, for publicity and to revive his flagging legal practice. And then, after months of waiting, the case finally began. Mamma had banished me from her house but still I was determined. I would win justice for myself, even if the sky fell.

Dublin Daily Sentinel
Tuesday 13 December 1864
EXTRAORDINARY CASE. LIBEL ALLEGED.
Law Courts Yesterday: Court of Common Plea before Chief Justice Monaghan and a special jury. *Travers* versus *Wilde*.
This was an action for libel. The plaintiff, Mary Josephine Travers, is the daughter of Dr Travers of this city and the defendants are Sir William Wilde and his wife Jane Francesca. Damages were laid at £2,000. Sergeant Armstrong, Mr Butt QC and Mr Edward J. Quinn were counsel for the plaintiff. Sergeant Sullivan, Mr William Sidney

QC and Mr Philip Ennis appeared for the defendants. The following jury were sworn to try the case: Thomas Simpson (foreman), John Fry, D. Redmond, James Brady, C.Wallace, Denis Kehoe, William Allen, R.J. Devitt, Caleb Palmer, Eustace Thorpe, James Leahy, Walter Ferguson.

The summons charged that the letter written by Lady Wilde to Robert Travers was a libel reflecting on Miss Travers's character and chastity. The defence pleaded that Miss Travers, who had been an acquaintance of Lady Wilde, took umbrage at some sort of supposed slight which she thought her ladyship had put upon her. This slight had taken place in Lady Wilde's home in Merrion Square in July of this year 1864, and, from that time forth, Miss Travers had conceived the desire of insulting and annoying her in various ways. Miss Travers had published a certain scandalous and immodest pamphlet under the title of 'Florence Boyle Price or A Warning' by Speranza, thereby causing the public to believe that such a publication was by Lady Wilde. Miss Travers made it appear that a person therein style 'Dr Quilp', intended to be read as Sir William Wilde, had made a violent attempt on her virtue and that in furtherance of her design, she had caused various diverse doggerel to be inserted in this newspaper and others, signing some of them Speranza. The defence also set forth that for the purposes of further annoyance and insulting the defendants, the plaintiff had on the occasion of a public lecture by Sir William at the Metropolitan Hall and for the purposes of exposing him to ridicule, caused a number of large placards to be exhibited in the neighbourhood and employed a person to ring a large hand bell. Miss Travers sold further copies of the same immodest pamphlet 'Dr Quilp', in which she would have it believed that she had had an intrigue with Sir William.

Following this attempt to upset the Wildes, the plaintiff pursued Lady Wilde to her house in Bray in the County Wicklow where she gained entry to the home and gave the Wilde children copies of the pamphlet and the letters. In the light of these provocations, Lady Wilde was compelled to write to Dr Travers and request his fatherly authority to curtail his daughter's persecutions.

Sergeant Armstrong opened the pleadings and stated the case for the plaintiff. She was a young lady whose name was Mary Josephine Travers, daughter of a gentleman well known in the city, particularly among the literary classes. Robert Travers was a man of distinguished literary accomplishments, a professor of Medical Jurisprudence in Trinity College, a lecturer in some of the medical and surgical schools in the city and a librarian at Marsh's Library. He believed that an acquaintanceship had existed between Dr Travers and Sir William Wilde. He then told them that the plaintiff was one of two daughters and that there was one brother, Arthur, the eldest, several years since emigrated to Australia to pursue his fortunes in that country.

Last year, the plaintiff, being afflicted by threatened deafness, applied to Dr Wilde as his reputation as skilled physician had long before attracted public attention and he had, no doubt, attained well-deserved celebrity. They would see Miss Travers in the box hereafter, with the traces of care and agitation marked upon her face, but they would discover in her a power and capacity and, at the same time, signs of outer beauty, which did not render it at all extraordinary that a man such as William Wilde should have taken in her a deep and what he (Sergeant Armstrong) truly believed was at the time an innocent interest. Dr Wilde examined her ears and it turned out that, after his professional interests ceased to be necessary, he apparently took the deepest interest in her welfare. Knowing of her love of all matters literary, Dr Wilde sent her books and, in one letter, even dubbed her with a name punning on a favoured novel. 'Why is a certain lady like one of Bulwer-Lytton's novels, and which of Bulwer-Lytton's novels is she like? Do you give up? *Ernest Maltravers.*' From this forth, he dubbed Miss Travers Earnest Moll. Occasionally, her father was not in a position to supply her with articles of dress of as showy and attractive a character as Dr Wilde would wish to see her dressed in. In several letters he wrote to her, 'I think you should have better gloves. Do you wear long shifts?' (laughter)

Sergeant Sullivan: I must protest against the course my learned friend is taking. I don't understand how these letters are evidence.

Sergeant Armstrong: I will show that he was giving Miss Travers money. Lady Wilde will tell us that the plaintiff was looking for money but I will show that Dr Wilde was constantly offering and giving it.

The Chief Justice: I will not stop counsel at present. I must take it on his word that these letters are to be tendered as evidence.

Sergeant Armstrong: In one letter, it is clear that Dr Wilde met Miss Travers on the street in Dublin and told her he had a great desire to go and see her father's home, which he did, accompanying her there. He went through the house and saw Dr Travers's study and, having seen all, found great fault with the house and told her that her father ought to have a more respectable place for her. She said that what was good enough for her father was good enough for herself. In another letter he asks, 'Would Robert come to dine, if asked?' Robert meant her father, his children being in the habit of calling him by his Christian name. That was the first time it was suggested that Dr Travers should ever be the guest of Sir William Wilde at a dinner party; the time had come for assuming an appearance of friendship. On one occasion, when Miss Travers called to inquire after the health of one of his children, she saw him in his study when suddenly he clasped her in his arms and refused to release her unless she called him William. She did not yield and so she then was forced to leave the house.

Miss Travers suggested that Sir William had her in such a state of fretting that she decided to break with him and travel to her brother in Australia. William Wilde took the greatest interest in these matters and supplied her with the money to travel, but when she went from London to Liverpool and boarded the ship, she found that her cabin onwards to Australia was already occupied by another person, and so she changed her mind and returned to Dublin. Sir William saw her soon after at his house in Merrion Square and she rebuffed him. He said to her, 'I know you will have your revenge. You may try the law and tell your father.'

Miss Travers tried to see Lady Wilde on this occasion, but was sent away. Miss Travers left the house, and wrote to Sir William in the following manner. 'I have come to the conclusion that both you and Mrs Wilde are of one mind with regard to me and that is, to see which will insult me most. As to you, you have treated me as I deserve for taking your money, but to Mrs Wilde I owe no money; therefore I am not obliged to gulp down her insults. I once thought so much of you: I thought you, at least, incapable of deceit.' In some anguish Miss Travers, now barred from the Wilde house, then wrote the pamphlet under the name Speranza. The pamphlet was entitled 'Florence Boyle Price or A Warning by Speranza' and was, to a certain extent fiction, but the object of it was plainly to put before the public a sketch of some of the passages between Dr Quilp (Dr Wilde) and Florence Boyle Price (Miss Travers), including a most distressful event involving the use of chloroform. The learned counsel read the pamphlet as follows:

Florence Boyle Price or A Warning by Speranza

A physician's office has always been held as sacred and his prerogative considered unlimited and it is sad to think that in this, the nineteenth century, a lady cannot venture into a physician's study without being accompanied by a bodyguard to protect her. Robert Boyle Price was a physician of some note who lived a secluded life with his only child Florence. While still in her schooldays, Florence contracted a delicacy of constitution that alarmed her friends. Dr Price sent her to a particular friend of his, a physician called Quilp. Dr Quilp felt such an interest in the lonely, unsophisticated and intelligent Florence that he constituted himself guardian, friend and even father to her. Dr Price's lack of worldly wisdom often caused his yearly income to be lessened so that Florence's dress allowance was often unpaid for months. In such cases, she might trespass on Dr Quilp's purse, which he cheerfully laid open to her at all times. On one occasion, Quilp said, 'Florence, I want you to make me a promise. You know I am your dearest friend. Will you promise me that you will never, under any circumstances, be induced to contract a solemn engagement or take a decided step without consulting me?' 'I will,' she replied. Dr Quilp had a decidedly animal and sinister expression about his mouth, which was coarse and vulgar in the extreme, while his underlip hung and protruded most unpleasantly. The upper part of his face did not redeem the lower part; his eyes were round and small – they were mean and prying and, above all, deficient in an expression one expected to find gracing a doctor's countenance.

Mrs Quilp was an odd sort of undomestic woman. She spent the greater portion of her life in bed and, except on state occasions, was never visible to visitors. Therefore, whenever she gave an entertainment, it was perfectly understood by her circle that a card, left by her guests on the hall table, was all she required of those who had enjoyed her hospitality.

The scene is changed to a doctor's study. The patients have been seen, prescribed for, and dismissed – all, save one, an intimate friend, whose throat requires to be touched with caustic. The trifling operation has been performed. Another is deemed advisable and an appointment is made for her to come the following day. She rises to say good-bye, but she is detained! The doctor asks her is she 'afraid' of him.

She answers – 'No; why should I be afraid of you?'

'You look pale,' he says – 'here' – and he places a handsome scent-bottle close to her face. She grasps it, and, pouring out some of the liquid, says: 'I will put it to my temples.'

He snatches the bottle from her excitedly, and roughly asks her why she has done that. No answer was needed. The bottle contained a strong solution of chloroform; the vapour filled the room rapidly, and she lost consciousness. When she awoke, with Quilp kneeling over her, she feared the worst. The scene was enacted in a shorter space of time than I have taken to write it. Florence rushes to the door, but is interrupted by the detected Quilp, who, flinging himself on his knees, attempts a passionate outburst of love, despair and remorse; but the horror-stricken Florence implores to be released from this dangerous place. She dreads to give alarm, knowing the irreparable disgrace, the everlasting ruin, it will entail. She fears he is mad; and begs to escape.

Some days later a letter from Quilp arrives, which read as follows: 'Forgive – I am miserable and very ill – utterly sleepless. Remorse and illness are doing their work. For God's sake see me and say you forgive me before I die!'

Florence knew that Quilp was sometimes at death's door with asthmatic and gouty attacks, and she could not help feeling concern for the unhappy man, now that he was stricken down with pain of both body and mind. She thought it too much sternness to refuse a death-bed request. She went; she hastened, as she thought, to the dying man. She was ushered into the study where she was surprised to find Quilp seated. He threw an agonised look at her as she entered. Neither spoke for a moment. Florence stood at the table by his side.

He spoke first – 'See my drawn features – my sunken eyes – my haggard face. Florence, have pity; oh forgive and forget.'

'I forgive,' she replied.

'You do not say that from your heart,' he said.

'Hush,' she said, 'or I leave you. I forgive, I must forget – forget I ever knew you. I esteemed you above all others; here our acquaintance ends. Farewell for ever!'

She left the house, as she thought, never to enter it again. Little she dreamed she would again enter it, and leave it again under very different auspices. Quilp recovered and made several ineffectual attempts to meet Florence. He called on her but at an hour when he knew Dr Price would be absent from home.

About this time, Florence had in preparation a long poem for publication, a portion of which had been left behind in Dr Quilp's study the day before the chloroform attempt. Florence considered that she could not demean herself by going to his house again but what could be done? She felt the necessity for the temporary compromise of her fears and so she was forced to call at his house.

Quilp's study again. Florence, with flashing eyes and scornful tone informed him, 'Never approach me again. I am no longer the credulous simpleton of old; your subterfuges will not mislead me. Disguise your handwriting, put false addresses on your letters to me, to deceive me into opening them if you will; "forewarned is forearmed". You tried all this before, but it will not succeed again. I never will recognise you on this earth; we are strangers from this hour.'

'Florence, Florence', exclaimed Quilp, 'I am no longer a supplicant for mercy from the passionless, unnatural woman that I have loved in silence, because I dared not strive to win her, but whom I determined to conquer. Florence, do not repel me: you must never divulge what has occurred.'

Florence thunders to him to open the door or she will raise an alarm, but Quilp says, 'I will turn the tables on you now – you are in my power. If you breathe a syllable of the chloroform attempt, you blast yourself by revealing it, for you should never have entered my doors after the attempt – my cleverness got you back. I am not in your power quite so much as you think.'

The crisis had come, the hypocrite unmasked himself, and there was no longer to be a spark of compassion for him. Florence recovered her presence of mind in a moment. She left the house and wrote the following note; 'Miss Price's compliments to Mrs Quilp. Miss Price considers it necessary to inform Mrs Quilp, in her husband's presence, of the immorality and the brutality to which she has been subjected by Dr Quilp, in his own house.'

The letter was duly posted and delivered, but Quilp found the means to intercept it before it could reach his wife. After some days Florence learned that her letter had never reached its destination. About the same time a rumour reached her that Quilp was artfully circulating a report that she was mad, and had suddenly and unaccountably taken a dislike to him, and indeed that he feared that she would become dangerous. Here was a master stroke by the too-clever Quilp! Mrs Quilp returned to town, when Florence called and sent up her card, requesting to see Mrs Quilp. Quilp (who was in the hall when she entered) darted upstairs to his wife. The result need scarcely be told; Mrs Quilp refused to see her visitor. Florence was thoroughly roused by this indignity, her blood boiled at the audacious affront; but this was not all she had to endure upon that memorable day. Dr Quilp came racing down the stairs, proclaiming to Florence, in exulting tones, 'Mrs Quilp will not see you; she does not want your acquaintance.'

The foregoing is merely an outline of events that took place many years ago; the details, many of which are painful, but important, are reserved for future publication. 'Hope' being the English for Speranza, I have assumed that name for its appropriateness, hoping this warning will be of use to more than

'SPERANZA.'

Sergeant Armstrong said that the account given in the pamphlet no doubt varied in some respects from details of the narrative that he had been instructed to present, but the observation should be made that the pamphlet was consistent with the great point of the case, a secret between herself and Sir William. 'Gentlemen, I will leave it to herself to tell you what followed. I will only say that "She went in a maid/ But out a maid she never departed." The case will resume tomorrow.'

Reading over these old yellow newspaper cuttings, so innocent-looking, I am shocked anew at the young woman I was and all I can I remember of myself then was sitting in that court, listening to the ugly tale I had concocted, the twisting of the truth of my time with William into something sordid but all I felt was a sense of power and of impending vindication. Already the newspapers knew what I had failed to grasp, that even if I won, I had already lost.

Morning News
Wednesday 14 December 1864
SPERANZA IN UNSAVOURY LIBEL CASE
There is a name mixed up with this case, one, high, pure and spotless; the name of one dear to the respect and admiration of all Irishmen and a suspicion is that a design to wound and humiliate her underlies this astounding legal action. This is merely the climax of a long course of insult and outrage towards her and

this has lent a painful impression to the proceedings. We scorn to pretend that *she* can be affected by any verdict of a jury, or weaken the esteem in which she is held by her countrymen.

Dublin Daily Sentinel
LIBEL CASE CONTINUES:
Packed Court – Miss Travers Gives Evidence
Wednesday 14 December 1864
The hearing of this case, which continues to excite an extraordinary amount of interest, was resumed at half past ten o'clock. The utmost anxiety was manifested to obtain admission and the court became densely populated in every part immediately after the door was thrown open.

The Chief Justice took his seat at the bench and addressed the jury. 'I wish to bring to your attention improper comments that have appeared in some of the newspapers in regard to this case. I do not know what newspapers have been alluded to and so I need hardly say that this is a case in which the jury should decide upon and that the gentlemen attending to report will do so without comment. I wish the press to attend to my remarks and refrain from overt judgment.'

Mary Josephine Travers was called and examined by Mr Butt QC. Chief Justice Monaghan addressed the court and told the female members of the public present that some of the testimony they were about to hear was of a most delicate and upsetting nature and that they should quit the courtroom if they doubted their ability to retain a composure in the face of such evidence. None took this opportunity to excuse themselves. Before Mr Butt began his questioning of the plaintiff, Sergeant Sullivan appealed to Chief Justice Monaghan to have the letters of Sir William Wilde ruled as inadmissible as evidence, but Mr Butt contended that since Lady Wilde had referred to an intrigue with Sir William Wilde in her letter, the correspondence and also the alleged incident in the study were clearly part of the plaintiff's case. The Chief Justice, with some hesitation, allowed Mr Butt to go on.

Miss Travers told the court that she had first met Dr Wilde in 1863 in the company of her father and then had been a patient of his in relation to an ear problem. She confirmed that she had become friendly with the entire family over the period of this last year or so but, unhappy with what she saw as Wilde's increasing interest in her, decided to travel to Australia to live with her brother. William Wilde had offered to lend her £30 for the ticket but when in England she decided not to complete her journey. On her return to Dublin, she called to Merrion Square to return the money, but William Wilde refused to see her. The following day she called to the home of Dr Wilde in Merrion Square with the intention of accompanying his young children to a nearby park for an afternoon's stroll, as had been her wont in the days before her trip to London, when she was met by William Wilde and asked to repair with him to his study, where he had a manuscript on Swift that he wished her to deliver to her father. While in his study, Miss Travers complained of a headache and he said he would prescribe some laudanum. Sir William expressed great concern about a burn on her neck. He removed her bonnet for the purpose of looking at her throat but he pressed her throat so tightly that she said, 'You are suffocating me.' He replied, 'I will suffocate you, I cannot help it.' A handkerchief was pressed to her mouth and she fainted away.

Mr Butt: 'Can you now state, from anything you have observed or known that, in the interval of unconsciousness you have referred to, your person was violated?'

'Yes. I came back into consciousness with him kneeling over me. I became hysterical and he called his servants to fetch me a cab to return me to my mother's house, and I left the house on Merrion Square as soon as I could, in a state of great distress.'

Chief Justice Monaghan said he would have the entire room cleared if the noise did not abate. Mr Butt then told the court that he had finished his questions.

Cross-examining, Sergeant Sullivan began his questioning.

'When did you first determine to execute your vengeance

against Lady and Sir William Wilde?'

'I had no vengeance against Lady Wilde, but I had a pique against her.'

'When did you first determine to execute your vengeance on Sir William Wilde?'

'In the second week of July of this year.'

'This was two days after this alleged outrage on you.'

'On that day.'

'You saw him afterwards.'

'I did.'

'Went to his home.'

'I did.'

'On the day of the alleged violation, did you realise what had taken place?'

'Yes.'

'Do you believe that he used the chloroform with the purpose of assaulting your person?'

'Yes.'

'What occurred when he attacked you?'

'My Lord, must I answer?'

Chief Justice Monaghan: 'Let there be no mock modesty: there is no room for it in my courtroom. People who come to court must leave considerations of that sort outside. State what occurred but do not state in general terms.'

Miss Travers stated that she was unconscious for a period of five minutes and that when she revived, with the assistance of Dr Wilde, signs on her dress and person confirmed her impression that she had been violated.

'Impression,' Sergeant Sullivan asked. 'Surely if you had been assaulted, you would have had more than an impression and by this flimsy evidence you intend to condemn a man for a most serious crime. You say you were unconscious. How could you tell? Did you consult a medical person?'

'I did not.'

'Did you confide in a close female relative, your sister or mother?'

'No. I was too distressed.'

'Yet not too distressed to return to the scene of the alleged attack two days later.'

'Yes.'

Sergeant Sullivan asked Miss Travers if she had sent the Quilp pamphlet to Lady Wilde. She denied it at first, but on cross-examination, admitted that she had, but only because Lady Wilde had tried to suppress it. 'I used the pamphlet to summon her.'

'You summoned Lady Wilde, although Sir William was the person to offer the explanation.'

'Yes. I would have summoned him if I could but he took very good care to evade me in every way he could.'

Sergeant Sullivan. 'Now listen to this verse, written by Miss Travers and pushed into the door of the Wilde house on Merrion Square, in the weeks after the alleged attack.'

Your Progeny is quite a pest,
To those who hate such critters,
Some sport I'll have or I'm blest
I'll fry the Wilde breed in the West
Then you can call them fritters
The name is not equivocal,
They dare not their mother call
Nor by their father, though he's sir,
A gouty knight, a mangy cur.
Signed with most affectionate regards.

'You sent it with most affectionate regards.'

'Yes.'

'To the man who had violated you.'

'Yes.'

'You put it in his letter box with a pin in it.'

'Yes.'

'What was that pin for?'

'It was a newly acquired habit. I sent a letter to him which the servants might read and see the reproachful terms I had used.'

'When did you first see the letter from Lady Wilde to your father?'

'About three or four days after it was written.'

'Did you take it without your father's knowledge?'

'I did.'

'Was the drawer out of which you took it locked?'

'No.'

'Did you find it by accident?'

'No.'

'Did you go looking for it?'

'I did.'

'Was it a proper way to get it?'

'Under the circumstances, it was. I consider myself justified.'

'Were you in the habit of taking laudanum?'

'I am. I had a fall on the stairs in my mother's house last year and as a consequence have suffered from back pain and sleeplessness.'

'Did you ever read *Confessions of an English Opium-Eater* by Thomas De Quincey?'

'I have heard of it, but I have never read it.'

'You spoke of your mother. Are you and she on speaking terms.'

'No.'

'How long have you been on such terms with your mother?'

'For a year or so, but permit me to add that I have sat at table with her and addressed her and she has answered me.'

'Are you aware of a family called Ellis?'

'Yes; they are relations of my mother.'

'Are they, in fact, your own first cousins?'

'Yes.'

'Did they bar you from their house earlier this year on account of your persecutions of the Wildes?'

'No, I withdrew my acquaintanceship.'

Sergeant Sullivan asked Miss Travers if she had submitted these two verses to the *Dublin Daily Sentinel* under the false pen name Speranza. She had used the name Speranza because Lady Wilde had no right to it and that she intended to take the name from her. Sergeant Sullivan read the verses.

The Occultist Cured

I give you my word
With his own bottle, too, I have dosed him.
I have sent him a drink,
That will set him to think,
Until his own blushes will roast him.

The Late Dubbing in Dublin Castle

The other day, with great surprise,
I saw it in the paper,
Great W.W. rose a knight
By touch of Carlisle's rapier.
The doctors have it their own way,
Though neither wise nor witty,
Not long ago 'Grey' got his tip
For watering our city.
Then why should not another man
'Gainst fickle fortune fight, sir,
And try by art of surgery
To be a belted knight, sir,
For deeds of blood and slaughter?
But now a man may win a name
By bottles of eye water.
The deaf can hear – the blind can see,
These are his triumphs great, sir.
The only wonder really is
They were discovered so late, sir.
Backed by our honest Dublin Press
By friendly puff and pars, sir.
Publicity he sought and found –
Oh! don't he bless his stars, sir?

—145—

> *For, perched upon a niche of fame,*
> *Dame Fortune opes her store, sir,*
> *And all with admiration gaze*
> *On him for evermore, sir. – Speranza*

Miss Travers replied that she had written these verses and also that she had dropped a copy of this poem through the letter box of Merrion Square.

'Is it true, Miss Travers, that on the morning of the alleged attack, you purchased a bottle of laudanum in O'Brien's Medical Hall on Westland Row.'

'No, I cannot recollect.'

'I have a copy of the purchase book here. Be so good as to look upon it and confirm your name on the right-hand column for the day in question.'

'That is my handwriting.'

'So did you purchase the bottle of laudanum on that morning, before your visit to Dr Wilde's study?'

'I may have done.'

'And is it true that a servant of Dr Wilde's, one Barney Dean, was summoned by his master to go fetch an antidote from the very same medical hall, at around two o'clock on the same day, telling the chemist that a lady had taken a dangerous amount of laudanum in Dr Wilde's study and needed urgent medical assistance.'

Mr Butt: 'Is this relevant to the case and will hard evidence be produced?'

Chief Justice Monaghan: 'Mr Sullivan, do you have witnesses to these allegations?'

'Yes, my Lord. I have the servant and the chemist here in court today, and they can be sworn in.'

'You may proceed.'

'Miss Travers, did you in fact take an overdose of laudanum in Dr Wilde's study that afternoon, and were your moments of unconsciousness, in fact, self-induced?'

'I cannot remember.'

'You cannot remember, but you have sworn on oath that chloroform and not laudanum was the agent of your swooning.'

Mr Butt: 'My Lord, Miss Travers has answered the question.'

Chief Justice Monaghan: 'No, she has not. Miss Travers, was it laudanum or chloroform that rendered you incapable?'

'I do not remember.'

'Yesterday you testified that you were made unconscious by Dr Wilde.'

'The afternoon was a fraught one for me. I fainted, and the events leading up to that loss of my mind are now unclear.'

'Am I to understand that you are now withdrawing the charge?'

'I am unsure.'

Sergeant Sullivan: 'I have no further questions.'

The further hearing of the case was adjourned until half past ten today.

Monday 10 June 1895

All is back to business on the streets of London today but I cannot face the library. I walked out for an hour or so this morning and had my lunch and now I plan to lie on my bed and read these papers. This hotel room seems too small to contain all the memories and thoughts unleashed for me. I can see it now, the torturous giving of my evidence, the gradual leaking away of my confidence and my bravado, the dawning realisation of what I had done. More than anything else, I recall the moment when I realised that I had condemned myself, pinned under the steady gaze of Jane's handsome grey-haired lawyer as he unpicked all my inconsistencies and then enjoyed watching me entangle myself in traps of my own making. I remember one of the men on the jury, a fair-haired young man with a strangely worn and tired face, nudging the man next to him, a large bearded man, and then the bearded man frowning and motioning the worn-looking young man to stay still. That was it: the fall from triumph and determination to fear, the lies I had been encouraged to tell by

Corney, now tripping me up. I knew only the wish to run away. I stood by and allowed my father be caught up and then made a fool of by the proceedings of this lumbering, unstoppable, mammoth legal case, rampaging through my life and his and Jane's and William's. I had unleashed it and was now incapable of stopping it. I read Emily's letter to Papa, a model of restrained sorrow.

> Percy Place
> Dublin
> *Wednesday 14 December 1864*

Dear Papa,
Mamma tells me that you are under sub poena to appear this week in this unnecessary libel case, to testify about Jane Wilde's letter. Last week, before Mary moved out to stay with Aunt Belle, Mamma and I told her in no uncertain terms that you wished to have nothing to do with all this unpleasantness and yet she has involved you in the trial against all our wishes. I am sincerely sorry you have been made part of this sordid trial and I will call to see you tomorrow evening.

> With fondest love,
> Emily

Dublin Daily Sentinel
Thursday 15 December 1864
MORE REVELATIONS. LADY WILDE CALLED TO THE STAND
Sergeant Armstrong began his case for the defence and called Lady Wilde to the stand. She was not in court and so the newsboy who had distributed the pamphlet was called in and examined. Lady Wilde arrived at half past one and was sworn and examined by Mr Sidney QC.

'I have known Miss Travers as an acquaintance for a year or so and for all that time she was received as a guest at the house from time to time, but the coolness with Miss Travers began when she called to Merrion Square in July of this year and, on being told I was unavailable to meet her, nevertheless made her way unannounced into my bedchamber. The next day, she staged a mock suicide attempt in my husband's study and was banished. As a result, Miss Travers kept up a severe quarrel and wrote innumerable letters on the subject and passed me very rudely on the street. I have never since saluted Miss Travers. I never spoke to her after this, but also in July of this year a pamphlet first came to my notice. One was sent to me through the post and then others were posted through my letter box. I heard in different quarters that they were sent to people, and that they were dropped on the Rathmines Road that week. I was with Sir William at the Metropolitan Hall where he was lecturing, the hall being crowded to excess and, as I was going in, I saw a boy selling pamphlets, and a large number were seized by one of our friends, who brought them to our house afterwards.

I remember going to our house in Bray on the day after the lecture. A servant handed me a pamphlet while I was at tea. I went out and found a boy with them outside my house. He told me that he had got them from a lady who desired that he sell them and cry out on the Esplanade in Bray. I took one away from him, greatly annoyed and frightened that they would be handed to my children. The next day I was informed by my older son that before I was up, there was a boy at my door selling the pamphlets. I immediately got my pen and wrote the note to Dr Travers.

Sergeant Armstrong: 'Did Sir William direct you to write that letter?'

'No, Sir William never knew I wrote that letter. He was in Dublin. I did not trouble him with such a matter.'

Mr Butt for the prosecution then questioned Lady Wilde. Lady Wilde denied any feelings of ill-will or malice towards Miss Travers.

'Ill feeling? I had no ill feeling. I objected to her conduct. I thought she had behaved badly indeed.'

'Did you like her?'

'No.'

'Did you hate her?'

'No.'

'Did you dislike her?'

'For her conduct, yes. I received her with great kindness before.'

'You were very much excited and angry when you wrote the letter.'

'Of course I was angry at the line of misconduct she was pursuing.'

'Would you have been so angry if you were aware that the girl had sworn that Sir William violated her in his own study that very month?'

Chief Justice Monaghan intervened to say that he would have the court cleared if the noise continued.

Lady Wilde: 'I don't know how I should have felt. I never heard that statement made.'

'You read the pamphlet; she implied an intrigue and the offer of chloroform. What do you, Lady Wilde, understand an intrigue to mean?'

'An underhand sort of love affair. She wanted to make appear that there was something wrong.'

'Don't you think that her father reading your letter would understand there to have been illicit intercourse between herself and Sir William.'

'He might judge for himself. I asserted nothing.'

'You stated that you did not believe that your husband and Miss Travers had an intrigue.'

'I did not believe in an intrigue. I complained to her father because I believed that the object of the writer was to give rise to the suspicion that there was an intrigue. I regard the whole pamphlet as a fabrication. I did not accuse her of it. I complained to her father that she had published certain documents that would suggest to the public that there was an intrigue. If she choose to disgrace herself by sending around such publications, and putting her name forward in such a suspicious way, and using my name on the pamphlet, she was disgracing herself, but that was not my affair. If I had believed in the intrigue, then it would have been very much my affair.'

Mr Butt said, 'I had expected to see Sir William here today in court.'

The court was adjourned and will meet tomorrow at 10 o'clock in the morning.

Merrion Square
Dublin
Thursday 15 December 1864

Dear Coz,

You are too kind to say that I was magnificent in court yesterday. I think that was the choicest performance since Catherine of Aragon confounded Henry VIII and all the bishops of England. That silly girl threw away her case yesterday with her evasions and her contradictions. We will have the victory feast in Merrion Square on Monday, mark my words!

Jane

Dublin Daily Sentinel

Friday 16 December 1864

CONCLUDING STATEMENTS IN TRAVERS CASE

The hearing of the case was resumed yesterday at the sitting of the court, which, as on the previous day, was densely crowded from an early hour, the interest maintained in this case increasing as it proceeds. Robert Travers was examined by Sergeant Armstrong.

'The plaintiff in the action is your daughter.'

'Yes.'

'Take that letter in your hand and open it. Did you receive that letter on 7 May of this year?'

'I did.'

'Did you open and read it?'

'Yes.'

The witness was not cross-examined.

Sergeant Sullivan summed up for the defence. 'Gentlemen of the jury, I never rose to advocate the case of a client more profoundly impressed with a deep sense of duty than I do at this moment. I very much fear from the manner in which this case has been conducted that your minds will have been drawn away from the real question that you have to try. You will find that from beginning to end, from the first moment she allowed this woman into her house, Lady Wilde is beyond impeachment and it is a grievous thing to have her dragged into court and treated in the way she had been because, stung by insult, she writes a letter to the plaintiff's father to keep her from doing further mischief to herself and to others. This is an action taken against Sir William Wilde, founded on no illegal action of Sir William's but based on a letter written without his knowledge after Lady Wilde had received at the hands of the plaintiff the grossest insults that a woman could receive and the direst provocation that could be offered. The letter was written in the impulse of a moment, and when her husband was away from the house.

And now, to come into court and to make outrageous and contradictory statements about laudanum and ask for damages on a letter she pilfered from her father's desk. This will give you a key to the sort of woman she is: excitable, vindictive, uncontrollable. There are no lengths to which this woman will not go in order to satisfy her passion and all because of a small transaction of no importance when Lady Wilde rebuked Miss Travers for entering her bedroom unbidden. I really do believe that in some senses the woman is unaccountable for what she has done and that she is one of those who have been described as afflicted with madness, the most dangerous and mischievous person that can afflict society.

She enacted her revenge by writing that pamphlet, and it is impossible that any man can regard this work with anything but horror. In this pamphlet, Sir William is represented as administering chloroform for a base purpose on one of his own patients in his own study and then Miss Travers alleged an assault, but by her own evidence she returns to the house, the scene of the outrage the very next day, and accepts tickets from the hands of her alleged assailant. She writes of this episode in her pamphlet as 'most unpleasant'. If a woman has proper ideas or notions as a woman, does she call the violating of her person an unpleasantness? Does she renew acquaintanceship with her attacker? Should she not look upon him with horror? Her pamphlet and her testimony are concoctions of the grossest manner and plainly meant to insult Lady Wilde, and therefore I direct that Lady Wilde's letter was a sincere plea to the plaintiff's father to corral and rein in a difficult and dangerous woman hell-bent on vengeance. How can we believe in the honour of Miss Travers, a woman who hints at a relationship with a married man, to discomfit his wife, with no regard to her own modesty?

Mr Butt stood up to give his concluding statement and expressed his concern that Lady Wilde showed little disturbance at the possibility that her husband had assaulted Mary Travers. Mr Butt said, 'Lady Wilde's letter to Robert Travers suggested that Miss Travers had sunk to the lowest depths of vulgar prostitution. The disgusting defence was that it was written in good faith to the father in order that he would interfere to prevent his daughter from exposing her own prostitution and extorting the wages of her infamy. I could understand Wilde coming into court and saying his wife wrote that letter under circumstances of strong irritation; it would have been a powerful appeal to the jury if that had been his course. Mr Sullivan, in his very eloquent address, told you that we have placed Sir William Wilde in a very embarrassing position towards his wife. I care not what honours may have gathered around the name of Sir William Wilde, what position Lady Wilde by her genius may hold, but the man who instructs his counsel to speak of the daughter of his friend as a perjurer and asks you twelve Irish gentlemen to find that on your oaths, while he does not pledge his own, is not worth much consideration. It is not the behaviour of a gentleman. If Miss Travers's story is not true, why did Sir William not come here to the court to contradict it? It would have been more satisfactory for Lady Wilde. Would you condemn her, while the man who asks you by your oaths to believe she is perjured, shrinks from coming in here and pledging his oath to that to which he asks twelve Irish gentlemen to pledge here.'

Mr Butt continued: 'Lady Wilde is capable of playing with the deep passions and with the higher feeling of our nature. You have heard Lady Wilde examined and it would be with the deepest sorrow and pain, far more than in anger, that I should comment upon her demeanour in that box?'

Mr Butt read out a letter from Miss Travers where she wrote: "'I went into your husband's study and took laudanum with the intention of committing suicide." And what does Lady Wilde write in reply to that awful intimation. Oh, shame! Shame on the heart of a woman and above all shame on the heart of an Irish woman. The intelligence has no interest for Lady Wilde. If she had the feelings of a mother, of a wife, and of a woman, then it would have been a Christian act in her to endeavour to raise up a fallen woman. Don't be led away with this tale of an outraged woman. For, remember this: for the past while Miss Travers has been the worshipper of Sir William. I believe she was unconsciously in love with Sir William but she was never his mistress, despite the hints from the other side. She was driven away from the house of him whose secret she had kept.'

In summing up, Chief Justice Monaghan said that the correspondence between Miss Travers and Sir William was of a very extraordinary character to take place between a married man and a young woman of her attractions. He discounted the absence of Sir William as being of little import on the case, but made the point that if the alleged assault had been the subject of a criminal prosecution, it would have been thrown out because of the failure of the plaintiff to report the occurrence and because of her contradictory evidence.

The jury took one hour and twenty minutes to decide that the verdict was that the letter was libellous, and the damages awarded to Miss Travers by Chief Justice Monaghan were one farthing, with Sir William Wilde liable for legal costs of £2,000.

The Lancet
19 December 1864

The case of *Travers* versus *Wilde* is in every respects an exceptional one. It rarely happens, in these kingdoms, that a young and prepossessing woman, not without pretensions to talent, is permitted to pursue a legal case in which she provokes mingled feelings of wonderment and commiseration, Miss Travers, on her own showing, admits herself to be indifferent to the obligations of her oath and indifferent to the truth of her sworn evidence. As a result, we must regard her as being excessively silly. Of Lady Wilde no one can speak except with sympathy and respect. If honest indignation and matronly scorn had well weighed every word, perhaps her communication to Miss Travers's father would have been more guarded. Why was Sir William Wilde not examined? He might have branded as perjury the wild imaginings of the unhappy plaintiff and thereby have added further to her self-created dishonour. Sir William Wilde has to congratulate himself that he has passed through a trying ordeal supported by the sympathies of the entire mass of his professional brethren in this city; that he has been acquitted of a charge as disgraceful as it was unexpected, without even having to stoop to the painful necessity of contradicting it upon oath in the witness-box, by the expressed opinion of one of the ablest of our judges, by the verdict of a most intelligent special jury, by the unanimous opinion of his fellow citizens, and by, what I am sure he will not value least, that of every member of his own profession.

Merrion Square
19 December 1864

Dearest Coz,
You, of course, know of the triumphant end of that law affair which has occupied us for the past week or so and thank you so much for you kind support in the courtroom. If you are asked by the avid gossips of Dublin, just say that the simple solution of the affair is this: that Miss Travers is half-mad and that her family is mad, too. She was very destitute and haunted our house to borrow money – remember how very kind we were to her because we pitied her – but suddenly, as you saw, she took a dislike to me amounting to hatred and then her only aim was her endeavours to ruin my peace of mind. I was forced to endure those series of anonymous attacks. Then she

issued such vile publications in the name of Speranza, accusing my poor William of assault. It is very annoying, but of course no one believed her confused story. All Dublin now calls on us to offer their sympathy and all the medical profession here and in London have sent letters expressing their entire disbelief in her, in fact, impossible charge. Sir William will not be injured by it and the best proof is that his professional hours never were as occupied as now! You have been a true friend and I send you my deepest gratitude. Come to dinner tomorrow.

Your dearest Jane

One farthing. How Dublin laughed. A memory came to me last night as I sought sleep in vain. The morning of the verdict, the day in which, as I believed, all my troubles would be vindicated and I would shine forth. It was when I heard of the award of one farthing and the bellow of crude male laughter in the courtroom and the round of derisory applause that something began to unsettle me. Mr Butt was jubilant, despite the meagre award, and kept shaking my hands into his and telling me how pleased I should be, and other men, lawyers and their clerks, kept coming up to him and telling him he was a man newly remade, and then, as if an afterthought, turned to me, bowed low and congratulated me. Corney Wall was by my side, insisting on taking me in his arms and embracing me, his sweat smeared on my face and even on my lips, his damp hand briefly on my back. Jane was surrounded by admirers, that cousin of hers, Maturin, all triumphant and all I kept wondering was William. Why didn't he come? Where was he? Mr Butt wanted me to talk to some newspaper man but I didn't listen for something was happening to me.

I began to fear that outside the courtroom, silent armies were gathering, ready with some steely intent to witness my destruction. I became agitated and tugged at Mr Butt's sleeve, asking if we could leave. He assured me that we could, that he had a carriage waiting to take me to a celebratory lunch, but people kept coming up to him and I could almost hear these menacing armies beginning to take their stand outside, so I pushed my way out of the court, Mr Butt calling my name behind me, and ran out into the clear afternoon air. At the corner I stood panting, ready to make a bolt for home. But which one? Papa had barred me from his and I had dared not go to Mamma since the trial began. Aunt Belle had given me shelter, despite some misgivings, and even my cousin Clara had come along to the first day of the trial but had not returned since my own day of evidence.

On that cold December afternoon, a few stray flakes of stinging sleet falling, I decided. As if pursued by furies, I ran towards Percy Place and pushed my way into the house despite the maid's protests. I had been barred from there from the outset of the trial. I ran into the sitting room and threw myself shivering at Mamma's feet. The rest of that day or even that month is still unclear to me. Straightaway, Mamma put me to bed, called the doctor and had a hot stone jar placed at my cold feet. I cannot say she nursed me with any show of emotion but she did what was necessary, keeping cold water by my bedside, changing the lavender compress on my forehead whenever the maid or Emily were away from the room, mixing the potent sedative that the doctor urgently recommended. That care, however grudgingly given, was enough for me.

As soon as I was better and was able to walk down to the drawing room, Mamma did consent to sit with me, but had nothing to say. It was little enough comfort but her physical presence was sufficient to still the massed armies that I still believed to be outside my window, awaiting a signal before bringing down utter destruction on my head. It was many weeks before I could contemplate dressing and leaving the house, and my first day out was pure agony, the streets around the canal awhisper with my name and the windows all around full of invisible eyes, all directed towards me.

Mamma's red rosary beads. In the first month after my collapse, she insisted, night after night, that Emily and she and Nora O'Hara, who was hired to watch me, would say the rosary. I objected at first, when I was still not able to speak, by turning my head away and squaring my shoulders, but Mamma said, 'If I am made responsible for your recovery, without any consultation, then I must be allowed to know the best means by which that recovery can take place.'

At first I hated it, and ground my teeth but, as the days went by and I began to recover the power of speech, I started to watch the turning of the blood red beads in Mamma's large, smooth hands. Each bead was like the burning threads of thought in my mind, keeping me from sleep, untiring, self-tormenting, prodding me wide awake at 4 a.m. every night. I came to depend on these nightly prayers, my room full of soft whisperings, the certainty of each decade, and the bright hope of the long-awaited reward of the 'Hail, Holy Queen' at the end. 'Turn, then, most gracious advocate,/ thine eyes of mercy towards us.' The steady caressing of the beads between Mamma's fingers, the quiet murmur of prayer, these became the quietest moments of those long months of illness, and I grew to depend on her dogged surveillance, particularly when the sleeping draughts were failing in their purpose and I begged for laudanum, William's magical potion. One evening, when Emily was out of the house, Nora in the kitchen, and Mamma slumbering alone by the small fire in my bedroom, when the thought of another night of half-dreams of William threw me in a fit of despair, I woke her and asked, 'Mamma, will I be mad for ever?' She looked over at me, momentarily off her guard because of her drowsiness, and then shook her head as if to clear it.

'Mary, you are not mad now. To ask such a question is proof enough itself. In ten years or so, you will pass him on the street and wonder: now who was that man?'

Now I know that she spoke the truth. I was not mad. Even my demented suitor, the poor mad Frederick, would never have asked such a question about himself. Regular sleeping draughts, no newspapers or letter-writing, no novels or poetry, but history books and travel journals permitted, light needlework and a hand or two of cards. Prayers, light food at the same times each day, and a warm bath most nights, with fresh bedclothes and linen. Slowly, all these had an effect and soon she set me at light household duties, shelling peas, polishing silver, and within the year I was taking walks along the canal alone, keeping my head down and my thoughts on each step, one after another. Mamma saved me.

All morning I have been tearing up the rest of Papa's papers and letters but a few I shall keep.

The Archbishop's House
Northbrook Road
Dublin
14 March 1865

Dear Dr Travers,

Dr Trench has asked me to inform you, with his deepest regret, that you have been unsuccessful in your application for the position of Keeper of Manuscripts at Marsh's Library. He is mindful of your long years of devoted service to the library and so asked me particularly to assure you of his continued good wishes and he hopes that you will retain the position of Assistant Keeper, and that you will assist the Reverend Maturin in his new role. As you know, the rooms you presently occupy on the second floor are specifically designated for the sole use of the Keeper and so I should be grateful if you would surrender your keys to him as soon as is convenient.

The Archbishop hopes that you will be free to attend his evening of sacred music at St Patrick's Cathedral next Monday and I enclose two free passes.

Yours sincerely,
Reverend Percival Neville
Private Chaplain to the Archbishop

Marsh's Library
Dublin
18 March 1865

Dear Papa,

We have just learned the deeply unfair news of your application for the post of Keeper. This is clearly the result of that dreadful case. I am very angry and will call to you tomorrow evening, if you are free to see me. Mamma sends her sincerest condolences.

Your loving daughter,
Emily

Fitzwilliam Square
Dublin
12 April 1865

Dear Dr Travers,

Thank you kindly for your letter and for the enclosed keys. I fear there has been something of a misunderstanding. I have no need for the rooms you presently occupy in Marsh's Library and you must retain your own set of keys and pray do continue to use them as you require them. It would be a great favour to me if you would continue your work at the library for I fear that the collection would lose a valued friend in you, otherwise, and I hope that we two can work together in the valiant struggle to maintain the integrity and independence of the library and resist any attempts to close it down.

Your friend
William Maturin

Merrion Square
Dublin
30 November 1865

Dear Cousin William,

Thank you so much for your kindness in calling yesterday. I was much too overcome to receive even so close and dear a friend, with the tragedy still so fresh upon us. In your note, you asked me to explain the dreadful news. The facts are simple and heartbreaking. On 31 October the local bank-manager, a Mr Reid, was hosting a private party at Drumaconnor House, near Ralph's home in Monaghan, despite the severe weather and the snow storms and our darling Mimi and Em were invited to attend.

All was well until, at the end of the evening's entertainment when the other guests had all departed, the host took Em for a final dance around the deserted floor while Mimi obligingly played on the piano. Em did so love to dance, the little creature. As they waltzed past the open fire, Emily's crinoline dress caught fire and her lion-hearted sister rushed to her aid, but soon Mimi's dress also became enveloped by flames. The host wrapped his coat about the girls and bundled them outside where they were rolled in the snow, but it was too late. The burns were very severe and, after suffering for nine days, Mimi was released from her torment and given the eternal bliss and reward that her love and bravery so clearly merited.

An inquest was due to be held on 10 November, but Sir William wrote to the coroner asking for an inquiry rather than an inquest, on the grounds that an inquest might have fatal consequences for Em, who was still alive, and blissfully ignorant of her tragic loss. Then, to break all our hearts further, poor Em died on Wednesday, 21 November.

Ralph writes to say that he will place a granite tomb with these words above our cherished angels: 'In memory of two loving and loved sisters, Emily Wilde and Mary Wilde, who lost their lives by accident in this parish, They were lovely and pleasant in their lives, and in their death they were not divided. II Samuel'. I cry every time I read those words.

While they were dying, Eily went down to stay with them and my William told me that her groans and lamentation could be heard by people outside the house. Our hearts are broken for these lovely girls and I do not know if Ralph will survive the shock. He has been taken with a severe palsy and cannot move from his bed.

I can write no more. I will call to see you next week and all my love to you and to your beloved Sophia. My William is overcome; I fear he will not recover.

Your sorrowing cousin,
Jane

Tuesday 11 June 1895

There they all are, the tangible proof of my foolish anger, now preserved in my diary. It was my fault that Papa was ruined, and I made my name a source of public ridicule. The dark sober-looking diary contains them all. Perhaps I will show them to Emily when I return to Cork. After all these years, she might now understand how I could tell such lies in public, in a court of law. And if she did understand, perhaps she could tell me. And the Marmosets. Did I will those dreadful deaths with my malice?

The George Hotel
Russell Square
London
Tuesday 18 June 1895

Today I find that I wish to write again after days of silence. For this past week or so, I was incapable of repose of any kind, could only prowl around the streets of London or sit with an unopened book in my lap in some genteel park, my mind all fever and memory, my trial playing and replaying in my mind. I have been in London for far too long.

Yesterday I received another letter from the Countess. She tells me that Emily has been taken ill again and that I am needed in Cork. I will return by the end of this week, after I have summoned up courage to see Jane.

I wonder if I have already gone mad. Yesterday something else happened. I saw the Doctor walking through Regent's Park, as if alive. It was early in the evening. Wandering with little purpose by the lake, I heard the sound of a brass band in the concert area and strolled over to sit down and listen. Despite the approach of evening, the sunlight was still in full glory and many seats were taken, but here and there the trees gave cooling shelter. Under a tall chestnut I was fortunate to find an empty seat next to a nurse and her baby carriage. The regimental band was lively and the songs suitably jolly and martial. I was enjoying the lively rendition of 'Sweet Lass of Richmond Hill', a favourite of Arthur's from his boyhood days and his sporadic piano-playing, when I noticed an uncannily familiar figure in the middle distance, emerging from behind some shrubbery and walking in the direction of the bandstand.

I blinked, and, despite the lingering heat of the day, felt something like a touch of cold breath on my neck. I looked away and returned my gaze to the band, forcing myself to concentrate on the music. After a few moments, when I dared to, I looked over at the figure. There was now no mistaking those familiar outlines. It was indeed the Doctor! Even after thirty years, I knew the shape of his figure, his walk, in an instant. For so long, on the streets of Dublin, I prowled around, longing for a glimpse of him, and here he was, a walking phantom coming towards me on a warm summer's day in this elegant park, filled with the fashionable of middle-class London, and only *I* could see him. I wanted to get up from my seat and run away from the approaching visitor from the grave, dead nearly twenty years now, but I was unable to move. He seemed to be walking towards me but then, as he moved into direct sunlight, something made him pause and he came to a sudden halt. In the strong sunlight, I could see him clearly. It *was* the Doctor, as I had last seen him thirty years before, but dressed in a modern fashion, his clothes unkempt, his hair too long. He stood there, rummaging through his pockets, and then, just as suddenly, resumed walking in my direction. I sat there, stricken, afraid of the moment when our eyes would meet but – and this made it even more ghastly – when the spectre passed close by me, so close I could have reached out and touched him, it was as if I did not exist. He was muttering to himself and intent on his purpose. I caught a strong whiff of spirits and then he was gone off in the direction of Regent Street.

I sat, my brow cold, my stomach uneasy and, as soon as I could, I stood up on legs that felt unsteady and slowly made my way back to my hotel and straight up to my room. I was anxious to escape the sunny park, the roses, the chattering children and the band, where a ghost could walk unchallenged through the idyllic scene, unnoticed by all but myself. I sit here in my room, writing to keep myself from shivering, and wondering if I had been nudged into the abyss of insanity, tipped over by all those letters and newspapers and the memories of thirty years ago.

Tonight, for the first time in quite a long time, I keep thinking of poor crazed Frederick, wondering if he is still alive in his asylum. He must be in his early sixties now, and Papa always said that, in his professional experience of mental asylums, lunatics can live for ever, nourished by the strength of their delusions and obsessions. Frederick seemed such a gentle soul when I met him first, in Cousin Clara's drawing room, the old school friend of Clara's prim husband, and it seemed inconceivable that a kind, handsome man might consider marrying me, given my tarnished name and the ribald laughter about Moll Travers. Perhaps he had never known of my past. I realise now, because his own preoccupations he had little time to know much of the outer world. When I first met him, Frederick was in his late thirties, two years older than me, but fresh-faced despite his prematurely white hair, and I could tell from the first that he liked me, staring at me over the tea cups in Clara's house when he thought I could not see him. When Aunt Belle called Mamma aside and whispered to her about his connections and his family, he was made welcome in our house in Greystones, Frederick the scion of a successful family of printers, nephew of a wealthy alderman uncle, with whom he lived in a big house in Blackrock.

On that first meeting, Frederick told me that he had retired early from business life to concentrate on his attempts to write a novel, and this plan had his uncle's blessing. Another man of letters, I sighed to myself, but I was nevertheless intrigued and very much attracted to his narrow shapely face and kind green eyes. As we sat and chatted about books and authors, he abandoned his gentleness for a moment to tell me, blushingly, that I had the fatal smile of Helen of Troy. Before he left Clara's house that afternoon, he asked if he could write to me and call out to Mamma's house at some time. He turned to leave. I noticed that, despite his neat clothes and hair and careful demeanour, he gave off a slight odour, but I thought little of it at the time.

Over the next few Sundays, Frederick was a regular visitor to the house in Greystones, pleasing Mamma and Emily with his quiet good manners and his small gifts of flowers or chocolates. Soon it was becoming accepted that I, in my mid-thirties and with my damaged name, had that most unexpected of things, a respectable suitor. Then one Sunday he plucked up the courage to ask Mamma's permission to take me for tea in the Shelbourne Hotel later that week. I smiled at the thought of myself as requiring such permission but, if it pleased him to think of me as some delicate flower under Mamma's vigilance, then I was not going to disabuse him of the notion. That afternoon, I was permitted to walk with him by the seashore, and, on the way home, in the growing dusk, I allowed him to kiss me as we stood outside Mamma's gate, sheltered by the willow trees, his tongue making tentative darts into my mouth, and desire beginning to flicker for me too.

After this, and in spite of myself, I began to permit myself to dream a little; perhaps it was not too late to marry him or even to have a child or two. A child! I wince now at my own lingering innocence.

On the afternoon of our tea in the Shelbourne I dressed with care; still youthful, as my mirror told me, and made my way to the hotel with a singing heart.

When we sat down and began our tea, Frederick, with a touching, childlike honesty, began to explain to me about his health. Choosing his words with care, he described his periodic episodes of darkness, a condition he had inherited from his late mother, recurring delusion and panic that came over him every few months or so. In that elegant dining room in the Shelbourne, surrounded by dowagers and majors eating cake, he told me all, how it began with an ache in his head, a first warning sign, then spreading to the rest of his body, resulting in days and days of intense grief and an imperative to stay in a darkened room, away from all human contact. As he talked on about his most recent spell of good health, a spell that had lasted for most of that year, I listened and smiled sympathetically whenever he caught my eye, but he barely noticed my smiles, intent on recounting the full details of his own condition faithfully. All I could do was wonder how soon I could escape. I wanted to weep for this lost man and for the end of my silly brief hopes. Frederick, talking on remorselessly, told me that he had lost his business because of his health and was now living with his aged uncle, dependent on him for money, but that he had hoped to return to a working life, with my help as his wife.

With that word, I stood up, and began to mutter about a forgotten errand for Mamma. He stared at me, uncomprehending, as I reached for my bag and my gloves and told him not to worry at all or concern himself with conducting me home, since I was meeting Emily within the hour. His kind face was baffled and confused as I hurried out.

It was later that week that Frederick's first letter arrived at Mamma's house, the first of many, a new letter each day, begging to meet me. I read only that first letter; over ten pages long. He described the home we would have, the children we would raise, the novels he had planned to write, with me at his side, and he assured me that he had kept himself pure for me, to be worthy of my love and our blessed state of matrimony. Again and again he wrote that I had the smile of Helen of Troy and that my presence kept him from harm and from darkness, because of my goodness and my pure nature. I thought of afternoons with William in the small cottage in Werburgh Street, and of Corney Wall's large, wet hands on my body in his locked office, and I confess that I laughed at poor deluded Frederick. I should have kissed him, taken away his useless purity; God knows, it was his sole chance for some physical pleasure.

As soon as I had finished reading his first letter, I burned it and I put all subsequent unopened letters straight into the fire. When these letters ceased, after a fortnight or so, I felt a temporary relief, but then, later that month, Emily woke me late one night, to point out the lone figure under the tree in our garden. It was Frederick standing in the pouring rain, staring up at our window. The next day Mamma and I called on his uncle, a harassed old gentleman, who spread his hands helplessly and told us there was nothing he could do. He feared for his safety and had taken to locking his own bedroom at night in the house in Blackrock.

For the next week or so, Frederick appeared regularly outside our window, during the darkest hours of the night. We decided to go to the police but the matter was taken out of our hands later that month when Clara called to us in Greystones, and told us that Frederick had been arrested outside Dublin Castle for public disorder. He had been standing there for two days, protesting and singing hymns. Clara said that he had been taken straight to an asylum, much to the relief of his sorrowing uncle. She cried and told us that she had known nothing of his mental state and of his demented obsession and begged my forgiveness. I told her there was nothing to forgive, and indeed there was nothing. It was mere justice. While the letters from Frederick came in, day after day, I thought, 'I have tormented Jane and William in a similar fashion and now I am being punished.' The sight of Frederick under our tree seemed to me to be only just, and I endured it as rightful punishment. He wrote to me from the asylum, asking me to visit him. I thought about it but Mamma advised against it. I would have liked to have gone, if it could have helped him. Poor Frederick. Perhaps I will try and find him when I return to Ireland and see if he is being cared for properly.

He was my last chance for escape and, after that, illness and death began to cloud our lives. It was as if Frederick had been a bird of ill omen in my life, bringing a cloud of misfortune and illness. Soon after,

Aunt Belle told us of the sudden death of William and Jane's young daughter, and about the fever that had taken away the precious, much-loved Isola before she had reached her tenth year. For weeks, I shuddered at the thought of this child being taken so early, tormented by my cruel poem and my dangerous stupidity in publishing such a work and the fear that I had provoked the fates to move against William's innocent child. Far worse was the news of the cruel burning of the Marmosets, the lingering agony, the shared grave, the perfect loyalty between those two sweet girls.

As if to punish me, Mamma's slow illness had already begun, a kind of second infancy, a decline that kept Emily and myself in thrall to her, eventually longing for her simply to be gone. This torture went on for nearly fifteen years, until we were both women well-advanced into our middle years and beyond any hope of marriage or independence from each other. My memory of these years in Greystones at Mamma's bedside now is of endless duty in the sick room. At least I repaid my many debts of sorrow and hurt to Mamma. With the onset of Mamma's illness, Emily and I became mothers and nursemaids to our child-changed mother, and as she grew more and more frail and distressed we were obliged to take on a professional nurse, an old nun, to assist us in our night vigils.

One afternoon, I turned quickly towards Mamma in the bed, to raise her up and give her medicine and she flinched, as if warding off a blow. I said nothing and continued to help her out of bed but I realised that this had being observed by the old nun. Thereafter, as if by accident, I never found myself alone with Mamma. Always, Emily, or old Sister Anna, or Nora the kitchen girl, were near at hand. Did Emily really think I would want to hurt Mamma? Maybe I will ask her next week when I return to Cork. Towards the end, when the illness had driven her into a state of dementia, Mamma became agitated and began to babble about a baby, abandoned outside in the garden, begging us again and again to fetch the baby in before the cold dew began to fall, and struggling to get out of her bed to retrieve the baby. We tried to reassure her but to no avail. When we were alone, Emily said, without looking at me, that Mamma must be thinking of poor Bobby, her youngest, a baby again, but we both knew that this was not true.

One memory remains when Aunt Belle carelessly mentioned the fact that William was said to be gravely ill and near death, some short years after the frightful end of his girls. Without letting Emily know, I plucked up my courage to make my way into Dublin, intent on calling at Merrion Square and asking William for forgiveness for my unwitting part in the death of his daughters. I had made it as far as Trinity College when I spied a familiar figure, dressed in black and heavily veiled. Eily. I followed her along the wall of the college as she made her way slowly toward the house in Merrion Square and I stood across the road and watched as she knocked on the door and gained admittance. Jane herself opened the door and embraced her. As the door shut, I stood and watched, and imagined Eily walking with that slow, defeated gait up that stairway and into the bedroom, left tactfully alone by Jane unseen but somewhere close at hand, to sit silently at William's bedside, a comfort for Eily, a torment, I imagine, for William. After a few minutes spent looking across at the house and the drawn curtains of the bedroom on the second floor, I crept away.

I have just realised! Yesterday it was Willie I saw in the park, now grown into a man and his father's double. He lives in London, too. I must pluck uo my courage and go and see Jane, but still I hesitate. I am afraid.

Thursday 20 June

It is inexplicable to me but, of all the damage I wrought on other lives, apart from my own – William, Jane, Emily, Mamma – the sharpest regret is for the real and lasting pain I brought to the life of my honourable, well-intentioned, ineffectual father. In our daily intercourse I treated him with direct, unvarnished contempt right to the end of his days, I ruined his chances of achieving the only position he ever coveted, and I made him an object of ridicule in his professional life. Never once did he reproach me. Now I have the grace to blush. It is too late. He has been dead for nearly eight years now, just after Mamma, and such remorse is of no use to him. After he died I did try to convert myself, from Goneril to Cordelia, a kind of penance for my undaughterly behaviour. My patient, useless father, never speaking forth his fear, his despair, keeping his unhappiness to himself so that mine might burst forth and overwhelm us all. I blush for myself, but now, too late, I learn to be proud of my father and be proud of the fortitude of his unspoken despair.

Did I love him? In his lifetime, certainly not, at his death, it is doubtful. It is only now that I can appreciate his courage in not speaking and do justice to the valour of his reticence. But justice is not love. I learned that in a Dublin courtroom, as the Doctor's son is now learning in an English jail. The papers still scream of his sins, his disgrace.

The moment has finally come. I am ready and will go and to see Jane; I need to provide what I can to her in this hour of darkness. I owe her my little reparation.

Friday 21 June

Early this morning I made my way to the post office in Russell Square and asked to see the London directory, to locate Jane's address. The helpful young post office clerk explained that the names of gentlefolk and distinguished persons could be found at the back section of the directory of addresses. He asked which name I required, in his zeal to be of assistance, but I assured him that I would be able to locate the correct names myself. I was glad that I did so. There were three names listed, Oscar at an address in Tite Street and Jane, with Willie, at another in Chelsea. Next to Oscar's name, in clear pencil, was traced a word, a biblical word, naming his sin. It was underlined twice. So, I thought, alike but unalike as father and son. I suspected as much with Mr Naylor's insinuations but there it is, as clear as day. Why did someone go to the trouble of tracing out such a blunt word of condemnation? I imagine some timid citizen, looking around him, taking his chance and writing down the word with his pencil, pleasurably stirred up his act of condemnation.

I noted Jane's address and returned the bulky directory to the clerk, with a smile of thanks. I asked him for directions to the street in Chelsea and he obligingly wrote out the route for me. As the day was fine, with a strong, mellow summer breeze and fetchingly fluffy clouds chasing across the sun, I thought I would walk. I needed the exercise to calm my beating heart and to decide on my course of action as I walked. In my purse I had a brown envelope with Jane's name written on it. It contained a hundred pounds in crisp new notes. This I would leave discreetly on her hall table. Forgetting the task ahead, I enjoyed the walk and made good progress and was near her house by midday. Noticing a cake shop on the corner, I stopped, refreshed myself with some cool lemonade and, on impulse, bought a large plum cake, to bring as a calling gift.

When I got to the house, checking I had the correct address, I knocked firmly on the door, giving myself no time to reflect. Almost at once the door opened and a young woman opened it, her face pale, her eyes strained. She peeped out, holding the door closed over herself and seemed surprised to see me, if she was expecting someone else. She said nothing, simply staring at me and so I asked, 'May I present my compliments to your mistress, and ask if Lady Wilde is at home.'

She looked annoyed as she opened the door partially. She was heavy with child.

'My mother-in-law has been unwell and has just risen.'

Daughter-in-law? I wondered. Surely Oscar's wife had fled the country? The woman stared back at me with little welcome, only weariness. I noticed a mark under her eye, a small bruise, turning yellow. She looked at the cake box in my hand and roused herself to appear more civil.

'I am Lily Wilde. May I give a name? I will ask Mamma if she feels equal to a visitor.'

'Anna Kingston,' I said.

The woman was turning into the house when I heard a scuffle behind the door. A man's hand pulled at the door. It was Willie. He was a replica of his father as I had last seen him.

'What do you want with my mother? She is unwell and this cursed trial has broken her.' He glared at me suspiciously. 'Are you one of those scavenging women reporters?'

I began to think quickly, relieved that he had not recognised me. After all, it was a long time ago.

'No indeed, I am an old friend of your mother's from Dublin and I was hoping to provide her with some aid and succour in this time of distress.'

I held the boxed cake up for him to see.

The young girl, Willie's wife, put her hand behind her back to poke at him. He glared at her but fell silent as she fully opened the door.

'And you are indeed welcome, Miss Kingston, and please come in. Forgive the ruinous state of the drawing room, I am near my time of confinement, as you can see, and unable to provide the domestic support I would wish for Mamma. She has been sleeping but should be awake by now.'

She pushed Willie away from her down the dank passageway and the hall echoed with his heavy footsteps as he stumped up a flight of stairs. She ushered me in and so I stepped down the hall. Even on such a warm, fragrant summer's day, the house smelt of rank water. These few steps had removed me from summer and into darkest winter. I placed my hat and gloves and my bag on the hall table and then turned back to her. She gestured me to follow her through an open door by the stairs into a large room. In this room, there was a single candle burning and I could see books everywhere, on the floor, on the long table covered with a greasy green baize tablecloth. Large mirrors stood against the walls, shrouded in dark swathes of fabric, and the windows were heavily curtained on this lovely sunny day, so we were plunged into deepest gloom. I had strayed into Hades. Next to a small coal fire, an old woman sat slumbering. I turned to the young girl and offered her the cake. She shook her head and nodded towards the old woman. Walking up to her, she raised her voice.

'Mamma, you have a visitor and look, some lovely cake.'

I started with horror. Jane, this shabby old crone! I turned to Lily to ask if I had been mistaken but she was backing out of the room.

'Miss Kingston, I will leave you with Mamma while I fetch us some tea.'

With this she gestured me towards Jane and left the room. Jane, this wrinkled old parody of Jane, struggled to raise herself. I was unable to speak. I wanted simply to turn and leave.

'Who are you?' she demanded, her voice familiar but now tired and a little hoarse.

'Please, Lady Wilde, do not trouble yourself, and forgive my intrusion. I call merely to pay my compliments.'

She peered up at me. Something of the old manner returned to her eyes and mouth but it was deeply unpleasant, as if Jane had been imprisoned in old, tired flesh and was struggling to be released. She was dressed in dowdy black; her bodice covered in an array of old tarnished-looking brooches and chains. An immense black mantilla was clinging uneasily to the neck and her shoulders, fastened into her hair by the clasp of a black-toothed comb. She smiled at me, as regal as ever, and gestured me into the dark red seat opposite her. I sat.

'An Irish voice. So few of my fellow-countrymen and women will call in these hateful times. Do I know you?'

I thought for a moment or two and then I decided.

'Yes, I am Mary. Mary Travers.'

Jane thought for a moment or two and something of the old beauty of intelligence returned to her eyes. She nodded.

'Mary Travers. Yes, I knew her. A mad poor girl. And so, can you tell me is she still alive? I have not seen her for many years. Someone told me that she was carried off to an asylum in the County Cork.'

'No. She died there, in her asylum. Last year. It was a sad life.'

Jane shook her head savagely.

'Good. I am glad she is dead.' I braced myself for a torrent of venom. I deserved it.

Jane sighed.

'She is lucky to be dead and she was always a sad, confused girl. This can only have been a release for her. I long for death, now that Oscar is in that cruel prison. How can people weep at death? To me, it is the only happy moment.'

She paused and looked into the meagre fire. Then she looked back at me and tried to remember.

'So Mary Travers is dead. She was so much younger than me, and a bright girl. And I am still alive. I was sorry to hear that her madness overwhelmed her. All those crazed letters and poems pushed in our door. Her brother died in a madhouse in Australia, I believe. Did you know her?'

'Yes, she was my cousin. She instructed that I come and visit you. To pay her respects and to give you this.'

I took the envelope from the cake box and placed it into her old wrinkled hands. I remembered those hands, large, plump, busy writing, or waving around as part of an anecdote. She looked down and a gleam came into her eyes. She opened the envelope and looked at the money. At once, a look of fear crossed her face. She hurriedly put the money into the pocket of her old, black dress.

'Don't let Willie see this,' she whispered. 'I will give some to Lily later, to buy supper. She is near her time, poor child, and needs meat and some porter to build her up. When I was waiting for my darling Isola to be born, I drank Guinness every day to fortify myself and she turned out to be such a beautiful child. She died, you know, just as Em and Mimi died. Much too young.'

I nodded but she was past caring for my reactions.

'I have asked them to call the baby Isola if it is a girl, but Willie says that will bring his child bad luck. He never spoke of his little sister after her death. And then Mimi and Em. All those deaths, they broke my William. Ralph put up a gravestone. They were lovely and pleasant in their lives, and in their death they were not divided. Eily was devastated, too. But not me. I endured. Unfortunately.'

She turned back to me. 'Who did you say you were?'

'Mary Travers. I am Mary Travers, the daughter of Robert Travers.'

'Yes. I remember her. We had to take her to court, you know, years ago. We won. She was clearly mad and got caught up with that awful cad Corney Wall and Isaac, too. My former beau.' She chuckled. 'Chivalry was never allowed to get in the way of a lucrative case. My William had to pay the lawyers over two thousand pounds, you know, and all she got was a farthing for her honour.' She laughed. 'Still, we won. I pitied her poor father. The last time I saw Oscar in the Cadogan Hotel just before they arrested him, I told him, if you stay, even if you go to prison, you will always be my son but if you run away, then I shall never speak to you again.'

Her face crumpled and all the old Jane went with it. She dwindled back into being an old woman. A tear wandered down her cheek.

'How could I have been so foolish to say this to him? Two years' hard labour. It will kill him. Those animals spat at him on the streets and at the railway station as he waited in handcuffs to go to his prison. My beautiful boy. Lady Queensberry had her son spirited out of town as soon as she could and advised me to do the same. I should have paid attention to her words.'

I roused myself to speak, if only for myself and not for her. The dark room and Jane's whisperings were beginning to unsettle me.

'I am very sorry, Lady Wilde, for your misfortunes.'

'Thank you, my dear, you are most kind and please do give your mother our deepest sympathies on your father's passing. It was very kind of you to call and tell us. Dr Travers was a most cherished friend of Sir William's. When did dear Robert die?' She smiled at me with some sympathy.

'Some years ago now.'

'Yes, we knew his daughter. Mary. A most unfortunate girl. We meant only to be kind, I'm sure. You look a little like her. A handsome girl and full of learning.'

I found myself unexpectedly tearful.

'And you were. Very kind. It is I who was most unkind.'

Jane smiled over at me.

'Not at all, my dear, not at all. It was not your fault. Pray do not blame yourself. Isola died of a fever; it was merely an accident.'

She pulled her mantilla around her and moved her hand towards the fire.

Something cold gripped my heart. I made to speak but she went on.

'No, it was simply that you were young and foolish. It is the duty of youth to be foolish.'

She looked at me. Jane. No longer the old crone.

'Jane,' I said, in a low whisper, 'Jane, I have come back. Can you forgive me, please? It's Mary.'

She looked at me, and seemed about to speak when we heard the rattle of cups on a tray.

'I hear Lily. She may have some tea for us.'

The young woman came into the room, a tea tray in her hand and settled the tray in a low table next to Jane. I rose quickly to assist her in bringing tea to Jane and in cutting the plum cake. I placed some on a plate and handed it to her, with her tea, and Jane began to devour the cake greedily, pausing now and then to sip at her tea. I took advantage of the diversion to whisper to Lily.

'Lady Wilde – is her mind quite … sound?'

Lily looked down at her mother-in-law with some asperity.

'When it suits her to be sane, she can be so. She and her sons are actors, first and foremost. They perform whichever role suits. She has some symptoms of mental decay but sometimes she can be as sane as you or I.'

I laughed at that and she smiled and nodded.

'Yes, indeed, Miss Kingston, if you or I can ever account ourselves sane. Mamma can wander at times, with all her recent griefs. We have had reporters and bailiffs dunning us and even hired thugs from Lord Queensberry, and you can imagine how unsettling it has been for her and now, if you will excuse us, Mamma needs to rest.'

I was being dismissed! It had been too short. I wanted to continue what I had begun. Forgive me, Jane. Every wounding letter, every rancid poem, they were simply my plea. Let me come back to you and to him. Do not abandon me. Do not live in the same city and walk the same streets and make others laugh or cry and behave as if I was now dead. That is why I did what I did. Your silence almost killed me.

Instead, I stood up and made to make my goodbyes to Jane but she was too intent on devouring her second slice of cake to do more than wave a regal dismissal. Like a child, she had extracted a large piece of plum and was sucking on it.

I walked out into the hall to collect my hat and my bag from the table. The hat and gloves were where I had placed them but the bag was gone. I turned back into the darkened room but Lily was intent on settling Jane on a chaise longue. At a loss, I stood in the hall for a moment and then a thought struck me. I turned down the hall and made my way upstairs.

On the first floor, a door stood ajar. I hesitated and then pushed open the door without a word. There, on a squalid, unmade bed, Willie sat, my bag open in front of him on the stained blankets. He had tossed

Mamma's red rosary beads and my last letter from Emily on the ground and, when I entered, he was shovelling the contents of my change purse into his pocket. My wallet, empty of the few pounds in it, was also on the floor. At my entrance he was frozen, and I started, not knowing what to do. He was the first to collect himself and his reddened face creased with rage.

'How dare you enter my bedchamber, you demented old spinster! Get out of my house!'

'And how dare you rob a visitor to your mother in her hour of distress, to feed your drinking.'

I knelt down and grabbed the rosary beads, the wallet and the letter and then stood up and held out my hand for the bag. He threw it at me and I caught it.

'Return my money or I will call a policeman immediately.'

Almost as soon as I had spoken, he jumped up from the bed and rushed at me. A sudden blow to the side of my face and I was thrown against the wall. I held on to the bag as I began to sink to the ground. He took my arms, to prevent me from falling, as I thought but, instead, gripping my arms and breathing into my face with his father's fetid breath, dragged me out of the room and onto the landing. With an oath, he pushed me to the edge of the stairs and then shoved me forward. I thought the fall would kill me but I slumped sideways, managing to clutch at the curtains of the landing window as I was pitched forward. I heard the bedroom door slam behind me and, as I righted myself by dragging myself up using the curtain, I knew only one pressing purpose. To quit that house. Recovering my footing, I picked up my scattered possessions somehow and scrambled down the stairs as soon as I could and out through the hall to the front door. As I passed it, I noticed that the door to Jane's room had been firmly shut. I had a moment of panic as I clawed at the handle to get myself out as soon as I could.

I was out of the door and down the pathway as quickly as I could and it was only when I reached the corner of the street and could lean against a low wall that I felt the moisture trickling down my chin. I put up my hand and it came away with blood all over my fingers. He had cut my lip with his blow. Panting hard, I sat there for a few moments and then, my terror returning, I struggled to my feet and made my way to the next street where I hailed a passing cab. The driver was coming to a halt when he saw my bloodied face and my disordered uncovered hair. Instead of stopping, he shook his reins and hurried his horse onwards.

I took my hat out of my bag, put it on and pushed my hair under it. Then I mopped at my bloodied face with my sleeve. The next cabbie stopped and, in the calmest of tones, I told him of an attack in the street by a thief and the loss of my purse. He was a kindly man, and when he was assured that I was neither drunk nor lunatic, he helped me into the cab, asked me if I needed a police station on the way and when I refused, he drove me back to the hotel where I was able to pay him well for his good deed. On the way, I closed my eyes and leaned back to ease the throbbing in my head and all I could see was Willie shoving money into his pocket with a delighted urgency. I remembered the small boy he had been, the afternoon I helped him with his painting lesson: his clean, bright, beautiful face, his shining eyes and blunt, happy questions to me.

When we got to the hotel, the housekeeper insisted on dressing my lip with iodine. She sent for some powders from the chemist. I explained to her that I had fallen in the street. In all the excitement, and with a throbbing head and sore arm, I failed to notice the telegram on my writing desk. It was only in the early evening, when the worst of the aching had subsided that it caught my eye. It had been delivered while I was out, that morning. I opened it. It read. From Anna, Countess of Kingston, Imperial Hotel, Cork City, Ireland. Regret to inform sudden death of Emily Travers. Please return home by earliest mail boat to Cork. Will be waiting in Cork. Deepest sympathy.

Imperial Hotel
Cork
Sunday 23 June

Tomorrow, for the second time in my life, I find myself giving evidence in legal proceedings, and, again, I am under an obligation not to tell the truth. Indeed, the legal advice is that I should lie. This time, I have little choice in the matter. Back in this hotel, I am now the guest of the Countess and she has proven herself to be unexpectedly decisive in relation to Emily's death and, in particular, about my evidence at the inquest tomorrow.

Last night on the train from London to the boat, I fell into a fitful sleep, my head still aching from the blow two days ago. Dreams assailed me. When I awoke, they had all fled, but I did remember one in particular: a nightmare about Jane, young again and full of anger, bursting into Eily's cottage in Werburgh Street and striking me. When I got on the boat, I was determined to stay awake. I paced the deck for the whole journey, pausing only to take more powders to keep the ache in my head at bay. I fought off my fatigue in this way, watching the white of the sea water ripple against the brow of the ferry and wondered, for the first time, where Jane had been on the weekend I had travelled to the County Monaghan with William. What had she been thinking? I imagined her putting her boys to bed, or reading, trying not to think of her husband and of this young woman, the girl she was determined to befriend. With such thoughts did I pass the hours of my sea crossing, resolutely ignoring the fact of Emily's death?

This morning, when I disembarked from the boat, I found the Countess waiting for me in her carriage. With a tact I greatly appreciated, she didn't embrace me or make any of that public fuss around mourning that so many women and not a few men enjoy so much – the elaborate ritual, more for their own enjoyment than for the comfort of the bereaved. In addition, she took care not to notice my bruised face. Instead, she took me gently by the arm and led me towards the carriage, explaining that she had reserved a suite of rooms for us at this hotel. Breakfast had been ordered, she went on to tell me, although the thought of food repelled me, and so, when I was rested, she told me, she would come over to my room and talk through the necessary arrangements for the next few days.

After that, we sat in silence as the carriage rattled up the Cork quays, an early morning of unparalleled summer beauty all around us, the air from the river fresh and caressing, a few boats out rowing already. The idea of Emily dead struck me again with all its unreality. I wanted to enjoy the crisp early morning air on my face and the delicate scent of lilac, but such were the circumstances that I felt I could not be seen to do so openly. When we alighted, the Countess led me up to my room, and, just before she departed, mentioned that the inquest on Emily's death would be held in the hotel the following morning. I was too tired to respond. It was only as I lay down on my bed for a brief sleep that the word came back to prick at me. Inquest.

I had a few hours of fitful sleep, the heavy curtains blocking out the sun and making a new night-time of the room, the chatter of the maids in the corridor outside jarring and faintly sinister, a low murmur in the next room sounding to me like the nightmarish mutterings of plotters. Just after a maid had woken me up with a lunch tray, a polite knock at the adjoining door announced the return of the Countess, armed with some flowers. I struggled to rise from my bed. She insisted that I lie back, firmly pressing me into the plump pillows and pouring me coffee. I drank and looked around the room as she drew open the curtains and let in the blinding sunlight and then fussed some flowers into a vase for me. Her finances may have been in ruins, but her title could still command a suite of the best rooms in the Imperial Hotel. I was uncomfortable to be lying down as she prowled around the room and so, again, I made to rise.

'No, no, you must rest. You have been travelling and need your strength for tomorrow. I insist.'

She took a seat next to the bedside table, having poured coffee for herself. The room was filled with summer light and a slight breeze filled the room with the scent of the lilies. Her slightly over-anxious solicitude made me uneasy and I determined to speak.

'Tomorrow?'

She put down her cup.

'Yes, indeed. The inquest. It will be held here in the hotel at ten tomorrow morning.'

'Must I attend?'

'I'm afraid you must. I have provided the necessary identification for the police, as has dear Miss Bowen, but my solicitor Mr Greene tells me that you will be called to give evidence.'

I felt annoyed by all this and trapped in the expensive bed.

'I don't see why?'

'You are Emily's next of kin.'

'Nevertheless, I have been away from home and have no knowledge of my sister's last hours. Indeed, I don't understand the necessity for an inquest.'

She answered patiently, as if I were a difficult child. 'It is always required in the aftermath of a sudden death.'

A discreet knock came to the door and, before I could respond, the Countess had called out 'Enter' in a tone of firm authority, a tone I had never heard her use in Mitchelstown. Miss Bowen, looking pale, glided quietly into the room, made her way over to the bed and took my hand, pressing it, without a word. I could see from her face how exhausted she was and I felt that I owed her some expression of gratitude or sympathy. After all, she had saved me from finding my sister dead.

'It must have been a shock to you,' I said, 'to have...found Emily?'

She nodded. Her deep, pleasant voice surprised me from this thin, rather bloodless-looking woman. I don't remember hearing her speak before, her taciturn ways of little interest to me as she and Emily and Anna gathered to make clothes and prepare baskets of food for the deserving poor of Mitchelstown.

'To be strictly accurate, it was the maid who discovered her but, yes indeed, when they came to fetch me, I had no idea what would await me.' A deep breath, almost against her will, seemed to well up in her chest.

'I can assure you, Miss Travers, that I could detect no sign of distress. I said a prayer, clasped her hands together and then called the doctor. She looked as if she was merely sleeping as she lay there.'

I wondered. I had seen both Mamma and Papa die and the moment of death was not always as angelic as Miss Bowen seemed to suggest.

'Lady Kingston.' I turned towards the Countess. 'Must we be subjected to the agony of an inquest? Is it necessary?'

Her ladyship answered more sharply than I had ever heard her speak. This matter had been forced upon her and even her smooth politeness could run a little thin at times.

'Yes, indeed it is. I don't think you quite grasp the gravity of the matter, my dear Miss Travers. It is always required in the wake of sudden death and, more so in your sister's case, when the person was alone.'

I shifted in the bed and wished I was standing. The implications of the next day's ordeal were beginning to make me restless.

'Emily's death comes as a great shock to me as well,' the Countess continued sympathetically, her eyes never leaving my face. 'She and I had become such great companions with our needlework and suchlike.'

Her grief was of no interest to me.

'What can I offer to the coroner by way of explanation? I am myself perplexed that a healthy woman in her fiftieth year should die so suddenly.'

At this, Miss Bowen moved away, walking towards the window, her back to us. The Countess stood up and followed her to the window, pressing Miss Bowen's elbow briefly and then turned back towards me. As they stood there, their shoulders almost touching, they managed to block out the bright light in the room.

'Why, indeed?'

The Countess sighed and looked uncharacteristically weary, her years more apparent on her pretty face than usual.

'That is why you and I must speak frankly. I was hoping to spare you some of these sad details, but I'm afraid I cannot.'

She moved nearer to me, to look at my face as closely as she could.

'Tomorrow Doctor Greene will testify that your poor sister died as the result of a convulsion, a fit of epilepsy, and you will be asked by the coroner to confirm that she had been suffering from this condition for the last ten years or so. I ask you to help me by confirming the nature of her illness.'

'Fits. But I knew nothing of this. Emily never spoke of her health.'

I felt a pang of remorse. I continued. 'Is that why she was removed to the nursing home for the last few weeks?'

'No.' The Countess sat down next to me. 'Sadly your sister had discovered early symptoms of the malady that afflicted your late mother. She moved into the nursing home for an extensive examination. The doctors there confirmed her suspicions and, of course, from experience, she knew too well the inevitable end of such an illness.'

This conversation had taken a deeply disturbing turn. The Countess continued her story, a little too quickly, as if it concerned some stranger and not my sister.

'As soon as her doctor had confirmed the nature and gravity of her illness, she wrote and asked me to meet her here in Cork where we spoke of her illness and of all the necessary legal and financial implications. She was most anxious that you should be spared any trouble in this regard and that all your money would be safely transferred into your sole custody.'

'This has all been done,' I said. Why was she wasting my time with this babble about money?

She was silent, watching me all the time. 'Epilepsy?' I said, hoping to prompt her to begin again. 'So what is this about epilepsy?'

She paused, took a breath and then continued, 'When I met dear Emily here last week, she also told me that she had made...arrangements.'

'Arrangements.' A thought struck me in horror. 'What kind of arrangements?'

The Countess took my hand and held it, keeping me firmly in her gaze. Her hand shook a little. I remember thinking: she is somewhat afraid of me, but not afraid enough to be deflected from her purpose. Two difficult husbands and an albatross of a castle had given this gentle woman sufficient steel for her task.

'My dear Miss Travers – Mary, if I may. You must help me and those around me to respect the last wishes of your sister. She was all too familiar with the protracted and painful course of the illness facing her and so she took certain decisions.'

She paused. I longed for her to stop, to unclasp her hands but nothing would deter her.

'To protect those who helped her, it is imperative that you tell the coroner you knew of her fainting fits and her attacks. You must not voice any doubts.'

She spoke with the clear enunciation of one determined that I would agree with her. I had a momentary glimpse, a memory. Mamma in her drawing room with William on that evening so long ago, grimly determined that I should obey her at any cost. It was an unpleasant sensation.

'But how was it done?'

The Countess darted a glance at me. It was not friendly.

'It would be better if you did not know.'

'I must know.'

'I believe that, following her own instructions, chloroform was administered to sedate your sister and render her unconscious. Then her suffering was brought to an end in the most humane way possible. She was found in such a way as to support the prognosis of a seizure. Such were your sister's wishes and I must see that they are respected.'

She fell silent. I turned into my pillow, willing these two women to leave. Yet they had suffered more directly than me in the matter of Emily's death. They had been kinder to her in life, and, even more so, in the manner of her dying, than I had ever been. Chloroform. The bottle she had requested.

'We should leave you now to rest but, before we do, you must accept that it is vital that you help me tomorrow, by answering as I suggest. Will you do so? Will you help me?'

I disliked having my hand forced, so I sat up and addressed them both.

'I do not know if I can bring myself to lie under oath.'

The Countess fell silent and looked away. Miss Bowen, still at the window, turned back towards the room and, although I couldn't see her face, a slant of light passed over her face, catching a glint of moisture under her eyes. Her voice, very low, came at me with the certainty of steel.

'Why not? You have done so before.'

I blushed.

'What do you mean?' I knew exactly what she meant.

'If you refuse to help the Countess, then I'm told that the solicitor will have no option but to cast doubt on your evidence. Your connection with another legal case, years ago, where you gave contradictory evidence, can be brought to bear on your reliability as a witness.'

I stared at her and then back at the Countess, who had the grace to look a little abashed. How much did she know about my old story?

Did Emily tell all? I had always feared this. Her face carefully free of all expression but the mildest of smiles, the Countess took my hand again and tried to ameliorate the harsh tones of her fellow conspirator.

'Really you need to say very little. The doctor is prepared to advance the prognosis of epilepsy, as is the matron in the nursing home. If necessary, I will take the stand. I would not wish to force you to do this for the world, but I know that when you reflect on this, you will see the justice of my request.' She looked again at Miss Bowen.

'This may seem harsh but time is against us, and our affection for Emily gives me no choice. I intend to live up to that obligation of our friendship.'

Despite her conciliatory words, I had never seen the Countess so determined and, in a way, I felt sorry for her. Why did she have to deal with such difficulties, two strangers left to her care?

'So, can we rely on you? Will you do this, to help me and to help your poor dear Emily in court tomorrow?'

I sank back on the pillow. I couldn't answer her. Emily had never been mine. The thought of another courtroom began to unsettle me, that feeling of being hunted, of a hostile multitude waiting in the wings to attack me. Despite the warm day, the soft blankets and satin coverlet, I began to shiver. I found myself asking, 'Why? Why this way?'

Miss Bowen spoke up again from her refuge by the window. She said a most peculiar thing.

'Mortuary inclinations.'

I stared at her. Was she losing her mind?

'That's what Emily called them. Mortuary inclinations. She was determined on this. She told me last week that if she was unable to secure assistance, she would take matters into her own hands. I was still unsure but last Sunday I found her contemplating the drop from her hotel window, a fall of some twenty feet. That decided me.'

I continued to shiver. The Countess came over to my side and took one of my hands in hers. Her hand was warm in mine. I felt a stab of pain, the merest dart behind my eyes, and put my hands up to hold my head. She whispered to Miss Bowen, 'Please, can you fetch my dressing case?'

She started to gather the blankets around me and to rub my hands.

She pushed the bell for the maid and, when she arrived, ordered some brandy. Meanwhile, Miss Bowen had returned with the case. The Countess took a slim bottle from the case and poured a little into her cupped hands and began to massage my temples. The stinging, sweet lavender, wet on my skin, tingled, and her fingers gently began to move the ache from behind my eyes. I felt near to tears and exhaustion.

She had won, and knew it. I closed my eyes and ignored her as she kissed my cheek lightly. Miss Bowen, her eyes a little red, came over and took my hand again. I don't remember her speaking. In a strange way, her strong words, her threat, had upset me very little. After all, she was a brave woman, but not so brave that she would risk prison. Only Jane's son had been that foolish.

'I am very grateful to you,' I told Miss Bowen and I was sincere in that. I would do as they ordered.

Mitchelstown
Wednesday 26 June
The inquest took place two days ago without any complications and then the Countess conveyed us both back here as soon as she could. Exhausted, we both slept in the carriage and then, almost before I knew it, I was back where I now dreaded to be, in the house in Kingston College but without Emily. For the past month or so I have been living in hotels and now, in the house alone for the first time, the silence is unnerving, so this evening I have opened all the windows and let in the evening sounds: the bird song, the lowing of the cattle in the field beyond the mill, the children playing outside on the green, the occasional passing wagon, and the fragrance of high summer filling the house.

On the morning I arrived, the Countess brought me down by carriage to my house and I was surprised to see Hannah waiting at the door, more than a little nervous. The Countess was in a hurry to return to the Castle, but insisted that Hannah should accompany me into the house, despite my firm hint that I wished to be alone. Once inside, I understood why Hannah was so nervous. I threw open the door to the front room and there, in a neat pile, I could see many of Emily's possessions, gathered up and stacked neatly on the small sofa and on the table. Hannah, following closely on my heels, was anxious to explain all.

'You see, Miss, it was Miss Emily. She wrote to me sayin' that, if, God forbid, anything happened to her, her clothes and things were to be packed up and taken care of, to save you any bother.' Hannah spoke rapidly, her eyes never leaving my face, swaying a little on her feet. 'I hope you'll forgive the impertinence, but she was very particular in her letter, and her ladyship tellin' me to do it, too. They wanted to spare you any trouble.'

I knew I should reassure her but it was making me so angry. Yet another person anxious to spare me trouble and taking liberties with my life and my home. *A letter from Emily.* I am not even sure that Hannah can read. I forced a smile, took her hand in mine and pressed it slightly, hoping she would leave, feigning speechless grief, whereas what I really felt was a kind of trembling anger. Hannah took this for gratitude and, in her relief, went babbling on about all the work she had done.

'She was most particular about the clothes, knowin' that you and she are different sizes. All the shoes and boots went up to the Castle, for her ladyship to distribute to the poor, and Mrs Brennan on the main street will buy all the dresses and the coats, and the money to be given to Canon O'Brien for his missionaries.'

Exhilarated by the thought of a task successfully completed, she took my hand and brought me down into the kitchen. Here, again, all was neat and tidy, if a little empty-looking.

'I've picked all the early gooseberries. Miss Emily was anxious about that, knowing full well that those birds would have had them all gone on us, and Louie's mother will have them made up into jam for you next week. The nets are spread over the strawberries....'

I could stand no more of this.

'Please, Hannah, my head. I am most grateful, but I must lie down or my head will explode. You have been more than kind.'

She looked a little forlorn and so I asked her to come back the following day, and we could go through everything then. Now the house is blessedly silent and I sit and write and wonder about all the time and care Emily took in planning every last detail. Gooseberry jam and boots for the poor. There was no letter. Even Hannah was told.

Thursday 27 June

The house is spotless, well-cared for by Louie and Hannah and now that I have settled back, a curious dread has come over me. I fear Emily in death as I never feared her in life. I dread that I will look up and catch an unexpected glimpse of her. Not that I believe in an afterlife or in ghosts; not at all. It is simply that I fear that the wall between the living and the dead becomes transparent at times like this and I dread that, unexpectedly, I will catch sight of Emily entering the room or at the foot of the stairs, or awake suddenly to find her watching me, quietly, calmly, without malice or anger. The spectre of her ordinary, everyday self is what I dread most, yet in my mind I know this to be irrational.

Now they have all gone – Mamma, Emily, Papa, Arthur in his Australian grave, Bobby buried somewhere in India, and I know that I will never see them all again.

Yesterday the solicitor came and collected me to go up to the Castle for the reading of Emily's will. With the verdict of the coroner, it seems that her will can stand and so her money is to be released and we can bury her. When we arrived, I found the Countess and Miss Bowen waiting.

'This will not take long,' the solicitor told us. 'The late Miss Emily Travers had assets of over nine thousand pounds in bank deposits, a half share in three Dublin properties with her sister', nodding to me, 'and also a policy on her life for the sum of one thousand pounds. The property and the bank deposits she wills to her sister, after death duties and some small bequests to the servants Hannah McGill and Louisa Collins. The money from her life policy she leaves to be divided between Lady Kingston and Miss Bowen.'

There was a look exchanged between the two women and the Countess spoke up.

'Mr dear Mr O'Connor, would it be possible for Miss Bowen and I to refuse the bequest?'

'I'm afraid that might be complicated.'

'Then perhaps we could direct that the money be used to erect a small memorial to the late Dr Travers at his beloved Marsh's Library, in the name of his daughters.'

He nodded. 'Let me see what I can do. Miss Emily has also left a sum of money to buy a plot of ground at St George's Church here in Mitchelstown, for herself and her sister.'

So Emily expects me to stay.

This morning Hannah called in again at my request and I told her of Emily's legacy. In return, she recounted the full details of a great commotion here in my absence and the fact that it involves Mr Naylor. The trustees from the English branch of the Kingston family have descended on the Castle office, demanding to see the rent rolls for the last ten years, concerned that the eventual inheritance of their young master, just about to come of age, may have been compromised by Mr Naylor's mismanagement. The young master over in Devon is the heir to the property, after the Countess, and little remains for him to inherit, except what may be confiscated from Mr Naylor's own estate. I can tell from Hannah that she is pleased to see Mr Naylor discomfited, although, as expected, he is blaming all around him: the innocent Dean of the College, the reputable old firm of solicitors in Cork, all have been sworn to be culpable but both of them clever enough to have committed to paper their qualms about his business decisions and so he has been made responsible in law.

I had the misfortune to encounter Mr Naylor yesterday as I walked up to St George's Church to make the arrangements about Emily's memorial service and burial next week. I was crossing the green in front of Kingston College when I spotted his carriage approach me and so I began to hurry, but before I could make my escape, he had thumped on the roof to make Kenneth stop the carriage. I waited patiently while he descended, his face a study in sombre, false sympathy. For the first time, I caught the full summertime scent of the lime tree under which I was standing. Emily will be in her usual raptures about the lime trees, I thought, before I remembered that the recently dead cannot be talked about with mild ridicule, even in our most private thoughts.

Mr Naylor descended, and took my hand and, for one terrible moment, I feared that he was about to embrace me, so I grasped his elbow sympathetically to keep him at bay.

'My dear Miss Travers', he shook his head mournfully, almost speechless with the sadness of it all. 'A sad blow for us all.'

Emily and he hardly spoke. I was always his real prey, Emily cleverly escaping off to the Countess. It occurred to me that she will miss Emily.

He looked around him, surveying the line of neat houses that constituted Kingston College and the pretty green space in front.

'A sad time, indeed, and now the trustees tell me that the estate may not be able to afford to maintain you all in the College. But let us not speak of heavy business matters on such a day.'

Why not today? I thought. Emily had armed me with sufficient funds to leave this place and I was no longer subject to his petty wrong-footing, his honeyed words designed to put me always in the wrong.

'But, as I understand it, Kingston College is funded by a separate trust,' I said. 'It has no connection with the everyday running of the Castle and the estate.'

A sharp look from his blue eyes and the face of weighty sympathy disappeared, as I had hoped.

'Where did you hear such an untruth? That trust earns little or no income. The College has been draining funds from the estate for years and now I am blamed and held to account by the Trustees.'

'Well then, maybe I bring you good news in such unsettled financial times. My dear sister consulted with a lawyer in Cork when she was making her will last year and she was informed of a separate trust, kept apart from the Castle accounts and funded by lands held in the County Waterford and the town of Dungarvan. If you have been indeed paying your own money into the upkeep of Kingston College, then I'm sure the trust will be able to repay you all your monies since I believe the annual income from these properties is over two thousand pounds.'

His face grew angry.

'Miss Travers, you have been misinformed, and let me remind you that it is owing to the kindness and generosity of my wife and myself that you have a roof over your head.'

I thought: I must put an end to this.

'Indeed it is not. You are not a trustee of the College, Mr Naylor, and therefore I must ask you to desist from any further discussion on this matter. My private finances are none of your business, and now, if you will excuse me, I must engage gravediggers and choose a coffin for my sister. Such are the pleasant day's tasks that await me while you tax me with obligations to you that do not, in fact, exist.'

I walked away. He was an enemy not worth provoking, but the thought of the money in the Cork and the Dublin banks had made me speak as I had wished. Money was indeed a freedom beyond all other freedoms.

Emily has made the papers and not I, as I feared.

We regret to announce the death of Miss Emily Anne Travers, daughter of the late Dr Robert Travers, of Trinity College Dublin and Marsh's Library. For some days past, Miss Travers had been staying in the Imperial Hotel in Cork City, whence she had come from her home in Mitchelstown. She appeared to be in the best of health and spirits and met her friends with the cheeriness that was characteristic of her. On the day before her death, she took a Turkish bath for medicinal purposes and then, at supper, had the company of her friend Miss Bowen. During the night she was taken ill and Miss Bowen summoned, but before a doctor could be brought to the hotel, she passed away.

Mr Coroner O'Sullivan (Cork) held an inquest on Miss Travers yesterday afternoon. A lady book-keeper at the Imperial Hotel confirmed that Miss Travers was a guest at the hotel. She arrived last Friday and intended to stay for a week. She went to bed at ten on Tuesday night and seemed in good spirits. Evidence of identification was given by Miss Bowen and Doctor T. O'Connor. The Doctor said that he knew Miss Travers well, because she had consulted with him in relation to regular fainting fits.

The Coroner to Dr O'Connor: 'Did you assist in the examination of the room?'

'I assisted in the search of the room and found nothing to show.'

The Coroner (interrupting) 'to suggest the cause of death?'

'Nothing in the world.'

The Coroner. 'Did you know her previously?'

'Yes.'

'Can you suggest the cause of death?'

'She was in the habit of getting fainting fits and would lose consciousness for a short period of time. She was leaning out of one side of the bed and she was smothered. Died of asphyxia.'

Miss Sarah Bowen, Mallow, confirmed the above evidence. 'Was there anything in the room to suggest cause of death?'

'No, nothing.'

Miss Mary Travers, sister of the deceased, confirmed that these attacks could come on very suddenly.

Coroner: 'If someone had been near her at the time, could they have put her in the right position?'

'They could.'

'She was not able to help herself.'

'No, the fits were very frequent. About every six months or so.'

In conclusion, the Coroner confirmed the verdict in accordance with the medical evidence and offered his sympathy to Miss Mary Travers.

Sunday 30 June

A dull grey morning. Emily's funeral last week. The night before, I went down to the church to bring a few of the roses that grow along the side wall of the house, to place in her coffin. I found Miss Bowen there already. The coffin was about to be closed and the undertakers had invited me to pay my last respects before the lid was slid into place. They left me there in peace for a few moments and I put the roses into her hands and took Mamma's rosary beads out of my pocket and dropped them into the coffin. It seemed only fair. I looked at Emily's waxy, composed face and her neat hair and thought how much she would have disliked the dull coloured dress they had put her in. I fidgeted until they returned, anxious to get away. Grief for Emily was something I was determined to avoid, a precipice I glimpsed now and then opening beneath my feet. As I left the church, I could hear the lid moving into place and I made Miss Bowen some excuse and ran back, and when the undertakers were looking elsewhere, I quickly kissed the smooth wood of the coffin and whispered, 'Goodbye. Goodbye'.

The service on the next day was a quiet affair: inside the church a few of the other residents of the college, some wan religious singing and then the burial in the churchyard in heavy, unseasonable rain, with the Countess always by my side, full of concern. Outside in the churchyard, after the service, I noticed quite a crowd around the graveside, all the servants from the Castle where Emily had been popular and some of the local shopkeepers, respectful of Emily's canny business ways and her hard bargains over chickens and fruit. Then a cold lunch in the Castle. It was civilised in every way.

I spent yesterday sorting through Emily's papers. I cleared out the walnut bureau, the one Mamma had inherited from her uncle, spread the contents on the kitchen table and worked my way through them. I had been dreading a final letter or a note, but, of that there was no sign, and so I swiftly disposed of Emily's endless bundles of patterns, knitting catalogues and select Catholic devotional journals, burning them in the open grate as I worked.

That done, I opened the strong box under the kitchen sink and took out everything. It had been tidied up and very recently. Emily had left all our cash in envelopes and money bags, and she had wrapped her own few jewels and trinkets into an old lace mantilla of Mamma's. I opened out the bundle and scattered the contents onto the kitchen table. I forced myself to pick through the few chains and lockets, reluctant to touch them. There was a heavy gold chain, with a beautiful thin crucifix on the end. Aunt Belle's. Emily had inherited it after Clara's sudden death and wore it from time to time. I thought about wearing it now myself but something made me shiver and I bundled all the trinkets back into the mantilla and placed them in the strong box. Everywhere I looked I could see evidence of Emily's care and foresight. All was in order. She must have planned this for months, quietly disposing of old clothes and useless papers, making our finances safe, all the time presenting the same placid, slightly blank façade to the world and to me. I shuddered again, grief opening up.

All that care, all that everyday iron courage.

JULY

Monday 8 July

I find I write less and less, as I struggle with living alone. At night, the silence is filled up with the thousand nagging thoughts of domestic trivia. The fruit unpicked and rotting on the bushes, the flowers dying of thirst, the house becoming more unruly and grim, the milk bill, the butter and bread bills. Is this Emily's revenge on me, to trap me in this domestic hell? Finally I decided: I will ask Louie's mother to come for a few hours every morning. She is nearly seventy and much less able than I to work but the family need the few shillings I can pay her.

Wednesday 10 July

Yesterday, a short note from Miss Bowen, who is still in residence at the Castle. Could she come and visit me for a few moments this afternoon? I have been avoiding her and so was tempted to write back, pleading a headache, or my continued need for quiet and seclusion – indeed, any such excuse – but I suppose that I owe her something and so I sent a short note inviting her to tea at four today. As chance would have it, yesterday Louie's mother had given the house a good cleaning, picking some roses from the garden and placing them in vases everywhere. This morning I decided to walk down to the bakery on the main street and buy a fresh Victoria sponge and some tea cakes. Then I set the table in the front room with Mamma's best china. When the knock came to my front door at four precisely, I was ready and was somewhat gratified by the quiet look of surprise on Miss Bowen's face as she took in the well-ordered tea tray, the fresh butter and cream and the last of Emily's strawberry jam. I fetched the kettle and made the tea, cut the cake and we occupied ourselves with bland chatter while both of us toyed with the cake and the bread and butter. As I knew she would, Miss Bowen wasted no time in coming directly to the purpose of her visit.

'You must forgive my intrusion, but I have one final duty to discharge, a service your...I mean dear Emily asked me to fulfil. She hoped that you would have these words inscribed on her headstone and insisted that I copy them out and deliver this note to you.'

There, on a slip of paper, I read, 'I Know That My Redeemer Liveth'. Was this all? I was relieved. I had had too many unpleasant revelations in the past month.

'Thank you so much; it was kind of you to remember. I will be calling into the undertakers next week to settle the account and so I will order that this will be engraved on her headstone.' I paused. 'I say *her* headstone but, of course it will be mine, too, in due course.'

'So you intend to remain in Kingston College?'

'I suppose I do. I have not give it much thought but, yes, this will be my home.'

I looked around. It seemed a grim prospect and I could not prevent myself from shivering.

Miss Bowen threw me a look of sympathy. 'I do hope that you will stay near to your friends. I hope also that you are not finding your house too sad and lonely, surrounded as you are by memories of dear Emily.'

All visible reminders of dear Emily had been removed, thanks to her own foresight and planning but I rather liked that Miss Bowen referred to her as dear Emily. Too often, the recent dead are called 'poor' this or that, and I have always detested it as a charade of pretended sentiment.

Looking at Miss Bowen, a thought occurred to me. I would test her.

I rose, excusing myself, went into the kitchen and fetched Aunt Belle's gold cross from the strongbox. I picked out an old lacquered box of Mamma's and put the jewel into it, returning to the front room.

'My dear Miss Bowen,' I said, handing her the box. 'Please do me the great favour of taking this small keepsake of my sister. I know she would have wished you to have it.'

She opened the box and took out the chain, unable to hide her pleasure in having the trinket. Yes, I was right! I wondered if Emily knew of Miss Bowen's tenderness for her. Undoubtedly, Emily had placed her in the greatest danger, knowing that she would be unable to refuse the task. Emily had thought of everything, I was beginning to realise, and a great anger grew up in me, such as I had known in my days of persecuting Jane and William.

I ran from the room and slammed the kitchen door shut. Miss Bowen must see herself out, I thought, as I looked around the kitchen for something to throw, something to shatter.

I did nothing. I stood at the kitchen table and looked out of the window into the small garden. Gooseberries bushes, beds of green strawberry leaves, pink roses all tangled over the back wall – I wanted to tear them all down, hack at them with Emily's garden shears. I stood still.

Presently, I heard the front door close as Miss Bowen made a discreet exit. I have my house to myself again. Tears threatened for a brief moment and I spoke out loud to her. 'Oh Emily, why did you trust me so little?'

Thursday 11 July

I made my way up early to the library for refuge. Within the hour of my arrival, I had a visitor, one I had long been expecting. The Countess made her way up to the tower room, followed by Hannah, carrying a tray for tea. The Countess rarely leaves me alone these days, perhaps afraid of the contagion of Emily's mortuary inclinations.

'I thought I might keep you company this morning, my dear.'

She sat down by the largest table and looked around in surprise.

'You have brought such order to the library; I don't think I've seen it so well cared for since Lord Kingston's death. I am indeed grateful to you.'

She paused and waited as Hannah slowly made her way out of the room, reluctant to leave such an unprecedented sight: her ladyship in the library.

'Mary,' the Countess touched my arm, 'if you will allow me. Mary, we are all so sad about your sister and at such a difficult time.'

I said nothing. I don't know if it was a sad time for me. I sipped my tea and smiled at her. Behind her I could see a grey cloud with grim-looking blue patches through the narrow turret window.

'Will you allow me to ask you something – something about the past? I owe you an apology. When we spoke of your sister's inquest, reference was made to your past life. Only the extreme circumstances could have justified such an intrusion.'

I nodded calmly. This day had been long due, my day of explanation and justification. She looked away towards the window.

'Lord Kingston and I knew Sir William a little and later I did hear something of the trial. I hope I do not intrude, but these present distressing happenings in London must be reawakening painful memories for you.'

'They do, indeed, my lady, and poor Mr Wilde was gravely mistaken in taking such a case, as we saw. It always ends unhappily, even if one receives a favourable verdict, as I did.'

Since she was forcing me to talk about my own past, I thought that I may as well remind her that I had been vindicated. I waited for the usual interrogation, the polite sympathy masking a ruthless desire to extract as many of the details as possible and find out any unsavoury detail left undetected by the newspapers and the barristers. In the years immediately after the trial, I developed a rigid system of snubbing those kind acquaintances and neighbours in Dublin who attempted such an interrogation. But a system of snubbing would not work with this woman. However, the conversation took an unexpected turn. She put down her cup and looked directly at me, almost apologetically.

'I met them at Dublin Castle, you know, when I was a very young girl. My late husband knew Sir William and Lady Wilde and I was very much taken with her. They were both gracious to me but his interest was not of a kind that a young woman would welcome, even as innocent a young woman as I must have been. But his wife! I found her to be a woman of great warmth and helpfulness to a timid younger woman and at a time when I needed such kindness, in the first year of my marriage and my first season in Dublin.'

She paused. I wondered why she was speaking in this manner.

'I went to see her, from time to time in the house in Merrion Square. Somewhere here, I still have a copy of her book of poems, inscribed with her encouraging words.'

She gestured vaguely towards the books.

Oh no, you do not, I thought to myself.

I gazed at her with unblinking politeness.

'That is why I was so surprised at her, shall we say, unfeeling behaviour towards you.'

I started at this. 'Unfeeling?'

I had to ask her, despite myself. I had become the Doctor's mistress and made Jane's name infamous and yet Anna Kingston could describe the Doctor's wife as being unfeeling towards me. She was firm, unusually so.

'Yes, unfeeling. I cannot judge the motives of another woman. She was a wife and a mother and her family naturally came first with her and so perhaps she judged it prudent to befriend you and bring you into her home. Nevertheless, to treat a young woman with such cynicism, particularly one with an estranged mother and an imprudent father, both of whom knew Sir William's history.'

She broke off. Emily had clearly been very forthcoming about our domestic history. I wanted the Countess to stop but I couldn't. She looked at me and then began again. I wished she were a million miles away.

'…to treat such a young woman without due care or protection, and then to abandon you, well, I suppose, I cannot judge, but it seems to me to be so unlike the woman I was fortunate to meet.'

She stopped talking and stayed looking at me, her fine hair falling over her forehead in limp, tired strands. No one had ever seen my behaviour in such a light. I could not trust myself to speak. Luckily she seemed interested only in speaking and not listening.

'Can I ask: how old were you when you met them?'

'The Doctor and Jane.' I had to think back. 'I was just twenty, I think.'

'Twenty. Such an innocent, foolish age. When I was twenty, my one wish was to marry my handsome cousin, the brilliant Oxford student with the golden hair but, well, it was not to be. One summer, he went away on a long study tour of Germany and, in his absence, the proposal of marriage came from Lord Kingston. At first the thought of marriage with such an old man filled me with horror. He was just forty.'

She smiled. 'The home I came from, the gentle parents, such disobedience seemed unthinkable and by the time my cousin had returned, I was a married woman. My married life was not as uncomfortable as I had dreaded. You know the old saying: a girl is a young man's slave and an old man's darling and I was indeed his darling. And, years later, quite unexpectedly, I did finally get to marry my handsome cousin, if after something of a delay.'

She must have noticed some impatience on my face.

'You must forgive my foolish ramblings. All this is to say that, in my experience, marriage exacts many necessary sacrifices. Indeed, it is built on such a process for women. Even so, I do not understand how Jane could have misused you so.'

Emily had once told me that she had been working late in the drawing room on some tapestry with the Countess and that Anna had been called away to deal with a crisis involving Mr Naylor, promising to return to her as soon as she could be spared. Time passed, the fire died out and Emily decided to gather up her sewing and make her way home. Trying to slip out as quickly as she could, she passed a room with a door ajar and, inside, she could hear Mr Naylor sobbing loudly, and saw him lying at his wife's feet and asking her, 'How will I survive this?' with his wife murmuring softly, patting his head, 'There, there, you will, you will.'

I wondered at her late marriage to her cousin. It seemed to me to be the worst kind of prison but her widowhood and remarriage were, clearly, for her, an unlooked for miracle.

She patted my arm and got up and left me, staring at the movements of grey cloud in the turret window. I got up too and looked down at my home, without really seeing it. I was seeing myself as she had described me and I hated the mirror the Countess had held up for me, a mirror fashioned out of her compassion and clear-eyed worldly kindness, meant only to absolve me from the withering burden of my own misplaced guilt and shame. I saw myself for the tormented young woman taken up and then dropped by the Doctor and Jane, unprotected by my indifferent father, and all that rage, anger and plotting simply the tantrums of a unloved girl no longer of interest to the older pair.

AUGUST

Sunday 4 August

Today, after a month or so of seclusion, I made my first appearance in public, wearing dark blue and not black. A few eyebrows were raised at this demi-mourning but they troubled me little enough. It was enough that I got through the day and managed to snub all attempts by visiting neighbours to pry about Emily, dressed up as concern and condolence. The Countess had told Hannah the story of Emily's fainting fits, with the intimation that she should talk freely to all the people of the town, and so the official story was now widely known. Today was the annual Castle garden party, and August opened last week with heavy, cold showers of rain. As I watched from my window, the day was so far precariously free from rain, but dark clouds seemed to lurk over the Galtees, and all the trees up to the Castle were dark with the wetting. There was a kind of windy grittiness in the air.

At three o'clock, I braced myself, put on my hat and gloves, grasped an umbrella and strolled up to the Castle, the gusty sounds of the hired brass band audible as soon as I stepped outside my front door and onto the green. Owing to the cold draughts everywhere, the Countess and her husband had decided to receive their guests indoors, at the far end of Big George's Gallery. Since the rain held off, guests were being encouraged to proceed outside where the band looked distinctly uncomfortable in their exposed place on the terrace, right in the line of the sharp wind that was blowing off the Galtees. Wind raced around the terrace, grit blew into the ices and the fruit punch and, after an hour or so, I tired of this pretence of a summer's day and made my excuses.

Tonight, I sit at my bedroom window, some cake from the garden party uneaten on a plate beside me, my tea going cold, and, in front of me, the unseen descent of the sun behind the clouds sharpens the too early, unnatural autumnal light. The band, having thumped out 'God Save the Queen', has packed up and gone home. Unwelcome autumn has come too soon to the County Cork. A high wind yesterday brought down the first of the leaves and already red berries have begun to appear in great profusion on the bushes. A bad sign for winter.

I will light a fire tonight. I have decided I will stay here until it is time for me to take my place beside Emily. Where the arrow falls, let it lie.

AUTHOR NOTE

This is a work of fiction based on the real libel trial involving Mary Travers and Jane Wilde. This is my version and is not a true account of their lives. The Wilde and Travers family existed as I have named them (although Emily Travers died of old age) and Isaac Butt, William Maturin and Anna Kingston are all historical characters. All other characters are fictional, including Anna Kingston's unpleasant second husband, Mr Naylor (her actual second husband was, by all accounts, a popular man). The poem by Speranza, the letter she wrote to Robert Travers and the Quilp pamphlets and poems all produced during the trial are original, but I invented all other poems, letters and newspapers accounts. Admirers of Elizabeth Bowen will notice her influence on the closing sentences of the novel; in particular, her account of the Mitchelstown Castle garden party in her 1942 family history, *Bowen's Court*.

In bringing this book to print, I was greatly helped by a Literature Bursary from the Arts Council of Ireland and by the encouragement, friendship and research of Dr Ciaran Wallace. Thanks are also due to Denis Kehoe for his perceptive reading of the manuscript. My thanks to Dr Muriel McCarthy and Dr Jason McElligott of Marsh's Library, Dublin, the Dean of Kingston College, Mitchelstown, Professor Claire Connolly, the School of English UCC Publication Fund and to the College of Arts, Celtic Studies and Social Sciences Publication Fund, UCC. Thanks also to Ross Higgins and Gráinne MacLochlainn of the National Library of Ireland, Becky Farrell of the Royal Irish Academy and Eamonn McEneaney of Waterford Museum and the Bishop's Palace.

Personal thanks for the support of my sisters Ria White and Oonagh Cooney, and to my friends Edmund White, Michael Dillon,   Dr

Noreen Doody, Dr John Bergin, Dr Carmel Quinlan, Dr Eve Patten, Dr Pat Crowley, Professor Siobhan Mullally and Anne Fitzgerald. This novel benefited greatly from the keen eye and the support of my agent Jonathan Williams and I owe him my grateful thanks. I am very grateful to Andrew and Jane Russell of Somerville Press for publishing the novel.

I dedicate this novel to the first readers, Donald O'Driscoll and Celine Walshe, with all my love. By caring about the story of Mary Travers as much as I did, they made this book come to life for me.